I0810740

Praise for *Past Redemption*

Vamp this!

"You were so blinded by the stars in your eyes for your lover, you forgot what we do, who we are. We're *spies*, Daphne. We're manipulators. You're valuable to him and his bosses. Sex. Love. Whatever it takes, he'll use it to get you to join them."

J's voice was hard, unbreakable, unwavering. He stepped close to me and leaned his face toward mine. "And despite the crap I've taken for doing it, I'd do it all again. Exactly the same way."

Just inches separated our lips. I'm a tall woman, but he is taller, and he bent down over me. I could feel his breath on my face. I could smell the woody, animal scent of his body. The first time I met J, I had been moved by the tremendous force of his masculinity. I had seen his cold control over his emotions at the same time I sensed the fires raging inside him. I felt them scorching me now. His eyes, ice blue and usually glittering with rage, held a smoky hunger he had never willingly let me see before.

A stirring began deep inside me, quickly turning into a tingling electric charge starting to spread across the surface of my skin. My breath pulled in with a gasp. An entanglement with J was a complication I didn't need—most of all, because it would be a personal and career disaster if I sank my fangs into his muscular, tempting neck. I had nearly done so once. That time my reason had stopped me. But would it again?

BENEATH THE SKIN

THE DARKWING CHRONICLES
BOOK THREE

SAVANNAH RUSSE

A SIGNET ECLIPSE BOOK

SIGNET ECLIPSE
Published by New American Library, a division of
Penguin Group (USA) Inc., 375 Hudson Street,
New York, New York 10014, USA
Penguin Group (Canada), 90 Eglinton Avenue East, Suite 700, Toronto,
Ontario M4P 2Y3, Canada (a division of Pearson Penguin Canada Inc.)
Penguin Books Ltd., 80 Strand, London WC2R 0RL, England
Penguin Ireland, 25 St. Stephen's Green, Dublin 2,
Ireland (a division of Penguin Books Ltd.)
Penguin Group (Australia), 250 Camberwell Road, Camberwell, Victoria 3124,
Australia (a division of Pearson Australia Group Pty. Ltd.)
Penguin Books India Pvt. Ltd., 11 Community Centre, Panchsheel Park,
New Delhi - 110 017, India
Penguin Group (NZ), 67 Apollo Drive, Mairangi Bay,
Auckland 1310, New Zealand (a division of Pearson New Zealand Ltd.)
Penguin Books (South Africa) (Pty.) Ltd., 24 Sturdee Avenue,
Rosebank, Johannesburg 2196, South Africa

Penguin Books Ltd., Registered Offices:
80 Strand, London WC2R 0RL, England

First published by Signet Eclipse, an imprint of New American Library,
a division of Penguin Group (USA) Inc.

ISBN-13: 978-0-7394-7916-2

To Theodora "Teddy" Bear

(1994–2006)

A gallant dog.

INTRODUCTION

This has been the winter of my discontent. Its cause is no mystery to me: My search for love has hit a dead end. Well, that's my excuse. The Buddhists say that to find inner peace, we must let go of "attachments"—all that good stuff that I really care about. My big "attachment" is to one hunky, sexy Darius della Chiesa. I guess, if I am ever to be enlightened, I need to "let go" of my dream of true love.

I've fallen hard twice now in my life. Neither romance turned out well. They turned out about as bad as relationships can get. The first time I went head over heels it was a disaster—and a tragic loss for literary history to boot. That was when I bit and killed Lord Byron. The second time I felt that zing-a-ling I learned not to trust a good-looking guy. Darius played dangle, and I was the danglee.

But, right now, as far as I'm concerned, Mr. della Chiesa can kiss my sweet ass. I'm moving on. I have more important things on my plate—like saving America. You see, I'm not just a vampire. I work for the United States government. I'm a spy.

CHAPTER 1

". . . yet from those flames
No light, but rather darkness visible."

—John Milton, *Paradise Lost, Book I*

A hand snaked out from the pink satin interior of the coffin and smacked down hard on an alarm clock's snooze button. The hand was mine. I was sleeping alone in the secret room behind the bookcases of my Upper West Side apartment. With more than a little sarcasm, I called this well-hidden nook the "crypt of the living dead," a place that admitted no light except for the garish red numbers of the digital clock.

The darkness around me mirrored the blackness within my soul, which had been damned four centuries earlier by the bloody kiss of a Gypsy king. Lost, wandering, without roots, I was a soul in torment, a fallen angel hurled headlong flaming from the sky to bottomless perdition.

Oh, yeah, right, I thought, as I climbed out of my coffin, my bare feet slapping against the hardwood floor. *Stop being such a drama queen,* I told myself. In point of fact I lived in New York City, which may be its own kind of hell, but I'm no fallen angel, rebellious or otherwise. It's not that I have never been good in my life. Unfortunately I have more often been bad. And like the little girl with the curl in the middle of her forehead, when I was good, I was very, very good, but when

I was bad, I was horrid. Agreeing to become a member of a deep black spy operation—an antiterrorist team that may or may not be part of the CIA—was one of the very good things I've done. The fact that I still lied, stole, occasionally killed without conscience, and drank human blood made a prima facie case that I was—despite my efforts at reform—still as bad as bad could be.

Being bad is my nature, inasmuch as some authorities call me an "undead creature." Since I am very much alive, it would be more accurate to say I am one of the long-lived, ignoble, and mysterious race called *vampire*. True, we are made, not born. Many of us feel our conversion is a rebirth that transforms us from human to something "not." Others feel the conversion is a living hell. We are neither demon nor angel, but we contain the capacity to resemble both. We live long. We often prosper. But we also have urges for passions and pleasures that my moral self resists but my dark side seeks out with no regard to rules or ethics. Most of the time, in the centuries since my birth in 1590, I had learned to control my erotic compulsions, or redirect them, letting them flow like a rushing stream around the rock, which is my heart, instead of uprooting it and carrying it off. Most of the time. But I had my slips, and they were often deadly.

Now, after a sleep haunted by nightmares, I rose when the sun slipped beneath the rim of the earth. I felt cranky and out of sorts. I would have preferred to curl up and return to slumber, but yesterday I had gotten a summons via a voice mail to come tonight to the Flatiron Building for the first meeting of Team Darkwing since the wrap-up of our last mission. We were supposed to be getting a week off. We had gotten only a few days. And after what had happened during that previous mission, I didn't feel like making nicey-nice. Part of the time I felt like resigning from the team. The rest of the time I felt like kicking somebody's butt.

I had my reasons, I thought as I padded over to the lever that swung open the faux bookcases that hid the doorway into the human world—my Manhattan apartment. This five-room flat in a vast pre–World War II building looked like hundreds of others in the neighborhood: It had high ceilings and huge windows, steam radiators that banged and hissed, and an old-fashioned bathroom with hexagon-shaped white tiles and a vintage clawfoot tub with a jerry-rigged shower. A casual look around my dwelling place would not arouse even the slightest suspicion that a monster—for indeed that was what I was—lived here. As long, that is, as no one peeked inside my refrigerator and saw the bags of human blood ordered from a blood bank under a phony clinic's name.

The blood was my elixir of eternal life. I needed it with such a fierce intensity that if I could not purchase it, I might be roaming the dark streets in search of prey. I had not hunted humans for decades, but I knew that without my FedEx delivery once a week, I'd soon be reverting to barbarism . . . to the horror that lay beneath my skin, always yearning to break free.

Enough of such morbid musings!

I shook my head to clear it as my malamute, Jade, who had been lying patiently in the hall like a sentry, barked a greeting. I gave her back a rub while my eyes squinted against the light, dim though it was. In a few steps I had passed from the impenetrable darkness of my lair to the murky illumination of the forty-watt bulbs that cast shadows and gloom throughout my apartment. I had gone from a phantasmagoria of dreams to the reality of this world, and even my nightmares were more appealing than what lay ahead of me this evening. Dreams didn't require any effort, or come with a shitload of responsibility . . . for as I walked back into my human life I remembered clearly what else the voice mail message had said: *We're in Code Red.*

Code Red meant a terrorist threat against the United States had been detected and was imminent. Was it a nuclear device? A bio-threat like anthrax or smallpox? Something worse? I didn't know, but I couldn't stand around guessing. The mundane tasks of life still took precedence over a national emergency: Jade had to be walked.

I passed quickly into my bedroom, where I do not sleep but where I do keep my clothes, and pulled on a pair of jeans and a black sweater (my standard "uniform"), then stuck my feet into a pair of UGGS. I dragged a brush through my hair to remove the tangles while my white rat Gunther chattered loudly in his cage. I grabbed a leather coat from my closet, one that had deep side pockets, then released Gunther from his prison. I put out my hand and he jumped onto it, ran deftly up my arm, and perched on my shoulder. He liked to come along on my nightly perambulations with Jade. He had always ridden in the pockets of his former owner, an octogenarian art dealer who went to pieces, thanks to a murderer's ax. Once we hit the streets, Gunther would scoot down from my shoulder to ride in an outside pocket. I had learned that when I'm walking a very big dog and have the head of a white rat peeking out of my coat, people look at them and not me. Those same people also kept their distance, which suited me just fine.

I'm a loner by temperament as well as by circumstance: My vampire state has made intimate relationships virtually impossible. As a result, I have been solitary for over four hundred years. Even the few nights that my last lover, Darius, stayed over in my apartment had proved problematic. Sure, the sex was great. I also loved cuddling on the sofa and playing footsie while we drank coffee at the kitchen counter. I loved his smell and the sound of his voice.

But we were incompatible in other ways. I didn't love picking up the wet towels from the bathroom floor after he took a shower or washing out the mug he left in the sink. Okay, okay, those were petty things, and all men need retraining. Every woman knows that. What I couldn't fix so easily was my resentment that he was an intruder in my space. Maybe I was too set in my ways. *Face facts, girl,* I thought, *use 'em, then lose 'em is your motto. You weren't cut out to be the happy homemaker. The happy hooker maybe . . .*

The sharp cold of the night air hit me hard in the face as my animals and I pushed through the glass doors of the apartment lobby and entered the streets of Manhattan at rush hour. March had come in like a lion. After a few balmy days that held the promise of spring, the weather had shown its fickleness. The temperature had dipped into the teens as a front known as an Alberta clipper blew in from the north. My spirit, buoyed by the hope of the approaching spring, plummeted with the thermometer. I turned up my collar and hunched my shoulders against the icy wind.

Phalanxes of people marched down the sidewalks in both directions, but everyone gave Jade a wide berth as we headed west toward the narrow dog park along the Hudson River. I shivered to think how much colder the damp air there would be. A subway rumbled beneath my feet as we hurried along Broadway. Horns honked. Steam rose from manhole covers. The smell of cooking meat escaped from the corner deli. After moving quickly along a few more blocks, Jade and I dashed across traffic-clogged West End Avenue. I stumbled and nearly fell when my boot struck the lip of a raised sidewalk. No one around me seemed to notice. Always wary, always more than a wee bit paranoid, I scanned the passersby and saw no familiar faces.

The crowds had dwindled to a few hardy souls by the time we reached Riverside Park, a narrow strip of green that runs along the Hudson River. Wet river air stung my flesh and stiffened my fingers. I focused on keeping my wits about me, not on the evening ahead or the days just past when I had lost so much. With the Darkwing meeting only an hour away, I didn't want to dally, so I kept Jade on the leash as she searched out her usual spots and did her thing.

The heartless wind lifted my dark hair. I cursed myself for forgetting a hat. I don't handle the cold well. Thin blood, you know. But my pace had slowed and despite my need to stay in the moment, my mind wandered and my thoughts kept returning to the meeting later tonight and the danger ahead.

In truth, except for my team and immediate superior, I didn't know much more about America's antiterrorist operations than the general public did. I had seen that the creation of Homeland Security added another level of bureaucracy but hadn't unified America's security agencies. The FBI and CIA remained rivals. Local police were kept out of the loop even when their city was at risk. The MIA, DIA, NSA, and other alphabet soup agencies duplicated efforts and got in one another's way.

Then there were the black ops, like Team Darkwing. A handful of people knew we existed. Congress sure as hell didn't. I wondered if the president knew, but I doubted it. Look at the Roswell UFO controversy; Clinton was never told a damned thing about it, as he readily admitted. Bottom line: I had strong hunches, but I still didn't know which agency had created the Darkwings or who else was out there on the front lines with us. Right now it scared the crap out of me to think that a team of vampires might be all there was between another normal evening rush hour in Manhattan and *kaboom* . . . .

Shivers racked my body from head to toe. Lost in thought—a mental state that can have deadly consequences for me—I was off guard when someone slammed into me from behind and I pitched forward, barely keeping my feet. With a growl, Jade lunged at the man who had bumped me, pushing him back. I fought to regain my balance and keep her from jumping at him again, this time with her teeth bared for attack. Another second and she could have torn out the asshole's throat. A burly guy in a black overcoat, he staggered backward, yelling, "Lady! Control your dog!"

"Well, watch where the frig you're going!" I shot back as he turned and rushed out of the gate of the fenced-in dog park.

He had no dog.

Now my senses were on hyperalert. This bump was no accident. What was the man about to do? I turned around and saw another fellow to my rear, standing inside the perimeter of the dog park, watching me. He looked quickly away. Dressed in a short blue jacket and wearing a Yankee baseball cap that kept his face in shadows, he appeared perfectly ordinary, except that he was at the dog park and he also had no dog. I have a good memory, and although I couldn't see his face, I had seen his Yankee cap and blue jacket among the rushing commuters on West End Avenue. Was I being followed? Was I being stalked?

Suddenly the man vaulted over the wire-mesh fence and ran up a path heading northward into Riverside Park. I decided to follow him. "Let's go," I called to Jade, and we took off at a run. The man had a head start, so Jade and I jogged around the outer perimeter of the fence, then started up the path in the direction the man had gone. Within seconds I could hear voices in the distance, chanting and cheering.

When I finally spotted the Yankee cap ahead of me, I slowed my pace and kept a half block behind him. He approached a small gathering of young people, and Jade and I soon found the source of the noise. About a dozen Columbia University students were gathered around a young man standing on a park bench and speaking through a bullhorn, his voice electronically distorted: "Two thousand dead for an unjust war; recruiters, we won't let you kill one more!"

"No more war! No more war!" the students yelled and clapped in response.

Then, megaphone to his lips, the student on the bench asked, "Should America be in the Mideast?"

"*No!*" the others yelled back.

"Well, then, what do we want?" asked the amplified voice.

"*Peace!*" the students answered.

"When do we want it?" came out of the bullhorn.

"*Now!*" the group yelled back, pumping their fists in the air.

I had heard the exact same slogans back in the 1960s, although this small group lacked the robustness of the antiwar demonstrations of that era. Then, too, the demonstrators against the Vietnam War weren't accessorized with iPods and cell phones. Other than that, these kids looked pretty much the same as those of the 1960s, right down to the denim jackets, low-cut jeans, and Frye boots.

Looks and slogans aside, this was a different age and a different war, I thought.

The earnest young man with the bullhorn started reading out names of American soldiers killed in the Mideast over the past few years, and the casual onlookers on the pathways around the students had grown, now numbering about fifty. A coed with very short cropped hair, a pierced eyebrow, and a fresh-scrubbed face wove through the crowd, handing out leaflets. She came up to me and offered me a flyer. As Jade sniffed her jeans, she said in a soft voice, "Please join us tomorrow."

I learn a lot about people from the way they react to Jade. This girl had no fear of my dog, which told me two things: One, she felt comfortable around dogs, and two, she was a fool, all too trusting as she ignored a large and potentially aggressive animal. She moved away and I glanced down at the printed 8½ X 11 sheet that gave information about an antiwar rally being held tomorrow by some organization called One Planet One People. Without reading the details, I folded the paper and stuck it in the pocket not occupied by Gunther. All the while I was trying to keep the Yankee cap in view.

I saw someone give my quarry a leaflet. Just then he looked up and I could clearly see his profile under the orange glare of the park's sodium lamps. He looked tough and street smart. He had a scraggly mustache, a wide pug nose, acne-scarred cheeks, and thick lips. His brow was low; his eyelids were heavy. He saw me staring at him, then turned his head as he seemed to hear something to his left. A dark form rushed in front of him, blocking my view. Then the dark figure ran off and I couldn't see the Yankee cap anymore. People started screaming. I shouldered my way through the crowd toward the screams, Jade in tow. Yankee cap lay on his back, thick red blood spreading out from under his body. His brown eyes were open and staring at the dark sky, but I was sure they saw nothing. As an expert on these matters, I know dead when I see it.

Heading back to my apartment, trying to make sense of what had just occurred and getting nowhere, I walked briskly, then broke into a trot. An acid taste filled my mouth; a knife blade of pain twisted through my gut. Although I had hightailed it out of the park before the police arrived, between chasing Yankee Cap and then witnessing his murder, I was going to be late for the Darkwing meeting. My perpetual tardiness was no biggie in itself. I'm usually late; all vampires are. But tonight I was concerned about the reason for curtailing our R & R. The last time a situation seemed this serious, a dirty bomb was being smuggled into the country in a ship's container through Port Newark. New York City had been less than twenty-four hours from another major terrorist attack. Were the bastards trying it again?

My front door swung wide as I pushed through it. Jade's nails bit into the parquet floor as she ran inside. Coming in right behind her, I spotted the light on my answering machine flashing red in the gray shadows of the room. Tension coiled tighter inside me. I hit the PLAY button.

I heard my mother's voice; it was taut, strained, and uncharacteristically tender.

"Daphne, *cara mia*. I am going to ask you to do something for me. You'll have to trust me that it needs to be done. I'll see you before dawn. Please keep an open mind. It concerns your father. Sweetheart, remember those days so long ago when it was only you and me? I need you to trust me now as you did then. I have a chance to find out what happened to your father." Her voice broke, paused, then, heavy with emotion, continued. "So please, just do as I ask."

What? I thought. *Why is she suddenly mentioning my father after refusing to discuss him for four hundred years?* My emotions surged between pain and utter confusion. I could not remember my father. He had died suddenly when I was still an infant, and in the days that followed, my mother had gone into hiding with me. Until I was nearly eight we had moved from place to place throughout the Italian countryside, sheltered by friends and followed by the dread of discovery. That was the time of "only you and me."

I never learned why we were being pursued, except that I had known from the start that powerful men in the Church of Rome wanted us dead. Since that time the Vatican itself has remained our bitterest enemy. My mother never explained what actually happened to my father. The history books say he died after a brief illness after he was elected pope. In the few days that he ruled the most powerful government in the world, he had passed sweeping reforms to help the poor and take from the rich—making him a real Robin Hood of popes. I sensed my mother's hand in his politics; they had remained remarkably consistent over the centuries. Maybe his radical ideas had moved someone to poison him, for his "illness" smacked of murder. And maybe someone had discovered the existence of his vampire mistress and the child she had borne him.

But whatever happened in the twelve days between his election to the papacy and his death upset and enraged my mother to the point where she could not discuss it. She always responded to my questions about my father with sad eyes, a shake of the head, and the promise that one day she would tell me what she knew.

That day had never come. My questions had remained unanswered. Now my mother's phone message not only aroused my curiosity; it reawakened my obsession to find out as much about him as I could. Perhaps every daughter who ever lost a father felt the emptiness inside that I did and had the perpetual longing to fill it. And perhaps, my more cynical self remonstrated, my mother knew that this rare mention of my father was the bait with which to catch my attention and gain my cooperation in whatever outrageous, unpleasant, onerous, or just downright repulsive scheme she had for me this time.

However, before I could process my mother's unexpected words, the second message started to play. My heart surged forward like a Thoroughbred pounding down the stretch. I heard Darius's voice, sounding far away. . . .

"Daphne? If you're there, pick up. Are you there? Shit, I guess you're out. Daphne, I only have a minute. I borrowed this cell phone. I'll get my own by tomorrow, then I can give you a number to call. I'm in Germany . . ."

I know, I thought as my breath caught in my throat and a flood of sadness washed through me. *I was supposed to be there with you.*

"I don't know how long we're going to be in this location. I can't say much more than that, except . . . well, I miss you. The situation here is . . . uh, tense. Maybe it's a good thing you didn't come along. I miss you, Daphne, but I don't know— Aw, fuck it. I hate talking to these machines." Then a voice, a woman's voice, called to him in the background, and he answered in a low, unintelligible voice. A few seconds later the message continued: "Hey, I gotta go. Call you later."

"You are such an asshole!" I screamed at the telephone.

That phone call summed up our relationship in a nutshell. Secrets and separations. Missed calls. Truncated communication. Doubts. Longing—and lies. Darius, who worked for a different security agency than I did, was posing as a singer with a band called Darius D.C. and the Vampire Project. At present they were off on a European tour, tracking down al-Qaeda-inspired terrorists and ducking vampire hunters half a world away.

His ex-girlfriend Julie, the band's singer, was right there with him. Did he honestly think that was okay with me? The bitch had tried to kill me. *No problem,* was the response I had gotten from some well-placed sources I had pumped for information about Darius's current mission. Officially, the word was that nobody told her *not* to attack me, and it was just a simple misunderstanding. *Give me a break!* "And," my source had said, "the Germany mission is important to national security." Since I had refused to go, it was too late to replace the agent. She had to be kept on.

Anger flashed through my mind, and I thought, *Lies color everything he says to me, and the color is cruel and black. Well, screw you, Darius della Chiesa. Once again you're lying to me by omission. You can call back, but hell will freeze over before I answer.* I was *so* frosted.

I was pissed at Darius. I was also pissed at my boss, J. At the moment I was pissed off at men in general as well as in particular. You know the old saying: "No man is worth your tears, and the one who is won't make you cry." Wrong! There is not one man walking the face of this planet who won't make a woman cry sooner or later. They all start off like Dr. Jekyll. *Oh, yeah, this one is a keeper,* you think. But it is just a matter of time before the sweet, easygoing doctor turns into the brutish Mr. Hyde. Lately the entire male gender was on my shit list. I hit the REPEAT button on the answering machine, and as soon as Darius began his message again, I hit DELETE.

Now if I could just delete him from my heart, I wouldn't be lying to myself when I said I didn't care.

At this point, making a six-o'clock meeting was impossible. The only unknown was how late I was going to be. Reflecting both my haste and my pissy mood, I simply exchanged my UGGs for my well-worn pair of Frye boots, didn't bother with makeup, threw my coat back on, grabbed my backpack, and went rushing out of my building into the icy embrace of the night. I might be over four hundred years old, but I looked as if I were in my twenties, tops. I was born a human, but I had been transformed into a vampire when I was still a teenager. Even at age eighteen, when my conversion took place, I had always looked mature for my age, and four centuries of living had made me an old soul.

Intellectually I had aged greatly. Experience had made me wary and sometimes world-weary. But I admit that with men my growth was stunted. My hormones still raged like a damned adolescent's. Most of the time I was able to suppress my constant state of horniness, and I affected an air of . . . well, what I considered sophistication and urban chic. As a result, I couldn't pull off looking eighteen anymore, and didn't want to.

Ironically, my mother still did look eighteen, resembling more a younger sister than my mother. But chalk up her dewy ingenue appearance to her skills at deception and expertise in disguise. She was not untried and innocent; she was one of the world's most powerful women. Marozia Urban—or Mar-Mar, as she was called by me and her dearest friends—had to be a thousand years old. I didn't know her birthday, since she was notoriously tight-lipped about her past. I didn't know who transformed my mother from human to vampire, or when it had happened. I had read the little bit recorded about her in history books and firmly believed it was all lies.

Those historical accounts report that Marozia died in 938, locked up in a castle in Rome by one of her sons. That sounds deliciously Gothic and fictional—and it was all bunk. She never died; she had been made into a vampire. She just moved on and hooked up with my father in Rome in the sixteenth century: my father, Giambattista Castagna, who became Urban VII, the pope. Okay, he never actually got to be pope; he died twelve days after his election and before his installation. His demise had been suspicious from the start. But if he had been murdered—and surely he had been—how and why remained a mystery.

Is that what Mar-Mar wants to talk with me about? I thought. *If so, why now, in the midst of a new terror alert?* The sudden death of Giambattista Castagna had taken place over four hundred years ago. Even though my mother still paled and trembled with rage when she discussed the Church, and even though I'd like to know the truth about what had happened at the Vatican on September 27 of 1590, now was neither the time nor the place. My job was to keep Americans safe and avert a national disaster. What did my father's death matter anyway? As Robert Frost wrote, *the past is a bucket of ashes.*

CHAPTER 2

"Et ignotas animun dimittit in artes."
And ignorant, he turns his mind to mysterious
things.

—Ovid, *The Metamorphoses* (Book 8, line 188)

After flagging down a Yellow Cab and arriving at 175 Fifth Avenue by six thirty p.m., I ran tear-ass into the Flatiron Building. I took the stairs to the third floor to bypass the maddeningly slow elevators and went flying toward the entrance of the ABC Publishers office. I sent the door crashing into the wall as I plunged through it. Then I froze in my tracks.

A stranger sat slouched in a chair across from my colleagues at the room's central conference table. His hair was long and curly, his mouth a slash of red beneath a dark mustache. With a languid sexiness, he turned his head and looked at me, amusement dancing like flames behind the ebony of his eyes. If the rebel god Prometheus had again descended to earth, he sat before me now: commanding, well muscled, lazily arrogant, and undoubtedly one of the best-looking guys I had ever seen in my life, all four hundred years plus of it.

Oh, shit! I said to myself. I hadn't even combed my hair after the walk with Jade. I didn't have on any makeup. I looked pale and wan, disheveled as a street person, and about like I did when I lounged around my apartment in an old

T-shirt and the bottoms of my cowboy pajamas. With this in mind, harnessing all my famous wit and skill with *bon mots*, I looked straight at Gorgeous Guy and asked in a loud, New York voice (the kind we all use to be heard over noisy crowds and traffic), "Who the *hell* are you?"

Gorgeous Guy gave me a shark's smile, showing sharp white teeth. My best friend and fellow Darkwing, Benjamina Polycarp, burst out laughing. Seated next to her, my other teammate, Broadway dancer Cormac O'Reilly, rolled his eyes. And at the head of the table, J, my boss and a man in dire need of an anger management course, turned the color of old bricks, brought his brows together in a frown, and said as if his teeth were clenched, "Agent Urban, you are late. Please take your seat."

I didn't even acknowledge J. I had a major beef with him. I still had half a mind to quit the team. I saw a manila folder on the table in front of an empty chair and figured it was mine. I dragged the chair away from the table, making sure I scraped it along the floor. I threw my backpack down; then I slowly peeled off my coat and hung it on the back of the chair, kept my hat on, sat myself down, and noisily dragged the chair back in.

That's me, Miss Urban Chic, all right. My behavior was juvenile, but I wanted to annoy J as much as possible and make an impression on the new guy. *Yeah, right, some impression! He probably thinks I'm a horse's ass. I don't care.*

What a crock! I did care, but no way J or anyone else was going to know it.

I had no sooner finished this little display when Benny, who was seated next to me, leaned over and put her lips very close to my ear. "Dibs," she whispered.

Okay by me, I thought. She saw the new guy first, and I had no intention of hooking up with anyone at the moment, so I winked at her and said sotto voce, "Sure." Benny was a beautiful natural blonde with huge brown eyes. She was tiny in build except for her Dolly Parton–sized breasts—and a man magnet if there ever was one. Unfortunately she attracted the wrong man over and over again. I guess she and I had that misfortune in common. Maybe Gorgeous Guy would be Mr. Right for her.

"Let's get down to business." The stern voice of J interrupted my thoughts. "The information we have is time-sensitive. But first, for the benefit of Agent Urban, let me *re*introduce our newest team member, Agent Tallmadge."

"First name?" I asked, lifting an eyebrow.

"Just *Tallmadge*," the newcomer responded with a seductive smile that created deep dimples in his lean cheeks and must have melted many hearts. Benny might have dibs on him, but he was openly flirting with me.

"Daphne Urban," I said as I stood and extended my hand across the table. When he took it with his, which was warm, a tingling shot up my arm and lit a fire deep inside me. Tallmadge was hot, and I felt his heat.

J cleared his throat, and I let go of Tallmadge's hand. "Moving on," J said, his angular face hard and taut. "Our mission is to stop an assassination." We all stared at him. Having gotten our attention, he paused.

"Whose?" I demanded impatiently.

"Joe Daniel's," he said.

That was a shocker. I thought maybe the president was at risk, or someone as crucial to the government as the commander of the armed forces. But Joe Daniel? Most of the millions of people who had been following his antiwar campaign on television for the last six or seven months just loved him, no matter what their politics. Daniel was a decorated war veteran turned antiwar activist, a Congressman from Illinois, and, some suggested, a modern-day Gandhi—but a prankster Gandhi with a great sense of humor and a warm laugh.

Last September Joe Daniel had become the most popular political figure in the United States almost overnight. He had broken into the national news when he and a dozen of his fellow veterans pitched tents and camped out outside the summer White House in Maine. They sang peace songs, skateboarded and hotdogged holding American flags, and paraded up and down the highway with a banner listing all the American dead in the current war. Within a week his miniprotest grew to a massive demonstration of over a hundred thousand people. Some of the crowds came to see the top music groups who showed up early on, such as Bono with U2, Pearl Jam, and Bon Jovi, turning the event into a spontaneous Woodstock for peace.

Daniel's message of "Stop the fighting and start saving the planet" made sense to more and more Americans. As for me, I was suspicious of do-gooders. I had seen so many heroes become demigods over the years that my natural dislike of politics had kicked in, and I had never become a Joe Daniel fan.

Just then Cormac's tenor voice said, "And how is a threat to a minor politician a Code Red situation? Sorry to be cynical, but you'd think the current administration would be glad to get rid of him."

I nodded, and as I did I saw Tallmadge watching me, appraising me with his eyes.

J responded to Cormac, his voice low and serious. "The information we have obtained concerning the assassination threat is so disturbing that it rises to a Code Red level." He paused, letting the gravity settle down on us hard, then added, "You'll find all the details on the CD in the folder in front of each of you . . ."

Like good little students in school, we all opened our folders to find an unlabeled CD and a single sheet of paper. I glanced up. Tallmadge's eyes were on me again.

". . . but in brief, this is what we know. In the first place, there is the real possibility that Daniel's killing will make him a martyr and cause a groundswell of popular support for the peace movement, which is the *last* thing the current administration wants to happen. They *would* like to get rid of Daniel, Agent O'Reilly, but by discrediting him, not by killing him.

"Second, the reason this reaches a Code Red level is this: We have information and belief that Daniel's assassination might be the first of a carefully planned series of killings of prominent African Americans, Latinos, and anyone of any color who steps up to take Daniel's place. His killing might be the start of a long-range conspiracy to destabilize the American government and plunge the country into widespread rioting. You might remember what happened in 1967 when Detroit, Newark, and Los Angeles went up in flames."

"Isn't your first scenario a bit far-fetched?" I asked. "Sort of a new kind of domino theory?"

J shot me a sour look and said, "Maybe. On the other hand, some analysts feel that killing Joe Daniel would quell any legitimate dissent to administration policy. That's a bad thing, because it would place a cork in the bottle of antiwar sentiment, letting the pressure of discontent swell until it exploded. The result, again, might be civil unrest.

"A third theory being tossed around is this: The ultimate goal of killing Joe Daniel might be to distract our security forces and so divert them by urban unrest so that a major terrorist offensive can be successfully launched before we know what hit us.

"But whatever the motive behind the assassination, the threat against Daniel is real and imminent. His death would, at the very least, cause the government embarrassment, and at worst cause a domestic crisis. That is why this is Code Red."

"Who's behind this threat?" Benny jumped in.

"Do you have hard evidence that any of your doomsday scenarios are real?" Tallmadge asked, his voice unexpectedly belligerent.

"Hold it! Let me respond. Starting with the matter of hard evidence," J began, shaking his head as if Tallmadge had asked the dumbest question ever. "In the spy business, Agent Tallmadge, the best information is humint—that's short for human intelligence—from double agents, informants, or drop-ins. And that's what we have."

Tallmadge's face registered his total contempt for J. "No documents? Electronic intercepts of conversations? Do we have anything like that?" he persisted.

"Quite frankly, no, we don't. Not at this time, anyway," J conceded.

"Well, it seems as if I've been 'recruited' to start tilting at windmills. I don't buy your theory that this is a terrorist plot; nor do I buy that it's the first in a series of assassinations. What seems obvious is that this guy has made enough enemies for somebody to want to kill him. But a matter of national security? Bullshit," Tallmadge said.

"Agent Tallmadge, you've been 'recruited' to be a spy in exchange for the opportunity to continue to walk on this earth. If you've changed your mind about your choice, just say the word," J said, glaring into the face of the newcomer.

Tallmadge looked back at him just as steadily. "I haven't changed my mind. This is just turning out to be more of a farce than I'd thought."

The shadows of the dimly lit room seemed to close in on me. An uneasy silence fell as Benny, Cormac, and I grew still and watched the exchange. None of us had volunteered for this job. We all had been given the same terms after we had been captured by U.S. agents: become a member of a new spying operation or be exterminated. I was resentful at first. I assumed Benny and Cormac had been too, but we soon believed in the importance of Team Darkwing. We had come to feel part of something bigger than ourselves, that our lives could be more than feeding on blood and pursuing pleasure. For the first time I had a positive reason to get out of my coffin. I had given myself, heart and soul, to keeping innocent Americans safe from terrorists.

I wasn't surprised that Tallmadge had not gone willingly into the good night of becoming a spy. I *was* surprised by his open defiance of J, since termination—or, to be less euphemistic, *extermination*—was the sword of Damocles above our heads. Darkwings couldn't quit. If we tried to run we'd be hunted down. If they caught us they wouldn't let us go. At that point there would be no forgiveness, just a swift, merciless wooden stake to the heart.

Yet Tallmadge was clearly in a pissing contest with J. From where I sat, I could see they were two alpha males vying for dominance. Right now J was top dog, but Tallmadge was refusing to back down. I wondered what gave him the balls to do it. Suddenly my heart squeezed hard as I acknowledged that I was attracted to him and that I was uneasy about that attraction. His exterior was sophisticated; inside he was all macho, a combination that appealed to me. I also sensed an amorality and a love of the dark side that matched my own. Tallmadge mirrored too perfectly the part of me I fought to suppress. Already I began to fear his influence on my fragile self-control.

J's voice interrupted my racing thoughts. "Tallmadge, you and I need to have a talk, but not here, not now," J said, and deliberately turned his body away from Tallmadge's side of the table and spoke to the rest of us. "To answer Agent Polycarp's question, we do not know who, specifically, is behind the assassination plot and conspiracy. There are several possibilities. One of your jobs will be to find out. But your primary mission is to stop the killing by locating the assassin and eliminating him."

"Are you saying you know who the assassin is?" Cormac finally spoke, his voice rising an octave higher than usual.

"Yes, we do know. And what's more, we know when and where the assassination will most likely take place."

"So what do you need us for? It seems as if this is a slam dunk for the FBI or any even *fairly* competent intelligence service," Tallmadge put in.

J didn't even look at him, but I did. Tallmadge's eyes were hard; a tremor in his jaw betrayed the anger barely restrained within him. He looked at me then, and the power of his rage both frightened and excited me. Not taking my eyes from his, I spoke in a soft voice. "Tallmadge does have a valid point." Then, breaking away from Tallmadge's burning eyes, I turned toward J. "Why us?"

J barked out his words. "Because this assassin is a man known to intelligence services around the world as *Gage*. Gage is an enigma. No one knows who he is or where he comes from. We only know one thing: If he is hired to do a hit, he gets his quarry, and no security force on earth has ever stopped him. His former targets may have included the president of an Eastern European country, the head of Britain's MI5, a former chief of our own CIA, the CEO of one of the biggest multinational corporations in the world, a Lebanese security minister, and the prime minister of an Asian nation. Now he's after Daniel."

"When and where is the assassination supposed to take place?" Cormac prompted.

"Daniel is coming to New York this Friday to formally announce his entrance into the presidential race. He'll be holding a series of rallies and media interviews over the coming week. The following Friday night he will formally kick off his campaign with a speech to some VIPs in Central Park at the John Lennon memorial. Then Daniel is supposed to move on to a huge public rally in Madison Square Garden. From what we've been told, that's when he will be killed."

"At Strawberry Fields or at Madison Square Garden?" I asked.

"That we don't know yet. We believe it will be at the Central Park location."

"Does Daniel know he is a target?" Benny asked, lowering her voice.

"He has been told there is a credible threat against his life, yes," J answered. "He either doesn't believe it or doesn't care. He'll appear as scheduled. And he'll die as scheduled—"

"Unless we stop it," I finished.

Just then something clicked in my mind. Maybe Daniel was the new Martin Luther King Jr.—a man whose potential to become powerful could withstand any attempts to discredit him, a man so threatening to his opponents that the only way to stop him was to kill him. That realization poleaxed me: It was logical, and it rang true. Martin Luther King Jr. never ran for president because he was cut down by an assassin's bullet. Bobby Kennedy picked up his banner and was stopped in the same way. Now Joseph A. Daniel, age forty-five or so, was about to become the first black American to run for president since comedian Dick Gregory—the difference being that Daniel actually had a chance of getting elected. He didn't have funds from any corporate backers or PACs. What he did have was a growing constituency of enthusiastic citizens, a lot of them young or people of color. With a groundswell of support quickly growing, he had a real chance at winning the race—and so somebody out there had decided he must die.

The meeting rolled to a rapid close. We learned that while Daniel had refused protection from any federal agency, he had agreed to cooperate with the New York Police Department. The single sheet of paper in our folders gave each of us our immediate assignment. Benny and I were to pose as campaign volunteers for One Planet One People, the group mentioned on the flyer I had stuffed into my pocket. They were sponsoring Daniel's New York appearances, and we were to show up at the headquarters they'd set up for Daniel tomorrow evening. Tallmadge was to focus on investigative work and maybe on how the Darkwings could best protect Daniel in the event we didn't stop Gage before a week from Friday. We were assured that the powers that be were trying to locate the assassin, and that we'd be briefed again soon.

That last little nugget of information didn't impress me at all, and while I was ruminating about how to track down Gage ourselves, Cormac slowly rose to his feet and flung down his manila folder so that it skittered across the table before falling to the floor. The blood had drained from his face, and I could see that his whole body was shaking. He spit out, "J, what the fuck! Where am *I* in this team? Am I in? Am I out? Why am I still assigned to Opus Dei? What the hell am I *doing* in this operation? Do you think I am so incompetent that I need to just sit night after boring night in the heart of a backward, ridiculous religious order I absolutely despise? What the hell do you people want from me?"

"Take it easy. Take it easy," J said, his hand up. "If it makes you feel any better, I felt you should be an active part of this operation. I fought for your teaming up with

Tallmadge right away. The higher-ups wouldn't budge. They said that you stay where you are."

"But why? *Why?*" Cormac insisted. "I'm not doing *anything.*"

"I don't know why," J answered. "If it makes you feel any better, I know you're going to be brought into this mission by next week, but for now, you just sit tight."

I couldn't restrain myself any longer. "J, you mentioned *they* and *higher-ups.* Don't you mean my mother? Isn't she behind this?"

"Look, Agent Urban, I told you before I cannot and will not discuss your mother's position in our organization. I said *they.* I meant *they.* I said *higher-ups.* I meant *higher-ups.* That's the end of it."

But it wasn't the end of it. Benny reached up and touched Cormac's arm. He looked past her, right at me. I understood that he was silently asking me to talk to my mother. I gave him a barely perceptible nod.

At that point J rose from his chair. "We're done for tonight. I'll be in touch. With *all* of you," he said, shooting a look at Tallmadge; then he turned to go.

"Just a minute, J," I said. "I need a word with you *now.*"

J stopped. "All right, Agent Urban."

I spoke to the others who were about to go out the door. "I'll catch up. Will you hang out for a couple of minutes downstairs in the lobby? I won't be long. Don't leave without me," I added, and gave Tallmadge a big smile.

He winked and replied, "See you downstairs."

I waited until the door had shut behind them, then looked at J. Before I could start talking he said, "I owe you an apology."

"At least that," I said, my voice etched with frost.

"Look," he began without apology, "first off, your

boyfriend, Agent della Chiesa, had no business barging into our last operation to blow up Bradley's drug lab. And then, without asking, without *thinking*, dammit, you were going to accompany him back to the city. Did you honestly believe I hadn't heard that his handler wanted to recruit you to work with his agency and quit the Darkwings?"

My face must have shown my surprise, because J crowed, "I knew it! You didn't know about his hopes to recruit you, did you? Della Chiesa was supposed to approach you about switching to his people that night. You were supposed to say yes because you couldn't say no to him about anything—"

"That's a crock!" I said.

"No, it's not. You were so blinded by the stars in your eyes for your lover that you forgot what we do, who we are. We're *spies*, Daphne. We're manipulators. I'm not saying he doesn't have real feelings for you, but wake up! You're valuable to him and his bosses, Daphne. Sex. Love. Whatever it takes, he'll use it to get you to join them. So yeah, what I did was out of line, but I knew *you* wouldn't listen to me, and I had to stop you. I had the 'red flag' you made from your underwear in my pocket, so I pulled a dirty trick and made him think you and I had been together." J's voice was hard, unbreakable, unwavering. He stepped close to me and leaned his face toward mine. "And despite the shit I've taken for doing it, I'd do it all again. Exactly the same way."

Just inches separated our lips. I was a tall woman, but he was taller, and he bent down over me. I could feel his breath on my face. I could smell the cleanliness of his uniform, and beneath it the woody, animal scent of his body. The first time I met J, I had been moved by the tremendous force of his masculinity, his blatant maleness. I had seen his cold control over his emotions at the same time I sensed the fires raging inside him. I felt them scorching me now. His eyes, ice blue and usually glittering with rage, held a smoky hunger he had never willingly let me see before.

A stirring began deep inside me, quickly turning into a tingling electric charge starting to spread across the surface of my skin. My breath pulled in with a gasp and became fast and shallow. I was stunned that I could react to him this way. An entanglement with J was a complication I didn't need for a lot of reasons. First of all, I didn't want to lose the respect I had for him as a stand-up guy who hadn't lied to me—yet. I didn't want to find out the hard way that J, too, might use me in any way he found effective.

But more important, it would be a personal and career disaster if I sank my fangs into his muscular, tempting neck. I had nearly done so once. That time my reason stopped me. But would it again? Sex and biting were so closely linked, I didn't know if I could separate the urges. And now I was pulled to J by an almost irresistible force. His lips moved even closer to mine. I wanted him to kiss me. My fangs pushed against the inside of my lips. I was losing control—

I quickly stepped back. Then I stepped back again, mentally shaking myself.

"Okay, I accept your apology," I said quickly, and even as the words spilled out my voice turned bitter. "In any event, I'm still with you and the Darkwings, not with Darius. So let's forget it"—I paused—"for now. But that's not what I wanted to talk to you about."

"What then?" he said, all business, as if nothing had almost happened. But we both knew it had.

"I was followed and accosted earlier tonight. Two men. I was in the dog park up on Riverside Drive near Seventy-second Street. A man in an overcoat pushed into me before my dog drove him off. Another, a Latino, was with him, and ran. I followed the Latino as far as a street demonstration, where he was approached by a third man and . . . murdered."

I had J's attention. He answered in an urgent voice, "What's your take on this? Were any of them vampire hunters?"

"I don't know. I don't think so. They looked more like drug dealers than vampire hunters. They were all shadowing me, I guess. I can't get a handle on it."

"I'll see what I can find out," J acknowledged as he picked up his papers from the table. As I turned and started for the door, he spoke again. He was watching me intently, never taking his eyes from me. "Daphne."

"What?" I asked.

"I . . ." he started to say. "Never mind. Just watch your back."

"Okay," I said softly, and walked out.

CHAPTER 3

You Gods who rule the spirits;
And you, the voiceless Dead . . .
Let me, with your help, describe
The Underworld beneath the dark, deep earth.

— Virgil, *The Aeneid*, Book VI

M y colleagues were not waiting downstairs in the lobby. They had remained in the dun-colored hallway outside the office door, lurking in the dim light. I don't know how much they'd heard of my conversation with J, but vampires have no scruples.

Tallmadge and Cormac were standing twenty feet down the hall near the elevators. Cormac was shaking his head while Tallmadge spoke intently, his face inclined toward Cormac's, his warm hand with its long, tapered fingers on Cormac's thin shoulder. Tallmadge raised his eyes as I stepped out of the office. I smiled and waved. He winked back at me—and Benny reached out like a striking rattler and grabbed my upper arm with a fierce grip. She dragged me off to the opposite end of the hall, as far from Cormac and Tallmadge as we could get.

"Ow!" I yelped. "What's that for?"

"Shee-it, Daphne. What part of *dibs* don't you understand?"

"All I did was—"

"All you did was put your skinny ass on the firing line back there in the meeting—for Tallmadge. '*Oh*, J, Tallmadge has a point,'" she mimicked. "You sure didn't give me a damn chance to hop in and play the hero."

"Benny, I . . . I didn't think. I mean . . . Look, I'm not . . . I'm not making a move on him," I sputtered. "Besides, Benny, he's not my type!"

"Sugar, get a grip. He's cocky, he's sexy, and he's trying to self-destruct. He's exactly your type."

My mouth fell open. "Benny, please believe me: I don't have the hots for him. Forgive me? Benny, come on; don't look so mad. You're a zillion times more important to me than any man. You know that, don't you?"

She kept her big brown eyes fixed on me for a few seconds longer, then broke into a grin. "Oh, shoot, girlfriend, I know that. Just back off, okay? I want to have a little fun, and this new guy sure seems like a party animal to me."

I looked over at Tallmadge. He was all smiles with Cormac now. He had stuck an unlit cigar between his white teeth and was languidly slouching against one wall. Just then, the elevator's DOWN light blinked green, and Tallmadge called out, "Ladies, our carriage has arrived."

After we all stepped into the tiny elevator car, I let Benny stand next to Tallmadge, and I do mean next to, as in, so close a sheet of paper could barely fit between the two of them. When the elevator car began its creaking, groaning journey downward, I asked, "Where are we headed next?" I felt that we needed to talk about our assignment, and we certainly needed to integrate Tallmadge into our team. *United we stand; divided we fall . . . to dust and oblivion,* I thought.

Cormac looked down at his hands and didn't meet my eyes when he answered. "To Tallmadge's club."

"Club?" I answered, my voice rising. "As in *vampire club?*"

A secret vampire underworld exists in New York, consisting of a network of private clubs, regularly scheduled raves, and invitation-only parties where unspeakable things happen, or so it is said. I had avoided this scene for decades. I had walked a similar path centuries ago, and it had jaded and corrupted me. But I had turned away from that life, realizing that mindless pleasure soon became an addiction, one that created a personal hell where cravings for new sensations and ever wilder experiences destroyed one's soul.

It's not that I'm such a Goody Two-shoes. It helped that I truly wasn't attracted to most male vampires. They were never faithful to a lover, and almost all of them were parasites of one kind or another. The idea of having sex with degenerates like that repelled me. Tallmadge proved the exception to the rule. I could imagine his kiss, his caressing hands, his body pressed close to mine. And if I dared to admit it to myself, I had avoided the vampire world of erotica and vice because I didn't trust myself to resist my race's greatest pleasure—the hunting of humans in order to drink their blood.

"No," I said sharply.

Cormac glanced back at Tallmadge. "I told you she'd never go."

"Daphne," Tallmadge said, "my club isn't like you think. It's not all Goth, like the Batcave in London. It's a place where we can talk in private, without worrying about others overhearing."

"How do you know what I think?" I said, my words cracking like dry sticks. "You don't know me."

"And you don't know me," he said in a kind voice. "I would feel safe to reveal myself there. And I have so many questions about you three and the Darkwings. Won't you please say yes?"

"Daphy, please," Benny asked. "We never had nothing like a vampire club in Branson, Missouri. Please, Daphy, can't you go? Just this once?" Her pleas melted my heart. Benny was such a pretty little thing, emanating the same sense of vulnerability as Marilyn Monroe and a likability that made you just want to hug her. She put her hand on my arm. I saw that she was wearing the West Point ring that belonged to Bubba, our former teammate whom vampire hunters had killed just a week ago. I had picked up that ring from the dust and given it to Benny, for she had loved Bubba more deeply than she had wanted us to know.

"Cormac?" I asked, turning to my longtime friend.

"I don't care." Cormac shrugged. "I've been to clubs before. It's no big deal. And it will be safe for us to talk there." So Cormac answered me, but didn't answer me, and his eyes stared at the wall, not into mine.

"I guess the majority rules," I conceded.

"Whoooeee, thank you, sugar!" Benny squealed, and gave me a huge smile.

"You may not thank me before the night is out," I answered grimly.

Abandon all hope, ye who enter here, I thought as we arrived at an elegant row house on Irving Place south of Gramercy Park. From the outside it didn't look like hell.

A young blond man in a tuxedo responded to Tallmadge's push of the doorbell. I noted that security cameras were aimed at us and had already revealed to the occupants of the mansion who was on their doorstep.

"Mr. Tallmadge, good evening." The man, evidently part of the club's staff, spoke with just a hint of a British accent as he greeted Tallmadge and said, "And it's a pleasure to have your friends visit us this evening. A private room has been reserved at your request." Then he addressed the rest of us, saying, "My name is Cathary, and I will be your facilitator this evening." Nodding toward another blond attendant, a Nordic god of a boy, tall and powerful, who had moussed his hair into spikes, Cathary continued: "Monsieur Dore Ducasse will take your coats if you wish; then please be so kind as to follow me."

Nothing looked extraordinary in the small foyer. A flight of stairs led to the floors above, and a gold-leaf table was topped by a large bouquet of dark red roses. I could see an empty sitting room to our right and a closed door to our left. A long hall stretched toward the back of the building. A hanging crystal chandelier fit with real candles, not incandescent bulbs, cast flickering shadows around the foyer and left the end of the hallway in darkness. Vampires prefer dim light, so while this fixture didn't surprise me, the gloominess along with the visible absence of other guests somehow increased my feelings of unease.

After I removed my jacket—and in my jeans and old black sweater I was definitely underdressed for the club's elegant ambience—we trailed after Cathary as he ascended the stairs. Tallmadge was at the head of our group, Benny and Cormac followed him, and I brought up the rear. Halfway up, I wanted to turn around and snatch my jacket back from Monsieur Ducasse, my instincts telling me I should flee instead of dutifully following Cathary up to the second floor like a lamb to the slaughter. Of course, the feeling was nonsense. I was in no bodily danger here in a vampire "safe house," no matter what lay ahead. It was my sensibilities and perhaps my morality that might be assaulted and put to the test. Did I think I would fail?

I reined in my imagination and continued climbing upward. It was only as the rest of the group reached the landing that I glanced back down to the softly lit foyer. Ducasse was nowhere to be seen. Instead, stepping out of the shadows was a man, his face hidden behind a black mask, his well-muscled chest bare, his leather pants skintight. He walked past the stairs and started to enter the sitting room. Just at that moment he glanced up. He saw me watching him, but all I could see of his eyes were pits of darkness. I shivered, for the kinds of games I imagined being played behind the mansion's closed doors were exactly the ones I feared.

The room reserved for Tallmadge was well-appointed, but decidedly ordinary. No masked figures stood in the corners; no drug paraphernalia littered the table set out with bottles of fine wines and spirits. Cathary asked what he could serve us. Benny and Tallmadge each had a glass of pinot noir; Cormac and I had mineral water.

"Please ring for me if I can get you anything else," Cathary said, and gave us a little bow. Then he exited, silently closing the door behind him. The room was almost dark and very warm. The air was lightly scented with citrus and sandalwood. Some tall white candles burned in wall sconces. Others of the same type sat in holders on the drinks table. A Bach cantata was being piped in over a sound system, loud enough to be heard but not to interfere with conversation. The room was lovely. So why did I feel so uncomfortable?

Benny sipped her drink and stared at Tallmadge as if he were a movie star. I could see she was falling, and falling hard and fast. Cormac, meanwhile, looked everywhere but at me as he walked around the room seemingly interested in the large paintings in gilt frames, which were barely visible on the walls in the low lighting. Then he went over and sat on the couch, slipping off his tasseled loafers and folding his legs beneath him in a lotus position. As a professional dancer, Cormac was thin and lithe. Now he sat there, holding a socked foot in one hand while with the other hand he thumbed idly through some large coffee-table book of photographs. Even upside down I could tell they were the arty erotica of Robert Mapplethorpe.

"Shall we all sit?" Tallmadge said, his voice mellow and silvery, the words like water over smooth stones. He was an attractive man in every way, from his manner to his physique. I wasn't surprised; most vampires were beautiful—on the outside, at least.

I opted to sit with Cormac, although I hugged one corner of the couch. Cormac and I were much better friends than we used to be, but neither of us was touchy-feely. Tallmadge lowered himself gracefully onto another couch facing us, saying, "Benjamina, my dear, please join me." With a radiant smile Benny sat at his side, putting her wineglass on the coffee table that sat between the two couches.

"Let me cut to the chase," I said abruptly, silently disapproving of the relationship developing between Benny and Tallmadge and thinking that all I really wanted to do was take care of business and leave. "Tallmadge, we're a team, and either you're with us or not. We all know you didn't come into the agency willingly, but you're important to us. We lost a good agent last week—"

"The best," Cormac said.

"Amen," echoed Benny.

"—so you have some big shoes to fill. What you do on your own time is your business, of course, but when the mission heats up, it's a twenty-four/seven priority."

"What does that mean, exactly?" Tallmadge said, holding his wineglass by the stem and staring into the deep red of its depths.

I was going to answer, but upon second thought I said, "Cormac, why don't you tell him?"

Cormac slowly raised his long, thin face and stared across the coffee table, pinning Tallmadge with his eyes. "It means that during a mission we are either physically together at a designated assignment, or in cell phone contact. If we're in different locations and any of us needs help, we get there no matter what. If we're attacked, we fight together. If one of us is captured or wounded, it is up to us to rescue him or her. No Darkwing is ever left behind," he said, adapting a section of the U.S. Army Ranger Creed.

"And Tallmadge," I added, "we have to trust one another totally. Trust needs time to build, but we don't have the luxury of time. So I'm asking you straight out: Can we trust you? Should we trust you?"

Benny looked up at him. "I think we can; can't we, Tallmadge?"

I wanted to reach across the coffee table and slap her. She was thinking with her hormones, not her head.

Tallmadge was quiet for a moment; then he responded. "I am a vampire first, and to the vampire race I owe my loyalty before king and country, before lover or child. You are vampires too. Because of that, I give you my allegiance and my solemn word that you can trust me. I will never betray another vampire. I will never betray you." He stopped here, put his wineglass down, then resumed speaking. "As for being a Darkwing . . . I didn't volunteer to be a spy. I care little for the government of this country."

"But . . . ?" I began.

Tallmadge held his hand up and continued: "But," he said with a charming, almost boyish smile, "I love liberty. I love America. I love this city. I have nothing but contempt for the terrorists who attacked it. I don't know if they are behind this assassin, this Gage, although it's possible they are. And despite being recruited through coercion under threat of death, I do feel a sense of privilege in being given an opportunity to be a guardian. I may reject human morality; I may live for the dark pleasures of my race, but I reject mindless violence and fanaticism. I am not entirely degenerate, you know."

"Of course not!" Benny said. "We never said that."

"*You* never said that, sweet thing. Miss Urban, however, is thinking it." With that, Tallmadge again took out a cigar from his inner pocket, and this time he lit it, pulling the smoke into his mouth and blowing it out in my direction. His lips were very red and his teeth were very white. "And Agent O'Reilly may be thinking it too, although I think he doesn't care very much."

"I have no reason not to think it," I said, folding my arms across my chest. "You belong to a vampire club, and, in fact, you flaunt your sybaritic lifestyle. Benny, forgive me, but you've been a vampire for only eighty years, and you spent seventy-nine and a half of those years in Branson, Missouri. . . ."

"And that makes me a hick, now, don't it?" Benny said with an edge.

"No, it makes you an innocent. And I love that innocence, but it leaves you vulnerable to . . . to the kind of things Tallmadge indulges in."

"Well, Miss Daphne Urban," she said, getting huffy, "maybe you think nights getting drunk in a shitty motel room halfway to nowhere with some rockabilly star with grease under his fingernails was a barrel of fun. Well, it wasn't, but it was all I had. Now, you know, I want to see more of the world, this world—a vampire's world. Is that so damned terrible?"

Cormac had put his head in his hands. He and I had been

where Benny was now, only it was centuries ago. He and I had lived the life, and, like me, he had left it. I guess I wasn't being fair to expect Benny not to taste it for herself and make up her own mind.

"No, no, it's not terrible. Not at all. Just be careful; that's all I'm saying."

"You know, Daphne, you can be a condescending bitch. I can take care of myself," she said, obviously pissed at me.

"I didn't mean it that way. I apologize," I said for the second time that night. *Two strikes*, I said to myself. *Three and you're liable to lose your best friend, so shut up!*

"Daphne and Cormac," Tallmadge said in his silky tones. "Let's not get off on the wrong foot here. I look at things differently, and I just ask you to keep an open mind." He tapped the cigar ash into an ashtray as he spoke, then took another series of deep puffs, watching the pungent white smoke sail slowly upward. "I don't see any reason not to experience as much pleasure as I can. I smoke. Why not? It poses no health risk to me. And I'll be up-front with you: I do indulge in other addictive substances, but not when I have work to do. I will not distract myself, I promise you, when we are on a mission. But as for the rest—the 'fun and games,' as I call them— what's the harm? We are not humans. Why should we behave like them? And Miss Urban, Mr. O'Reilly, can you honestly tell me you do not, that you have not recently, drunk human blood?"

"Of course," I said dismissively. "All vampires do."

"Oh, Miss Urban, you know I don't mean blood you have bought from a blood bank. I mean warm, living blood from a human's sweet neck. Can you look me in the eye and tell me you have not. . . and that you don't think about, dream about, hunger for it?"

Cormac didn't bother to deny it. I had never delved into

his vampire habits, but I knew him to be discreet and selective. If he drank living blood, it was from a lover or willing partner, not from a victim; that much I did know. And I? I had bitten my lover Darius and made him into a monster that he loathed. But I said, lying to Tallmadge by omitting that one slip in a century, "I may think about it, I may even dream about it, but I choose not to do it."

"Oh, Miss Urban, why? Why do you deprive yourself of the ultimate pleasure? Humans want to be our slaves, you know."

I did know. I had long ago decided not to prey on that weakness. I believed that since I was more than human, I could be better than humans, and I certainly had the power to use my strengths and my gifts to be something more than a corrupter . . . or worse, a killer. But all I said was, "We can debate this again sometime, Tallmadge. For now, let's just agree to disagree. I have somewhere else to go tonight, and before I leave, I'd like the team to talk about this assassin Gage, and what we're up against."

"And what are we up against, in your opinions?" he asked the three of us.

Cormac answered: "We don't have much to go on at this point. We have to find Gage and stop him—in a little over a week. We know that much," Cormac said, "but do we know anything more?"

"We know who else has been killed. Is there any connection between the victims?" Benny jumped in, proving once again she was no dumb blonde.

"I can take on researching that," Tallmadge offered, stubbing out his cigar.

"Perfect," I said. "Any other ideas?"

"Do we have any surveillance photos of Gage?" Benny added.

"Maybe they are on the computer disk," I guessed.

"And maybe they aren't," Tallmadge said with sarcasm. "I'll look for photos of the other assassinations. Maybe the shooter was caught on camera. The victims were shot, weren't they?"

"I think so, but maybe one of them was blown up," I said.

"I'll check it out," Tallmadge said, "and see if any organization took credit for the killings, too."

"Some of this may be on the disk," I pointed out. "Don't duplicate effort more than you have to."

"Agent Urban, you have a lot more faith that what's on those disks will be helpful than I do. So far I think calling our organization an intelligence agency is a contradiction in terms. And you can stop me when I'm lying."

I didn't respond, but I was thinking that Tallmadge's negativity could become a problem.

"Daphne and Benny can try to find out if anybody in Daniel's entourage is behind the plot," Cormac spoke up. "I can't. I'm still in purgatory. Oops, I mean Opus Dei's headquarters, but same difference. Daphne, I do need you to talk to Mar-Mar—or to get me in to see her."

"I'll do my best, Cormac. I don't know if my intervention will help, but I'll try. I mean that," I replied.

"Look, tell her I'm ready to quit. It's not just the huge crucifixes on the depressing dark-paneled walls, the chanting, and worse, the self-flagellation with the whip they call 'the Discipline' and the cilice digging into their thighs that give members of the order a smug, self-righteous expression—as if I didn't know they're getting off on their secret pain. It's that I'm isolated. I'm sitting on my hands there. Bubba showed me that I am a warrior, not a wimp. I can't play the fool anymore. This is eating me up, Daphne. It really is."

"I'll talk to her, I promise, Cormac. She's supposed to see

me before dawn. I'll call you. I will," I said, reaching out and lightly touching his sleeve. Cormac, the pouting, spoiled dilettante, had changed. I saw something immense and good happening to him. I didn't want him to act stupid and screw everything up.

"Daphne, let's meet up tomorrow and head to Daniel's headquarters together. I'll stop by your building around six, okay?" Benny said, breaking into my musings.

"Sure. Sounds good," I said, taking the olive branch being offered.

"What else should we be doing?" Tallmadge asked.

"I honestly don't know," I said, lying again. It's a habit I can't seem to break, but right then, there were things I didn't want to reveal to Tallmadge about me and my family. Maybe I could trust him, and maybe I couldn't. To me, the jury was still out. I intended to talk to Mar-Mar about some people she knew, the kind of people who could put me in contact with a local hit man. I figured if anybody knew who Gage was, it was another assassin. For all I knew, Mar-Mar was thinking exactly the same thing.

"Well, let's touch base by phone if we need to. If not, let's meet again tomorrow—late, after midnight. Will that work?" Tallmadge asked while he took out his wallet. "Here's a card with my phone numbers on it, cell and home." He handed cards to Benny, Cormac, and me.

I took mine and said, "Where will we meet?"

"Here," he said, smiling and sweeping his arm to encompass the room. "You've seen for yourself, Daphne—there are no opium dens, no orgies. Just comfortable, safe, and very private surroundings. I'll have dinner ready for us. Cormac, can you get over here from Opus Dei on a break?"

"Sure. What are they going to do? Fire me? I should be so lucky," he said bitterly.

"Okay, Agent Urban. Are you in?"

Benny had fixed me with her eyes. I knew what she wanted. "It's against my better judgment, but all right. Here. Midnight," I said, and stood up. "Benny, Cormac? Are you guys ready to go?"

Cormac unfolded his legs and stood, slipping his loafers back on. "Yeah, I've got someplace to go too."

"Benjamina, if you don't have any other plans, why don't you stay and dine with me?" Tallmadge asked, turning his charm full blast in her direction.

"Why, thank you, Tallmadge. That's right kind of you. I sure would like to stay," she cooed.

"Benny . . ." I started to say, but she sent me a look that said, *Butt out,* so I did. I wasn't happy about leaving her here. Not happy at all.

Tallmadge picked up a house phone and told someone that Cormac and I would be leaving. Very quickly Cathary appeared at the door, our coats in his hands. "I'll show you out," he said as we put on our outerwear.

I took a last look at Benny as Cormac and I walked out of the room. She and Tallmadge were standing face-to-face and very close together. Her skin was glowing, and her eyes were so fixated on the good-looking vampire before her that she didn't even say good-bye.

I didn't see any other hooded men on our way down the stairs, and on the ground floor the open sitting room was empty and quiet as a tomb. Orgies? I was sure they were going on here, and what else was occurring I could only imagine. To confirm my suspicions, the front door hadn't quite closed behind us when I heard from the dark bowels of the mansion a man's muffled groan. . . not a groan of pain, but of ecstasy.

*   *   *

A few minutes later I entered a small private hospital in
Chelsea through the emergency room entrance. It was past
midnight and visiting hours were over, but I had pulled some
strings and a pass was waiting for me. St. Julien Fitzmaurice,
a Secret Service agent, was in a high-security area of the fa-
cility, and he was, I had been informed, still in serious condi-
tion, but slowly improving. I had wrangled a fifteen-minute
visit, and was told they'd throw me out if I stayed a minute
longer.

For me Fitz represented, as far as intimate relationships
go, a road not taken, or not yet taken. When I met him I
thought he was one of the world's sweetest guys. Then I believed he was a drug dealer, but he turned out to be a Secret
Service agent investigating some highly influential U.S. offi-
cials who'd played a pivotal role in importing a lethal recre-
ational drug to the United States. My agency was
investigating the same drug, and the lack of disclosure between agencies nearly got Fitz killed when he tried to protect
me. As it was, he had been grievously wounded, and the road
to recovery looked like a long and rocky one. I owed him a
visit, and probably an apology. I seemed to be doing a lot of
that tonight.

I passed through two checkpoints where armed guards
scrutinized my pass and government ID. Finally I started
down a long hallway lit by fluorescent lights. The white
linoleum tile on the floor was so highly polished my eyes
ached in the glare. My stomach churned from the smells of
disinfectant, illness, and death that hung over this place like
a miasma. I let out a sigh. If only I had known who Fitz really
was, so much pain could have been avoided. I was truly getting tired of no one being who he appeared to be.

All my life I had had to lie about who I was. I had a string
of phony identities. I wore a mask every time I stepped into

the street. I appeared to be human; I wasn't. I appeared to be young; I was not, although I was physically stuck in late adolescence, and as I said, my hormonal drive had gotten me into trouble again and again. It also made me moody and recalcitrant, rebellious and sometimes just plain wild. But after centuries on this planet I was developing a powerful yearning for honesty. As much as I lied, I wanted to know someone who did not. As much as I dissembled, I wanted someone I could believe in. But I had to face facts: In the spy business, my chances of meeting a person like that were slim to none.

I had thought, for a short period of time, that Fitz was that person. Once again I had been proven wrong. At the end of the long corridor I found his room and slipped inside, shutting the door behind me. A night-light illuminated the head of the bed, and the green glow of the monitoring machine's LED readouts gave his long, handsome face a sickly pallor. He appeared to be sleeping. I pulled up a chair next to the bed and sat down, just looking at him. I reached out and gently put my hand on his.

"Your hands are still cold," Fitz said. His eyes opened, and stared at me.

"Thin blood, remember?" I responded, and smiled. "I'm sorry I woke you up."

"Don't be. I'm happy you're here. I wasn't really asleep. I doze on and off all night, and all day too. There's not much else to do," he said, his voice thready and weak. Curls tumbled down across his forehead; the deep cleft in his chin was a dark hollow in the stubble of his beard. His body lay broken and bandaged, with his legs under the white sheet. Tubes tethered him to machines that beeped with the rhythm of his heart. Yet my eyes drifted to his clearly defined pecs, the six-pack of his abs, the tattoo on his shoulder. Fitz was big and strong-boned, of black-Irish heritage with an Irishman's love of risk and whiskey, although from his size, I suspected Viking blood ran in his veins as well.

"How do you feel?" I asked.

"Alive, and that's all that counts," he said, turning his hand over and folding his fingers over mine.

"I came to say I'm sorry about getting you shot," I said.

"Daphne, you didn't have anything to do with it. Rodriguez was already suspicious of me. If you hadn't been there to call for help, I might be dead. Don't apologize to me. You don't *ever* have to apologize to me," he said, his voice suddenly stronger than a moment ago.

"Yes, I do. About a lot of things, and for misjudging you," I said, sadness turning my words into broken pieces, making them catch in my throat and mingle with the tears I never shed.

"You couldn't have known what I didn't want you to know. But I was going to tell you I was working undercover. I didn't want to keep lying to you, and I knew I could trust you."

"Fitz, you can't," I said bitterly.

"Can't? Can't trust you? Why?"

"Because there's a lot about me you don't know, and I don't know if I'll ever have the courage to tell you," I said, more open than I had ever been with a human before.

"What makes you think I don't know your secrets already? I know you have, or had, a lover. I know he's gone. And I know a lot of other things about you," he said, his voice hard. His hand tightened on mine, and, with a strength I didn't know he possessed, he pulled me out of my chair and close to him, until I was leaning over him, our faces inches apart. "Don't you understand, Daphne? Those things don't matter. I've seen your loyalty. I've seen your passion. I know how you were when we were together. I know there is goodness in you."

"No—" I started to protest.

"Yes. I don't know who hurt you so much that you don't believe in yourself, but Daphne, I'm not going to hurt you. And I believe in you."

"Please don't. I'll only disappoint you. You don't know . . ." I went to step back. His grip on my hand held me close to him. For a wounded man, he was unbelievably strong.

"Daphne," he said in an urgent voice. "Listen to me. I'm not asking anything of you, for *now*. All I will ask is that when I'm out of here that you give us a chance. Give *me* a chance to treat you like you deserve to be treated. To love you like you deserve to be loved." His steel gray eyes looked steadily at me. His lips were inches from mine. What else could I do? I lowered my face to his and kissed him. His other hand, with its IV line, came up and held the back of my head as his lips devoured mine, hard and hungry, his tongue pushing into my mouth. Desire made my stomach clench. The room started to spin. I wanted to stretch my body out on top of his and feel the length of him beneath me. I wanted to touch him naked from chest to toes. I wanted to seek out his neck with my teeth and—

Just then his hand left the back of my head and slipped under my sweater, sliding up my stomach until his fingers found my breast. I stopped thinking. I was breathless. With our lips still locked, his hand gently left my breast and stroked down my torso, leaving a burning trail that was consuming me with fire. He quickly unbuttoned my jeans and pushed them down far enough to give his fingers access to my wet, hungry center. I moaned into his mouth. My legs were beginning to tremble, but I had the presence of mind to push my jeans free from my hips until they fell around my ankles.

Fitz broke the kiss, but kept an iron grip on my hand as he whispered in a hoarse, urgent voice, "Take them off and come to me."

"I'll hurt you," I protested.

"My face isn't going to be hurt," he said, finally releasing my hand. "Kneel on the bed on either side of my chest and lean into me, Daphne."

My passions raging, I didn't have to be asked twice. I yanked off my boots, stripped off my jeans and panties, and mounted the bed. I spread my naked thighs over him, and, grasping the iron bars on the headboard of the hospital bed, I leaned forward until his mouth met my nether lips, slippery with my fluids, throbbing with need. His teeth grazed my bud, sending shock waves of pleasure through me. His tongue licked and searched as his hands came up and between my legs. His fingers spread my lips, allowing him entrance to the sweet, dark tunnel, which he opened with his thumbs and entered with his tongue. I moaned and shuddered as he plunged into me again and again. My fingers tightened on the bars and my back arched.

Then Fitz moved his hands to my bare ass and pulled me harder against his mouth, as he licked upward to my bud again, and this time he closed his lips around it, pulling and sucking on me as I moaned, "Ohhh, ohhh, ohhhh, don't, please, please, don't, don't stop, don't stop." With my head flung back and my eyes closed, I was all feeling, reveling in the unbelievable pleasure. My moans came faster and faster as the delicious sensations washed over me. I pumped myself in and out against his mouth and, shaking, I came, long, warm streams of pure pleasure pulsing hard, racking me from head to toe.

Only when I stopped moving did Fitz relax his hold on my ass. Carefully I pulled myself off of him and the bed. I stood up, looking at him with eyes heavy lidded and half closed with fulfillment.

Sated and stunned, I was breathing heavily. My lips—all of them—felt bruised. And good, so very good. Fitz watched me, never taking his eyes from me.

"That was . . . was . . . incredible," I said softly. "Thank you." I leaned over and picked up my underwear and jeans, pulling them on. Then I sat in a chair and put my boots back on.

Fitz kert looking at me all the while. Finally he said, "Daphne. I want you. I've wanted you from the moment I saw you."

"And now you've had me, but you're making a mistake," I said sadly. "If you knew me, you wouldn't want me. You're a wonderful man, Saint Fitz, and I'm not who you think I am."

"Why do you think so little of me, Daphne? I'm telling you that I can not only accept *who* you are, but I can embrace *what* you are. Let me prove it to you," he said, and struggled up to his elbows.

I left my chair and put my hand on his shoulder and carefully pushed him back. I took a tissue from the bed table and moistened it from a pitcher of water. Gently, tenderly, I wiped his face clean of me. Then I brushed my lips across his and said, "Fitz, one thing I know about you is that you're not going to take no for an answer." I was smiling now. "So save your strength to get out of here, and we'll take it from there. You've made me greedy, and I want more, please. Agreed?"

He collapsed back on the pillows, his biceps trembling a little from the exertion of holding me. When his eyes closed, his eyelids had a bluish tinge. Whatever strength he had was used up, but he was smiling.

"I'd better go now. Get some rest," I said softly. "I'll come back when I can, but some stuff's about to jump off. I might not be able to get here right away."

Fitz opened his eyes and lifted them to my face. "Daphne, I know you're on a mission. Don't ask me how I know. I have my sources, as they say. It's not important to visit this place. What's important is for you to survive and live to get the bastards. When I'm better, I'll find you and make good on my promise. And Daphne . . ."

"What, Fitz?" I said in a voice barely above a whisper.

"You deserve better than Darius. Yes, I know his name. I intend to show you how much better," he said. "Remember that."

A great sadness opened up inside me. Was it really possible Fitz could love me once he discovered I was a vampire? Could I ever love Fitz when Darius had an adamantine hold on my heart and soul, his blood in my veins and mine in his? I just didn't know. I did know, however, that a door to desire had been opened, one I could not easily close. "I'll remember, Fitz. Just get better, okay?"

His eyes had shut again. "One more thing—you heard about my mother?"

"Just what I read in the paper. She killed Bradley because she thought he murdered you."

He smiled, his eyes still closed. "Who knew Delores Fitzmaurice would turn into Dirty Harry? She's okay, by the way. They've stashed her in a posh sanitarium in Florida. Her lawyers are preparing a defense that she went crazy with grief. That's not true, you know."

"Having met your mother, I can say with some assurance that she's about as crazy as a fox," I said in a light voice.

"Daphne, since you have already met my family, I don't

know why you're worried that your secrets would shock me," he said, still smiling with his eyes shut.

"That's because you haven't met *my* relatives yet." I laughed. I leaned over him and brushed my lips on his; then I kissed his eyelids. "Go to sleep, Fitz. Sweet dreams."

"I'll dream of you," he said as I quietly slipped out the door.

CHAPTER 4

Non-cooperation with evil is a sacred duty.

—Mohandas Gandhi

As I walked through the front door of my apartment, my phone was ringing. My land line has an encryption device on it. For security reasons, my mother refuses to call me on my cell phone unless it's an emergency. Ditto with J. Depending on what's going on in our lives, Darius calls me on either one. I hoped he wasn't calling. I had just cheated on him and felt no shame at all. I felt exhilarated and hoped the chains that had bound me to him had broken. But, to tell the truth, I wasn't ready to find out. So for once I was glad when I discovered the caller was my mother, Mar-Mar.

"Daphne. I can't see you tonight," she said, the words tumbling out in a rush.

I mentally shrugged. Emotionally exhausted by the intensity of my lovemaking with Fitz, I was relieved that she wasn't going to show. "No problem. Everything all right?" I asked distractedly while I thumbed through the mail I had just picked up from the lobby.

"I'm in the middle of a project. But listen, I need you to do something important for me."

I forgot the mail; my senses went on full alert. "What's going on?" I asked, suspicion immediately forming and making me wary.

"You have to get hold of Cormac, and not by cell phone."

At first I was surprised by her request; then I figured J had spoken with her after the meeting, and that she knew Cormac had reached his limits of frustration. "I'm going to see Cormac tomorrow," I offered.

"It has to be tonight. We're running out of time," she ordered.

"Time for what? Is this about Joe Daniel's assassination?"

"No, it's about your father," she said, her voice hollow.

Frustrated and confused, I burst out, "He's been dead for over four hundred years! Why are you bringing him up now? You never wanted to talk about him before."

"Maybe it is time to talk to you about him. And I will. But right now you need to tell Cormac to locate a vault or some kind of security room in one of the subbasements at Opus Dei's headquarters."

"Why?" I asked, suspecting by now that she had been planning something with Opus Dei for a long time. In truth, I wasn't completely surprised by Mar-Mar's interest, since ties between the secretive sect and U.S. intelligence had surfaced in the media a few years ago. Former FBI director Louis Freeh was said to be a member. Even Supreme Court Justices Antonin Scalia and Clarence Thomas had been linked to the strange group after FBI intelligence expert Robert Hanssen, an Opus Dei supernumerary member, was arrested for being a longtime spy for the Soviet Union. Another odd fact had surfaced that linked all the men: Hanssen, Scalia, and Freeh all attended Mass at St. Catherine of Siena parish in Great Falls, Virginia, a Mass still offered in Latin despite the Vatican's orders against doing so.

I didn't believe in coincidence. A web of association and belief entwined all these men, and Opus Dei hid more than it revealed about what they did and who they really were. If I had bothered to think about why Cormac had been planted there, I might not have been so floored by what Mar-Mar said next.

"We need to break in there tomorrow night. We need to get our hands on Vatican files that were given to Opus Dei in some kind of trade."

"Files? Are they about my father?" I asked.

"Yes. At least, I'm that's what I'm hoping."

I couldn't believe what I was hearing. My quick temper rose before I could stop it. "Excuse me, but are you out of your mind? We have an assassination to stop. We don't have time for this right now."

"Daphne, listen to your mother. This needs to be done, and done as quickly as possible. After all these months, Cormac should seem like a harmless fixture at Opus Dei. No one will suspect him of anything if he goes snooping around. This is urgent. You need to trust me on this."

"Judas Priest!" I yelled. "Do I have any choice? What are you not telling me?" My hand tightened on the phone receiver.

"Daphne, take a deep breath. I'll explain everything when I see you. Just do what I ask. Please. No more questions. Just go."

I stood there without speaking, wanting to refuse but not able to say no. Mar-Mar was my mother and, God help me, some kind of director in the agency I worked for. She was my boss in every way possible. I sighed in resignation. Opus Dei headquarters was at Thirty-fourth Street and Lexington, relatively close to Tallmadge's club. I felt as if I were backtracking. It was late; I wanted to walk Jade, review the material on the computer disk, then slide into my coffin for a good day's sleep. I thought, *What a pain in the butt.* I said, "I'll go down there now. I have to take Jade out anyway."

"That won't work," Mar-Mar said flatly.

"Why not?" I said, figuring I didn't have all that much time before dawn.

"Women and men are strictly segregated at Opus Dei. Cormac is in the men's section. Even if he meets you outside, it would attract less attention if you looked like a man. A young priest would be optimal. Showing up with a large dog that looks like a wolf is not a good idea."

I had to say something about her expecting me to ask, "How high?" when she said, "Jump." The best I could blurt out was, "Mar-Mar, I'm not happy to be doing this right now."

"Your happiness is not an issue here, Daphne. This isn't about you," she said brusquely.

I saw that we were headed for an argument, so I decided to end the call. "I'd better get going. I only have a few hours left before dawn."

"I agree. I'll be in touch—love you," Mar-Mar said, and hung up.

Jade wanted to go out. No matter how pressed I felt to create a disguise and get down to Opus Dei headquarters, some things—like time, tide, and a dog needing to pee—do not wait. I slipped Jade's choke chain over her huge head while she grinned, her pink tongue lolling out of her mouth. Gunther stood up in his cage, gripping the bars with his pale rat hands, wanting to go with us, but I just said, "Sorry, pal, not tonight," as Jade and I rushed out the door. Even rushed and preoccupied, I have no excuse for what happened once we got to the park.

The night in its darkest hours had draped Riverside Park in funereal black. Not another soul stirred. The only noise was the wind whistling through the trees. The dog park was officially closed, but I went in anyway. The area being empty, I slipped off Jade's leash and watched her amble around, sniffing the "good spots" where other dogs had marked their territory. The wind raced down the Hudson River from the north, carrying with it a damp, merciless cold. It sent my long hair streaming out behind me. I sank my hands into my pockets and focused inward, trying to remember where I had put the priest's cassock I had picked up in Ireland a half century before. Its black fabric had turned rusty with age, but it would do.

Oblivious to my surroundings, I looked up only when Jade began barking wildly. I saw two men vaulting the fence. While one of them threw a net over my dog, the other jabbed her with a hypodermic needle. I started to rush forward, but I didn't get anywhere. I was yanked backward by my hair, landing on my ass in the dirt. A big-bellied guy wrapped fat fingers around my neck, pushing on my windpipe, trying to crush me into the earth. With a hiss I showed my fangs and grabbed his face with one hand, pressing into his eye sockets with my thumb and forefinger. He pulled back, screaming, "You little bitch!"

As soon as the pressure left my neck, I jumped up and hit him hard in the temple with my elbow. His tree-trunk legs crumbled under him and he went down, stunned from the blow. I looked over to where the two men were now lifting the limp figure of my dog in the net over the fence and lowering her to the ground on the other side. Before I could move toward them, the man I had hit regained his senses, grabbed my ankle, and pulled me off my feet. Once again I hit the ground, this time face-first; I barely broke my fall with my arms. I spit dirt out of my mouth. This guy was getting annoying. I needed to put him out of commission.

I looked over my shoulder. He was coming at me with a

knife in his hand. I rolled to my right, sprang up, and butted him in the stomach with my head, pushing him backward. The wire-mesh fence clanged as his back smashed into it. The knife flashed as he stabbed upward, but he missed me as I jumped to the side and decided to follow the slam into the fence with an uppercut I was aiming to land right under the guy's chin. I flexed my legs and my fist came up with tremendous power. His head snapped to the left from the force of my blow. It was a classic one-punch knockout. His eyes rolled back in his head, and he slumped to the ground.

Okay, one down, two to go, I thought as I whirled around. The men and my dog were gone.

As desperation took a grip on my heart, I ripped off my clothes in the frigid night to transform into the creature I was within. The cold no longer mattered as a swirling vortex of energy surrounded me, lighting up the night with flashes of color. I grew in size to over ten feet in height and, with a rustle that seemed to issue from the depths of hell, wings emerged from my back. My fingers became claws, and my pale white skin turned into a sleek, dark pelt with prismatic hairs that caused shimmering colors to dance over its surface. While my face retained its human features, my eyes turned into golden orbs—animal, not human eyes, yet vastly different from the deep black ones of the chiropteran that I resembled, but was not. Now, with the monster within me released, my dark side became manifest. Euphoria filled me. I was beautiful; I was powerful; I was terrifying.

And I was deeply angry. I leaped into the air and flew off, searching for the men who had stolen my dog. Dodging the trees, I gained height until I spotted them loading her into the back of a green van parked nearly a block away. As I swooped toward them, the men jumped into the front seat and began driving off. But not for long. I went into a dive and landed on the top of the vehicle, causing a loud bang as I hit the metal.

"What the . . ." one of the men yelled as he hit the brakes, perhaps hoping to shake me off.

It didn't work. I simply reached down with my clawed hands and tore the driver's-side door from its hinges. The passenger-side door flew open, and both men bolted from it into the night. The van rolled gently into the curb and halted. I sprang into the air once more, and the dog thieves ran as if the devil pursued them. With a high-pitched whistle I barreled into the driver, knocking him down with my shoulder, then landed in front of him. He started to get up until, seeing me, he fell to his knees. His body trembled like a leaf in the wind, his eyes wild with terror.

"Who sent you to do this thing? Is my dog to be held hostage to stop my investigation?" I hissed at him, but he seemed insensible and unhearing, struck dumb with horror. When I reached out and grabbed his shirt in my claws, lifting him as if he were a rag doll, he fainted. *Some tough guy.* I dropped him to the pavement. He stank. He had shit himself as well.

I sailed back over to the van and flung open the back doors. Jade lay entangled in the net, breathing raggedly but beginning to stir. I gathered the edges of the net in my talons and became airborne again, Jade hanging below me in a kind of sling. Returning to the dog park in seconds, I carefully lowered my burden and fluttered to the ground. With a howling rush of encircling winds and another blast of energy that sent strobe lights bouncing off the tree branches, I became human again, naked in the winter air and now cold—cold as death.

I dressed quickly. Jade was trying to stand, and I hurried to her and pulled the net away. I steadied her, talking with her, encouraging her. For me to carry a 120-pound dog all the way to my apartment would be possible, but uncomfortable. Once she regained her feet I found her choke chain in the dirt and slipped it over her great head, which she shook, trying to regain her balance. On shaky legs she took one step and then another. Although our progress was slow, we made it home, and with each step a bright, hard flame of hatred grew in me. I would find out who had tried to take her. And I would destroy them.

After I had given Jade fresh water, she settled into her dog bed in the kitchen and closed her eyes. I didn't know if she was capable of hating the way I did, but Jade was a formidable opponent. I felt that she would not be taken unawares again. Her enemies had made themselves known to her by their scents. I vowed that it was only a matter of time before they became known to me by their names.

Which brought me to the task that lay before me. It was already past three a.m. I had precious little time to get to Cormac, deliver my message, and return before dawn. I was not about to be caught by the light and be forced to spend the day hiding at Opus Dei or bunking with Cormac in his shoe box–size Greenwich Village apartment.

I spent a hasty five minutes doing a computer search of Opus Dei. Forewarned is forearmed, I always say. Then I scooted into my bedroom and pulled a priest's cassock from a storage box beneath my bed. It smelled musty and faintly like someone's Old Spice aftershave from long ago. Bulking up my figure with a thermal shirt and sweater, I pulled on the long cassock, hid my hair inside a wide-brimmed hat, donned a pair of tinted eyeglasses, and even found a fake mustache to wear in my top drawer. I often needed disguises; I could have opted for a full beard. No need, I decided when I looked in the mirror. My own mother wouldn't recognize me.

Then I picked up the phone and called the number I had for Cormac at Opus Dei. Using the phony Italian accent he and I had used back in the 1980s to throw *SNL* lines back and forth—during those occasional periods when we were friends—I pinched my nose and said in a nasal tone: " 'Ello? Pippistrello Pizzeria, calling abouta da order."

"Huh? It's after three in the morning. Who ordered it? Father Gordo again?" Cormac said in an annoyed voice.

"We be down dere in twenty minute. Where I take?" I asked, dumbfounded that Cormac was so frigging dense.

"Ring the buzzer at the men's entrance. On Lex," Cormac said, and hung up.

Terrific. You're a crackerjack spy, all right, Cormac, I thought, and headed for the door.

After a fast cab ride downtown, during which the tired cabbie never gave me a second glance or said a word after asking where to, I stepped onto the empty sidewalk in front of Opus Dei's arched wooden door. I rang the bell, and stood there until I felt the cold cement through the soles of my boots. I rang the bell again.

Cormac finally flung the door open, a scowl on his face, saying, "Keep your pants on— Hey, who are you?" he asked. "I thought you were the pizza guy."

I kept my voice low—Opus Dei is such a secretive organization they probably even had the doorstep bugged—and said, "Pssst, Cormac, it's me."

"Heh? I can't hear you! Speak up, Father," he demanded, opening the door wider. "Who did you say you were? Where are you from?"

Oh, my God, I thought, then took a deep breath and said in the most pompous voice I could muster, "I am Father Guido

Sarducci, from Roma. I am supposed to have a room waiting in the men's quarters." With that I pushed past Cormac into the vestibule, which wasn't much warmer than the sidewalk, whispering, "It's Daphne, you idiot!"

As I entered the stark, small lobby, my boots struck sharply against the linoleum tile floor, echoing with every step. Everything in the room had hard edges and drab colors. I felt confined and threatened, as if this were a prison, not a religious institution.

Cormac's eyes widened. "Uh, Father Sarducci, come over here to the desk and let me check whether there's a note left about your arrival," he said, acting solicitous. As we walked, he whispered back, "What are you doing here?" When we reached the desk, Cormac leaned over as if to pick up a pen and leaf through a register book while he surreptitiously turned up the sound on a small portable TV.

I bent over the wooden desk too, keeping my face toward the wall, hoping the cameras that were scanning the lobby saw only my back. When Cormac put his head close to mine, I began to speak quickly. "Mar-Mar wants you to find files stored in a vault or secure room in one of the building's sub-basements and figure out how we can get them."

"What! When?" he breathed.

"Tonight. We're going to bust into it tomorrow."

"No way. That's crazy," he said, his voice rising and taking on a hysterical edge.

"Way, Cormac, way. You've got maybe two hours before dawn. Now get me the hell out of here."

"Father," Cormac straightened up and announced. "As you can see, there's nothing here in my book about a room being prepared for you."

"How annoying. Totally incompetent. Father Echevarria will be told of this, " I said, remembering the name of the order's prelate at the Vatican from my recent Googling of Opus Dei. Pursing my lips beneath my mustache while pulling my hat lower over my eyes, I continued: "But perhaps I'd better seek a hotel tonight and straighten this out in the morning."

"That would be best," Cormac agreed. His face had paled, and a worried frown formed parallel tracks between his brows. He rushed over to the door and pulled it wide open for me. I bent my head down against the wind and walked out as fast as I could, preferring the cold night to the oppressive atmosphere inside Opus Dei.

I got back to my apartment without incident. Jade was peacefully sleeping off whatever drug had been injected into her, breathing regularly and making doggy snoring sounds. I still had some time before dawn, so I slipped the CD J had given each of us into my computer. I hoped to find some kick-ass intelligence about the assassin.

I opened the file marked GAGE and discovered a surveillance camera video that, even if it was enhanced, didn't reveal much. All I could see was a figure in a long coat and ski mask moving through a hallway carrying what appeared to be a large, deadly-looking rifle. Text accompanying the grainy pictures didn't identify the figure. It identified the weapon as a Barrett Model 95 M107 ten-round .50-caliber semiautomatic, the same gun officially adopted by the United States Army for use in the war in Afghanistan and Iraq. Specifically the M107 was the weapon of choice for sniper teams for precision long-range fire. It appeared to be a fine weapon for an assassin. Since the text also noted that the M107 weighs nearly thirty-five pounds, I could deduce that Gage was no flabby hit man but a trained soldier.

Who trained him? I wondered. As far as I was concerned, Gage had Special Forces written all over him. One person who would know that for sure was my own Darius, former navy SEAL and current undercover operative for— I'm guessing about this—the Department of Military Intelligence.

But I wasn't guessing about the fact that he had lived among the tight coterie of elite fighting men called Navy SEALs and Army Rangers for a long time. He must know if any of them had turned rogue. I was sure he could tell me something about the mysterious assassin. I wanted to discuss my ideas with Darius so badly that a wave of longing washed over me. If he called on the encrypted landline, I intended to ask him. I just didn't know exactly how to work it into a conversation that was probably going to start something like, *You bastard! Why didn't you just tell me Julie was over there with you?*

Okay, after what happened with Fitz tonight I probably had no business getting on my own high horse, but I wasn't going to bring that up. I could rationalize that I did what I did out of sexual frustration and a subconscious need to pay Darius back for hurting me again. I could say that, but I didn't know if it was true. My emotions had been whirled around in a food processor and I couldn't sort them out. To be honest with myself, I had to confess that if he walked through the door tonight, I might scream at him in rage, but I would still want him. Oh, yes, I'd still want him no matter how drawn to Fitz I had been. I still loved Darius, as stupid and self-destructive as it might be.

I knew the two saddest truths in life: There is no Santa Claus, and sex is not love.

Bringing my wandering thoughts back to the information on the CD, I finished reading the file on Gage. It took maybe two minutes. Basically, it was this:

Age: unknown
Nationality: unknown, but believed to be American
Whereabouts: unknown
Background: unknown
Associates: unknown
Modus operandi: gunshots from an M107, or plastic ex-
plosives detonated precisely at the right time to kill the
target (something very difficult to achieve)

Add to that "helpful" fund of knowledge the agency's ad-
mission that no one knew how Gage bypassed security to get
close to his victims.

I scanned the other computer files on the disk. One was on
Joe A. Daniel. It gave a standard bio, similar to the material
found on a dozen Web sites, including Daniel's own. In brief,
it summarized that Daniel was a retired Special Forces master sergeant with combat experience in Desert Storm and
Afghanistan. He had survived a helicopter crash in Kuwait
when he was thrown free before the Black Hawk exploded.
His teeth had been shattered (he now wore dentures), some
ribs and his pelvis were cracked, but he was otherwise unharmed. The crash killed everybody else.

Ten years later, he had earned a Silver Star medal, the
army's third-highest award for military service, in the moun-
tains of Afghanistan, in a lawless tribal area on the border
with Pakistan that the locals call Wziristan. In 2002 he had
been badly wounded by a roadside bomb in Kandahar and
lost a leg. Despite his injuries, Daniel insisted even as he was
being medevaced out that he knew it wasn't his time to die.
He talked about beating death twice for a reason, although he
didn't know what that reason was.

After some time in Germany, Daniel was flown back to the
States for series of painful surgeries. During his rehab, he

read the words of Mohandas Gandhi and experienced what he called an epiphany that awakened his mind and transformed his soul. He came out of the hospital with the zeal of a true believer that war was wrong and the only answer was peace. He had come to believe that we were killing not only one another, but our planet.

Only months later he ran for Congress in Illinois as a Green candidate. He stunned both the Democrats and Republicans by winning, and winning big. Now he had dedicated his life to changing minds and hearts. Nobody had a bad word to say about him, even his ex-wife. He seemed to have no vices. He was beloved by his staff and by his army buddies. Some called him a saint.

That's interesting, I thought. Despite my conviction that an opponent wanted Daniel dead, I had to consider the possibility that someone close to Daniel wanted to further the cause by making him a martyr. And dead saints were easier to manipulate than live ones.

I quickly read through the four other bios—one on Daniel's ex-wife and three on his top staff members, James "Chip" Rogers, Ginny Ford, and LaDonna Chavez.

The shortest file was on Daniel's former spouse, Barbara Daniel. It gave her birth date, the date they were married, and the date their divorce became final. It noted that they had no children. She gave the press no interviews. She refused to talk to anyone who contacted her. She left no paper trail—no credit cards, no mortgage, no car loan, no driver's license, nothing. There was no current address. That raised a red flag in my mind.

A slightly longer account concerned Chip Rogers. Connecticut born, he came from money, but he had dropped out of Yale to join the army. He was married to his high school sweetheart. They had six kids. Chip had met Joe

Daniel in boot camp. They served in the same unit. They both got chosen for Special Forces. They trained together. They had been in combat together. Chip might be Sancho Panza to Daniel's Don Quixote, but they were brothers in a band of brothers. When Daniel left the military, so did Chip. He spent weeks at the hospital watching over Daniel. In service, out of service, Daniel depended on Chip, and Chip never left his side.

Ginny Ford, a housewife, grew up in upper-class Lake Forest, Illinois, went to Lake Forest College, married into a well-to-do family, and became the abused spouse of a corporate bigwig. She had been married to this loser for fifteen years when one day, while Joe Daniel was home on leave, they met in a mall parking lot in a Chicago suburb. Daniel was a passerby when Ginny's husband was beating the crap out of her next to their Lexus. Joe Daniel intervened.

The account on the CD was a little short on detail, but following that incident Ginny got a protection order, then a divorce. She ended up with her house, the kids, and a big chunk of change. Her ex-husband moved to the other side of the country. I assumed Daniel had something to do with his decision to leave town. Ginny had worked on Daniel's first political campaign. She was a one-woman fan club. When she said publicly that she owed Joe Daniel her life, she meant it literally.

Then there was LaDonna Chavez. The thirty-five-year-old lawyer came from a family of California activists and was distantly related to the renowned Cesar himself. She evidently went ballistic about corporate wrongdoing after the *Exxon Valdez* disaster. She volunteered to work for Greenpeace and soon was a lawyer on their paid staff. Her brother, Roberto Chavez, had been in Afghanistan around the same time Daniel was, only her brother came home in a body bag. LaDonna joined Daniel's team while he was running for Congress and had been instrumental in his presidential run. Nothing raised my suspicions there.

Daniel had had a Damascus conversion from war to peace. His closest advisers all looked totally legitimate. But something didn't sit right, or some piece of crucial information was missing—I just couldn't spot it.

With that thought running through my brain, I opened my fake bookcase, peeled off my clothes, climbed naked into my coffin, and pulled the pink satin coverlet over me. The darkness descended quickly, but I slept fitfully. I dreamed of someone wearing a Kabuki mask and putting poison in a cup. I dreamed of Fitz in a room calling out to me as I walked out the door. I dreamed of how I had bitten Darius and how ecstatic the experience had been. . . and I dreamed of biting him again.

CHAPTER 5

We must become the change we want to see in the world.

—attributed to Mohandas Gandhi

"Why, sugar, don't you look . . . uhh . . . don't you look, Green, I guess," Benny observed as I met her in the lobby of my building. Dusk had fallen on a gray city. A brisk wind with a cold bite was rattling windows and blowing paper down the street. I had dressed to look like a tree hugger. My jeans were artfully torn at the knee and thigh. My feet were tucked into a pair of German clogs. I had exchanged my Louis Vuitton backpack for a handwoven pouch from Guatemala. My earrings were from India, my silver rings from Mexico, and my hat was alpaca, striped and hand-knitted, from Peru.

"Geez, Benny, I thought I looked both cute and multinational," I muttered.

"You do! It's just that you usually don't dress like this," she said as we headed out the door.

"We're spies, Benny," I said in a low voice. "We *do* disguises. We are about to insinuate ourselves into the Joe Daniel presidential campaign."

A look of alarm passed over her perfectly made-up face. "I should have thought of that, Daphne. I swear, you'd think my head weren't nothing but a hat rack sometimes."

"Benny, you look fine. You're Southern. I don't think you're allowed out of the house without a matching handbag and shoes."

"You know, Daphy, I think you just insulted me, but I'm not sure why looking presentable for company is an insult," she said. "And *my* mama taught *me* manners, at least."

Our doorman, Mickey Kay, a red-faced Dubliner prone to napping on the job, was missing in action, so I left Benny on the sidewalk and stepped out into the street to hail a cab. I looked over at her and said, "Benny, I'm just teasing you. You look fine. Classy," I noted, referring to her pink cashmere turtleneck and white wool slacks with matching jacket. Her bag and boots screamed Prada, and they did match—they were both pink.

After a Yellow Cab careened across three lanes of avenue traffic and stopped in front of the building, we ducked into the shadows of the backseat. "So what happened after I left last night, or shouldn't I ask?" I said to Benny after I told the driver where to take us.

During the space of a microsecond a look of fear passed over her face. Then she was grinning and saying, "Girlfriend, I will give you all the details, but not here." She looked meaningfully at the taxi driver. "Let me just say that Tallmadge can rise to the occasion and fulfills all expectations. Mmmm-hmmm, he's good. I also met this interesting woman. She's a real countess. I'll try to introduce you tonight."

"Oh, yeah, tonight. I can hardly wait," I said, and slumped down, my hands jammed into my vest's pockets.

The Manhattan headquarters for Joe Daniel's campaign was on West Twenty-ninth Street, near the historic Marble Collegiate Church on the corner at Fifth Avenue. As Benny and I climbed out of our cab, we saw long yellow, blue, and green ribbons tied to the railing surrounding the church, their graceful streamers fluttering in the cold, cruel wind. The ribbons reminded me of Buddhist prayer flags, but their movement was frantic, not joyful, and they reached out over the sidewalk like pleading hands.

Benny walked over to the church and read a sign explaining their significance. "Daphy," she called out, "each yellow one has the name of a soldier in the Mideast; the blue and green ones represent prayers for peace. Isn't that lovely?"

"Lovely? Colorful, maybe, but to me they're like tears—ineffective."

"Daphy, they're symbols, and beautiful ones at that. Are you always so cynical?"

"No, sometimes I'm worse," I said. I put my head down, stuffed my hands into my pockets again, and stomped away toward Daniel's storefront headquarters, not sure why I felt so angry.

A huge peace sign superimposed against a background of red and white stripes hung in one illuminated window of Daniel's headquarters; in the other a large photo of the Earth as seen from space formed the background for the announcement, VOTE GREEN! VOTE ONE PLANET ONE PEOPLE! WE'RE ALL IN THIS TOGETHER. JOE A. DANIEL FOR PRESIDENT.

"I guess this is it," I said to Benny, who was a few steps behind me.

"I think it's a safe bet," she yelled to me above the wind, which had increased in force and tore down the Manhattan street with a vengeance, pushing Benny's blond hair forward and fluttering her pant legs. I tried to open the door. It was locked. I rapped on the glass. A guy in a cheap gray suit opened it, blocking the way with his thick body. He had *security* written all over him.

"ID," he demanded.

I rooted around in my Guatemalan bag for my wallet, and

Benny dove into her Prada purse. We handed him our government photo IDs from the Department of the Interior. He
raised an eyebrow, pursed his lips, shook his head, and
handed back our cards.

"National Park Service," I added.

"Yeah, right," he said, rolled his eyes, and muttered,
"More goddamn spooks," under his breath. He moved aside,
and I gave him a dirty look as we stepped out of the cold into
a shoe box of a room. Brown folding tables sat around the
perimeter. Campaign materials were stacked on most of
them, and a half dozen people were stuffing envelopes. Two
people had iPod buds stuck in their ears; the others listened
to an old boom box set on a table and tuned to WPLJ-FM.
The envelope stuffers were all dressed pretty much like me.
Another guy in a suit with a bulge under its armpit stood with
his back to the wall.

At the table closest to the front door a slender, light-
skinned African American man sat cross-legged. He wore a
White Sox baseball cap backward on his short-cropped hair
and a frown on his face. He was trying to do "Rock the Baby"
with a fancy butterfly-design yo-yo that said DARK MAGIC on
it. He looked up and the frown vanished. He smiled then, his
face radiant and his teeth very white. "Can I help you?" he
asked.

"We're here from the Scarsdale chapter of Save the Trees,"
I explained. "Marozia Urban sent us down to help out. She
talked to somebody named Ginny."

"Ginny's in the back on the phone. It's right through
there." He nodded toward a white door, stopped playing with
the yo-yo, and hopped off the table. I gave him a closer look
and started to say, "Aren't you—" when he introduced himself. "I'm Joe Daniel, by the way. Thanks for coming down."

His voice was bigger than his slight frame and held the street sounds of Chicago.

He shook my hand, and I noticed that his was like a boxer's, its knuckles flattened, its grip muscular and solid. All the while, Daniel gave me his full attention, searching my face with eyes that were so light green, they looked like lake water in the sun. Laugh lines fanned out from their edges, and so much energy poured off of him that in that instant he became incandescent. I liked him right away and had to smile back.

"Daphne Urban," I responded, "and this is my friend Benny Polycarp."

When Daniel turned to Benny, she said, "Why, this is such a surprise, Mr. Daniel. We didn't think you'd be in town until Friday."

"Call me Joe," he responded as he pumped her little hand up and down in his big one. "Officially I'm not in town yet, but you won't tell on me, now, will you?" he asked teasingly.

"Your secret is safe with us; that's for sure," she said.

"Isn't there a big press conference planned for your arrival?" I asked.

"Plans change." His smile vanished and he moved away from us, his gait a little awkward. I remembered he had lost a leg in combat. With a quick, agitated movement of his arm, he started to do "Walk the Dog" across the old wooden floor with the yo-yo. After a few seconds his disquietude passed and he stilled the toy, bringing it back into his fist. He looked at us. "We're going to have a rally a couple of hours from now with OP, up in Riverside Park."

"Opi?" I asked.

"One Planet One People. Everybody calls them OP for short. Sometimes I call them OPOP. Reminds me of *Star Wars*," he added, looking up at the ceiling and thinking out loud rather than talking to us. "We didn't even tell the media yet," he said with a sigh. "I think that's what Ginny is doing."

Just then the white door opened and a whip-thin guy, his light brown hair in a buzz cut, came out with a fistful of papers. He rushed over to Daniel. Right behind him, a cell phone glued to her ear, was a stocky, well-dressed black woman.

"Joe, here's your speech for tonight, and the latest casualty list from the Mideast. We need to look it over," the man said, ignoring us.

Daniel put his hand on the man's shoulder and turned him in our direction. "Chip, these are some new volunteers, Daphne and Benny," he said. "Daphne, Benny, this is my top aide, Chip Rogers, and that's my campaign manager, LaDonna Chavez."

Chavez gave us a little nod but didn't stop talking into the cell phone. Rogers stuck the papers under his armpit and shook our hands. "Glad to have you on board," he said. "You talk to Ginny yet?"

"No," we said in unison.

"Go right through that door and you'll run into her," he said, then turned his attention back to Daniel.

"Talk to me later, Chip," Daniel said, shaking his head.

"There's not much time, Joe. We can't put it off," Chip urged.

"Later, okay?" Daniel said, his voice sounding tired. His good-looking face, so familiar from television, looked serious, and his eyes were sad. Almost as if he had forgotten we were all there, he started playing with the yo-yo again, doing "Around the World." The Black Magic yo-yo made a huge arc with Daniel at its center. Both Benny and I stepped back. So did Chip and LaDonna. To me, Daniel was pushing us out of the room with the flying disk.

Benny and I exchanged a look. Darkness had moved over Daniel like a rain cloud. He was a man with a world of hurt on his mind.

We went through the white door into an overheated room. At more brown folding tables lining the far wall, a half dozen young people were packing cardboard boxes with leaflets and campaign buttons. A chubby woman spoke urgently into a telephone. She looked up, spotted us, and held up a finger to indicate she'd be with us in a minute, then went on talking fast into the receiver. Then, from somewhere to my right side, came a voice.

"Of all the storefronts in all the towns in all the world, she walks into mine." The voice was annoyed, the face was black, the mouth was unsmiling.

"Huh?" I said, sparkling with wit, as my old nemesis Moses Johnson, an NYPD plainclothes cop, reached out, grabbed my arm, and pulled me aside.

"Detective?" I said. "Are you working this case?"

"Brilliant deduction, Sherlock," he said in a low voice. "Call me Johnson and try not to blow my cover. And you, Miss Urban? Here on spy business?"

"As you said, *Sherlock,* try not to blow my cover," I whispered back, and pulled my arm away. The man had taken an instant dislike to me when we first met, but at a moment of crisis he had saved my dog. I thought that act of kindness meant something had changed between us. It hadn't.

Johnson gave me a hard stare with cold eyes, and after a beat or two of silence he said quietly, "Look Miss Urban, you're a spook. You're a fed. You're on my turf. That's three strikes. And being within ten feet of you gives me a bad feeling." He paused, searching my face with eyes that were bloodshot, tired, and filled with disgust. Then he glanced over at Benny, who was waiting and watching near the door. "You have obviously been brought into this, and I guess I have to put up with you until I can get you out of here."

I stared him straight in the face without flinching. "I'm not going anywhere, Detective, so stop pulling my chain. Why don't we work together? It might make more sense," I suggested.

"I'd rather sleep with a rattlesnake," he said. "Just stay out of my way." By then the woman on the phone had finished her call and was rushing over to Benny and me. Johnson nodded at her and went over to a water cooler. He pulled a paper cup from a dispenser, but he never took his eyes off of us.

The woman had a pen stuck into her hair, which was pulled back with a rubber band. Her skin was so fair it was almost transparent. A blue vein throbbed in her temple. All her clothes were too tight, as if she had suddenly put on twenty pounds and was still wearing her "skinny" wardrobe. Squeezed into jeans and a denim jacket, she looked like a blue sausage. "Are you Daphne?" she asked.

"Yes."

"I'm Ginny Ford. I spoke to Marozia about your joining us," she said in a voice that was tight and filled with stress. "And you must be Benny? Thank you both for coming down on such short notice."

"Pleased to meet you, ma'am," Benny said. "How can we help?"

Tears sprang into the woman's eyes. Her palms were damp when she grabbed one of our hands in each of hers and squeezed them. In a voice I could barely hear, she said, "Keep him alive. Just keep him alive."

So she knows we're not really volunteers, I thought. *But who did Mar-Mar say we were?* I wondered as the phone chirped again. Ginny's eyes darted around the room. In a loud voice she said, "We appreciate your organization's support of Joe. We'll be leaving for the rally in a couple of minutes. Come along, won't you?" As she turned to return to the phone, she said softly, "We'll talk afterward, okay?"

I nodded. Benny did too.

Without hesitating, Benny left my side and joined the staffers packing cartons. All smiles and running her mouth a mile a minute, she was a born mixer. I was a born loner. I figured I'd put a stick in a hornet's nest. I walked over to Johnson at the water cooler.

"Why don't we kiss and make up," I said as I reached over and pulled one of the little white cups from the dispenser. I filled it and took a sip.

"Buzz off," he said, and watched the room.

I finished my water in one swallow, squashed the cup in my hand, and slam-dunked it into a nearby wastebasket. I moved toward Johnson, who was standing with his arms folded across his chest, staring at the staffers. I came close enough to count the pores in his nose. He did not move back even a fraction of an inch.

"Back off," he said.

I did, and smiled. "Now, Detective," I said in a saccharine voice, "as you observed, I've been sent down here. I'm on the case. At those tables you're watching so intently—how many more of those so-called volunteers are agency people? CIA? NSA? FBI? Two? Three?"

"Yeah, so?"

"And maybe one of them is on the other side, helping to set up Daniel to get a bullet through his head."

"I doubt it," he said, still watching them.

"Why?"

Johnson didn't answer me at first. Then he said, "Because whoever wants Daniel dead won't recruit college kids or housewives. If there's a traitor, he or she is already close to Daniel. Bet on it."

"Nice theory," I said. "Got any proof?"

"I don't share," he answered.

"Look, Johnson, you don't have to like me. But we're both here. We both want the same thing."

"Says who?"

"We both want to keep Daniel alive, don't we?"

Johnson looked at me with a face of stone. His breath smelled of coffee. "Look, Miss Urban, what *I* want doesn't mean dick. The *NYPD* wants to keep Daniel alive while he's in New York City. They don't give a rat's ass what happens to him after he leaves, and personally, neither do I. We know how to protect VIPs and bigmouthed politicians with a lot of enemies. We do it all the time. It's our job."

"You didn't do such a great job with John Lennon," I said. "Or Malcolm X."

Johnson's lips pressed together and his eyes narrowed. His face got even harder. "That's ancient history. We learn from our mistakes."

"I hope so; I really do. But the fact is, you've got an assassin out there somewhere, one who's never been stopped. One nobody can identify. It seems to me you need my help."

Johnson started to say, "When hell fr—" Then he stopped himself. "What exactly are you offering?"

"An exchange of information. I get anything on the assassin, I pass it on. You get anything, you return the favor. I uncover the viper in the nest here, I tell you, and vice versa. Just to keep on the same page. You'd be pissed if we took somebody out when you were secretly getting good shit from them. It would piss me off if you made an arrest at the wrong time—"

There was a bang. I turned my head fast. Somebody had

dropped a heavy carton onto the floor. The workers had
started putting the filled boxes on hand trucks. It looked as if
it was time to leave for the rally. Johnson pulled a cell phone
from his pocket. As he placed a call, he said dismissively to
me, "Okay, okay. You've made your point. I'll keep you in the
loop."

Why didn't I believe him?

Benny and I rode in a yellow school bus up to Riverside
Church along with the rest of Daniel's people. During the
trip, the security people made a list of names and handed out
badges identifying us as staff. At One Hundred Twentieth
Street near Columbia University, where the huge church
complex covered two blocks, the bus pulled into a well-lit
parking lot and we all got out. A huge banner was draped
across an exterior wall. It said, MARCH FOR PEACE AS THE
DRUMBEATS FOR WAR GROW LOUDER.

Benny and I followed the rest of the group into the assembly room, a large, Gothic-style space with stone walls sup-
ported by stone pillars. The room would probably hold five
hundred people. Its vaulted ceiling made the place look like
a cave. Our footsteps echoed when they hit the stone floor.
Once the place filled with people, the noise was going to be
earsplitting. A space inside a big old church that looked like
a cave wouldn't have been my choice of a venue to announce
a successful presidential candidacy. I was a vampire, after
all, the ancient enemy of churches and the clergy who have
tried to exterminate us for centuries. But Joe A. Daniel had
aligned himself with the peace movement, and that meant
standing shoulder-to-shoulder with liberal Christians. I
didn't know how those good folks would feel about standing
so close to me.

At one end of the room a stage held a podium bristling

with microphones. There was a line of folding chairs behind that. The rest of the room was devoid of seating, standing room only. Daniel's people quickly became worker ants, getting tables set up near the front door. We had come in a rear entrance, and Daniel, surrounded by his staff, had disappeared into a side room off the stage.

"Let me take a look at security," I said to Benny.

"Right. I'm going to keep mingling with the volunteers," she said.

I walked across the large room, through an entry hall, and out a door where a sea of blue uniforms seemed to form a human wall. A couple of burly cops were wrestling with a standing metal detector. Handheld wands were being laid out on a table by a policewoman. I didn't see Johnson. He was probably backstage someplace. A channel two, CBS-TV van pulled into the parking lot. Young people were starting to drift into the area as well. I ducked back inside. TV cameras from the networks were already being set up to the side of the stage and in the back of the room.

I made my way to the stage, dodging TV people and reporters. Benny had finished her volunteerism and joined me, and we both focused on watching the people filling the room. I didn't see anyone acting suspicious or sense anything dangerous. Some reporters had gathered, hoping to get backstage to talk to Daniel. LaDonna Chavez, the campaign manager, handed them a prepared statement and told them there would be a press conference tomorrow, but tonight Daniel wouldn't be answering questions. The noise level was rising in the room; an electric charge of excitement was building in the air.

I heard somebody ask why Daniel was in town a day early. LaDonna gave them all a warm smile and told them that Daniel had an invitation to appear on the *Today* show, so she was accelerating his schedule. Evidently the press hadn't heard any rumors about an assassination plot. That was a good thing.

A rainbow coalition of Spanish, black, and white local politicians came from backstage and occupied the chairs behind the podium. I sensed the anticipation in the crowd, which seemed to me to be extremely young, pierced, long-haired, and the kind of kids more likely to be at a rock concert than a political rally. I pegged some older folks as labor leaders. I'm no psychic. Their AFL-CIO VOTES FOR DANIEL campaign buttons were a tip-off. But I am a vampire. And suddenly, somewhere in the room I could smell fear . . . and hate.

The clamor of voices grew steadily louder and bounced off the stone walls as a middle-aged black man with an Afro and thick-rimmed plastic glasses stepped up to the podium. He looked like that Princeton professor, Cornel West. Joe Daniel slipped onto the stage from a side entrance. A roar went up from the crowd.

"Dan-yell! Dan-yell!" some of the crowd began chanting like cheerleaders. On cue, another group began to yell, "What do we want?"

"Peace!" was the response.

"When do we want it?"

"Now!"

The black man at the microphone held up his hands and called for silence. A blast of static from the speakers kept me from catching his name, but the crowd seemed to know him and watched him with rapt attention. A technician ran up and made some adjustments to the sound system. "Welcome to a historic night!" the speaker bellowed. The crowd cheered.

"Tonight we are announcing to the world that we are restoring the American dream!" he said. "E-qual-it-y! Dem-oc-racy! In-teg-rit-y! Gener-os-it-y! We are taking this country back from the oil men. Back from the lumber men. Back from the corporate in-hu-men who have put greed in power and sent young men to become cannon fodder. The same corporate in-hu-men who pollute the water and poison the air." The crowd cheered again.

"Tonight we have with us the man who will lead the way. He is no slip-slider. He says what he means; he will say it tonight; he will still be saying it next week—no matter how the polls respond between now and then. He stands up. He doesn't lie down. He's a soldier who fights war no more. He's a man who battles not with bombs but with the sword of justice. He's a patriot who steps unafraid into the line of fire. He has sacrificed much and will willingly sacrifice more—to steer this country away from its course of disaster! To change this world! To save this planet! To save innocent lives! Ladies and gentleman, I give you Mr. Joe A. Daniel, the next president of the United States!"

The crowd went wild, clapping and screaming, "Dan-yell! Dan-yell! Dan-yell!"

Dressed in a simple white sweater and jeans, his head bare, his chin held high, Joe Daniel strode to the podium and stood before the cheering crowd. I sensed in him a high level of excitement and something I can describe only as love.

Gripping the sides of the podium with both hands, Joe Daniel began speaking in a quiet voice. "Brothers and sisters." A hush fell over the crowd. "I am not here to cast blame. I am here to give hope. I am not here to hate. I am here to love. I was once a solider and I have seen war. I can tell you that war is failed diplomacy. War is a travesty. War is an abomination. War is unnecessary in this world. We must fight war no more."

The crowd interrupted him with a round of cheering. Benny whispered to me, "This guy is asking to be offed. Too many folks are buying into his position." I nodded as Daniel began speaking again.

"No more precious lives must be lost. No more precious children killed. No more precious sons and daughters slaughtered. For what great cause have they been killed? For freedom? No. For democracy? No. There is no 'great cause' in this war. Our sons, our daughters, our husbands, our wives have been slaughtered—for oil. They have been killed—for money. They have been maimed and tortured for selfish schemes by sightless men who cannot see the evil that they do. And if they do see, they choose not to understand. These men are on the brink of a chasm. They are about to fall into that chasm—and take our planet with them. But even if they cut off my hands, I must pull them out and save our planet.

" 'How can we save the planet?' you may ask. We do it by taking the path of nonviolence. Do not mistake me, brothers and sisters. I am not calling for passivity. I am not calling for surrender. I am calling upon you to fight the toughest battle of your lives. But to fight it with the weapon of your determination. The sword of justice. The olive branch of peace. I am calling upon you to use the power you have inherent in you when you say *no* to war. And say *no* to killing. Then you must say yes to a *fundamental change* in the way we live our lives. Will you say yes?"

The crowd screamed out, *"Yes!"*

Daniel held up his big boxer's hands for silence and went on. "What do I mean by fundamental change?

"First, I mean we must recognize that we all live together on this earth. It is by cooperation, not confrontation, that we will survive. Will you say yes to cooperation?"

"Yes!" screamed the crowd.

"Second, we must change our patterns of consumption. We must *stop* depleting our resources and *start* conserving them. We must clean up the water and air. We must take the poisons from our soil. We must respect all life—and all things, even the rocks themselves, are alive. We must become stewards of this planet and not destructors of it. We must put our resources not into building bombs, but into building clean energy. Will you say yes to a green world?"

"YES!" screamed the crowd.

"Third, we must remain strong and protect our people. Not by nationalism. Not by bullying. Not by trying to force the rest of the world into submission. We must lead by example. By being a people committed to the common good. A people committed to life. A people who do not tolerate children living in poverty. A people who do not tolerate citizens living without medical insurance. A people who do not tolerate lies and greed and lawbreaking . . . in the White House. In Congress. In the courts. Will you say yes to honesty, yes to compassion, yes to commitment?"

"Yes! Yes! Yes!" the voices in the audience yelled.

"Then you are ready for what I am here to tell you," Daniel said with a huge smile. "I am here tonight to announce my candidacy for president of these United States. I warn you now that my opponents will slander me. They will say we cannot win. They may even try to kill me. And perhaps they will." His voice was low and hushed, his face solemn.

Some people in the crowd groaned and said, "No, no," in soft voices.

"But they cannot kill our will. They cannot resist the tide of change. I tell you that this message cannot be silenced. It cannot be stopped. You must carry the banner. You must spread the word. You must have the courage to stick to your principles even if a bullet cuts me down.

"Time is running out, brothers and sisters. The polar ice is melting. The sea is rising. Tornadoes rage across our plains.

Category-five hurricanes ravage our cites. We must stop global warming . . . before it is too late to reverse the ecological changes already at work. We must stop waging war . . . before war leaves even one more family in mourning. And if old men, comfortable in their limousines, try to send *our* sons and *our* daughters—and it is never *their* sons and *their* daughters—to the killing fields of battle, you must say no as I say no. I say a new day is dawning. I say we are that new day—"

A man's angry voice shouted loudly from the back of the room, "You support the terrorists! You'd let them kill us all!" A phalanx of blue uniforms rushed across the room and descended upon the heckler.

"Wait! Let that man be!" Daniel yelled. "He is afraid. I don't blame him for being afraid. Terrorism must be stopped. Those who would kill innocent Americans must be stopped. But this war isn't stopping them. I was there. I saw. I know. We have the ability to catch al-Qaeda. Ask yourselves why we haven't! Sir, I will stop the terrorists. But I won't do it by invading Iran. Or Korea. Or Syria."

Despite Daniel's request that the heckler be left alone, the man was being hustled out the door by the uniforms. While that drew everyone's attention, there was the noise of breaking glass. The stench of rotten eggs began to permeate the assembly hall. "Stink bomb!" somebody yelled. The cops moved in quickly with a tarp and threw it over the device. The smell was unpleasant but not unbearable. But that made two incidents that security had not stopped. I was worried that a third could be violent.

"People!" Daniel yelled out, smiling broadly, lightening the mood. "We all know something smells in the current administration! They didn't have to prove it to us!" The audience laughed in relief. "I want to thank you all for coming here tonight. We need your support. We need your activism. Please join us! Keep checking our Web site for updates! We all agree it's time for some fresh air, right?"

"Right!" the crowd responded, and clapped.

"Well, then, thank you—and good night!" Daniel was grinning and raising his fist in the air. A sound system began playing the Beatles song "Revolution." The audience started filing out. The sulfur smell dissipated too. I looked at Benny; then we both looked over at Daniel as he headed off the stage. He wasn't smiling anymore. His head was down and he looked as if he were in pain.

At that moment I turned to give a last look at the nearly empty room. A small, pretty woman was approaching the stage. She saw that I had spotted her and waved to me.

"Oh, shit," I said.

"What's wrong?" Benny asked.

"My mother's here."

CHAPTER 6

*The trick to being happy is not to get what you
want, but to want what you get.*

— Anonymous (old saying)

From the shadows at the side of the stage Ginny's voice called out. "Oh, good, Marozia is here!" Emerging from the gloom, Ginny walked over to Benny and me. Tendrils of hair had escaped from her rubber band and were clinging to her perspiring forehead. She looked frazzled and worn. I hadn't forgotten that she had suggested we meet after the rally. I just didn't know my mother would be included.

I clenched my teeth and noted that Mar-Mar was rosy cheeked, bright eyed, and downright bushy tailed as she bounded up onto the stage. She certainly didn't look like a thousand-year-old woman, dressed as she usually did in bell-bottom jeans and a tie-dyed T-shirt now mostly obscured beneath a fringed Western jacket. Her feet were clad in high-top sneakers.

Mar-Mar had embraced the 1960s with a vengeance and never let go. During that rebellious decade of "Make Love, Not War," she had been accepted without question for the first time in her long life. Her nocturnal habits, her aversion to garlic, even her coffin bed were seen as totally cool, man, really groovy. She loved the protests and the politics, and above all she loved the Mary Jane. The ganja. You know, the pot.

Her retro clothes and hippie ways had embarrassed me for decades. Now she was totally in fashion again. She was also deeply embedded in the American intelligence community, something I had found out only a few months back, after I had been recruited into the Darkwings. Lately I had the idea that she had been in that shadow world of spies since the time we had gone into hiding after my father's death. My earliest memories include men appearing in the dead of night for whispered meetings and the exchange of documents. Once Mar-Mar arrived in the New World in the early eighteenth century, leaving me in England, she had met a very young George Washington—I still have letters, now faded and brittle, that she wrote—and I suppose she went back to what she did best to help him beat the British. However, Mar-Mar doesn't talk about the past, so I might never know the details.

At the moment I was dismayed to see that not only had she gotten a very butch haircut, but—*oh my God*—she had an eyebrow pierced. I didn't want to know if she had pierced anything else. I only hoped to holy hell that she wasn't into tattoos.

"Daphne," Ginny was saying to me as my mother approached, "you and Marozia are related, aren't you?"

Before I could answer, Mar-Mar showed up at my side and said loudly, "Hey, there, Ginny, you've met my cousin Daphne?"

Now I cut in before Ginny could respond. "Oh, yeah, we've met. I didn't know you were going to be here, *cuz,*" I said sarcastically. That earned me a dirty look.

Since no other staffers were around, Ginny suggested the four of us pull some folding chairs together. We made such a tight circle that our knees touched. We leaned forward so our faces were just inches apart. If anyone saw us, they wouldn't think a thing about it. Women always do stuff like that.

Ginny's eyes darted from face to face. She looked as if her head were on swivel as she started talking rapidly. "I want to thank you for offering to help us pro bono. I think it's just marvelous that there's an all-woman security agency like the Protectors. And located in Scarsdale! Who would guess? It's just so perfect. When that second official—the one with the ponytail—came up from Washington, I thought he'd be angry because Daniel wouldn't change his mind about refusing federal protection, but, you know, he was really nice. He gave me the number to contact you folks—*off the record,* he said. That was so thoughtful of him. It's not that we think the city police aren't good. It's just that hiring our own *private* security is so important. We just don't trust the people down in Washington. I mean, the CIA killed Allende—"

As Ginny's words rushed along, her voice got higher and higher. It was almost a squeak when Mar-Mar cut her off. I was speechless myself. It might have been nice if my mother had let Benny and me in on this cover story before we showed up at Daniel's headquarters. I was silently contemplating throttling her when this meeting was over.

"Now, now," Mar-Mar said reassuringly. "You did just the right thing by calling us in. We're women. We understand. But Ginny, to tell the truth—"

That would be a first, I thought.

"—we don't think the CIA is behind this. That's why we need to talk with you."

"Are you sure?" Ginny said, her pale eyes opening very wide and her voice shooting up another octave. "I mean, we know our phones have been tapped for months. We're not just paranoid. We've felt positively harassed even though Joe is a member of Congress himself. It's an outrage—"

"Of course it is!" Mar-Mar said, and took the woman's trembling hand. "Tapping phones is all too common these days. But Ginny, all my sources have told me that the government isn't behind this threat against Mr. Daniel. So we have to look elsewhere. You understand?"

Ginny pulled a wilted tissue from her pocket with her free hand and dabbed at her perspiring forehead. "Well, I guess a lot of people want to get rid of Joe. You know, the oil companies and big corporations that he attacks all the time. But we never thought they'd go this far." She let out another big sigh.

"Well, yes," Mar-Mar agreed. "But we have to rule out every possibility. Is there anyone close to Joe who has a grudge?"

"What? No! Chip and I have been on the campaign team since day one, when Joe ran for Congress and didn't have a pot to piss in. Well, we still don't have a pot to piss in, but we're starting to receive lots of donations. LaDonna volunteered about that time too. People *love* Joe. *Everybody*, and I do mean *everybody*."

"What about his old army buddies? Are any of them angry at his change in position about the war?"

"No, nobody! They might not agree with his position, but they support him right down the line, to a person. He was a hero in the war, you know? His men trusted him, you know? Privately they all say the war is a farce—not enough men or weaponry. They go out looking for al-Qaeda, and whenever they get close they're called back. A lot of them feel their friends have been killed for nothing. You should hear them!"

Mar-Mar cut in. "Okay, but it's hard to believe *everybody* loves him. What about Daniel's ex-wife?" she asked.

Ginny giggled, then started laughing and soon sounded close to being hysterical. Every time she tried to talk, she cracked up again. I looked over at Benny. She shrugged.

While Ginny laughed, Mar-Mar was trying to mask her annoyance, but I could see from the lines around her mouth that she was fuming. Finally she said, "Maybe you could explain why the question is so funny?"

Ginny held up her hand. "I'm sorry. Give me a minute." She took some deep breaths. "Sorry. It's just such a ludicrous idea. Barbara hiring an assassin? You'd have to know her, I guess." Ginny started to giggle again, and gave herself a little slap right in the face. "Oh, Lord, let me get hold of myself. Okay. Okay. You see, the whole idea is crazy. First of all, Barbara left *Joe*, not vice versa, when he was overseas. She was fed up with the war and him choosing to volunteer for all sorts of assignments and never being home. If anything, she feels guilty about bailing out on him, especially after he lost his leg and became so antiwar. The irony was, you see, that Barbara . . . How can I explain? About the same time Barbara split up with Joe, she became a Jainist. She started to wear a surgical mask so she wouldn't inhale any bugs and accidentally kill them. She freaked out if she killed anything, even a spider. She became a vegan and moved into a treehouse—no kidding, she lives in a frigging tree in Northern California. She doesn't have a phone. She doesn't drive. She doesn't have a credit card. She has a compost toilet. She grows all her own food. She doesn't file taxes, since she lives on, like, five hundred dollars a year. She wouldn't take a dime from Joe when they were divorced. Hire an assassin?" Ginny's mouth started twitching again, but she managed to say, "It's . . . it's . . . ridiculous."

"You know, Mar-Mar," I said, trying to keep the impatience out of my voice because questioning Ginny was getting us nowhere, "Ginny is right. None of the people close to Joe seem to have the funds to hire an assassin—and if they wanted to kill him, why would they need a hit man? They could just do it themselves. I think you're way off base."

Mar-Mar glared at me. "We are just trying to eliminate suspects, Daphne; that's all."

"So consider them eliminated and stop wasting time. I think Ginny might be on target when she mentioned big corporations, some gung ho right-wing military group, or maybe a gun group. But the bad guy has to be someone with deep pockets; that narrows the field. And it doesn't eliminate the government."

"I told you, it's not the CIA, NSA, or FBI," Mar-Mar said sharply.

"Well, that leaves the MIA, DIA, ATF, and Treasury Department, among others, now, doesn't it?" My back was up; she and I were close to getting into it.

Mar-Mar stared hard at me. "I can assure you this threat is not coming from the American government," she said frostily.

Benny had held her tongue since we sat down. "Okay, girlfriends, both of you all have made your point. From where I sit that makes the bad guy another government, like maybe one of those A-rab countries, or some nasty corporation. But do you all think we should be spending our time trying to figure out who hired the assassin, or trying to find the assassin? Maybe, like my mama said, we're putting the cart before the horse. Maybe we should be concentratin' on keeping this Gage person from killing Daniel?"

"If we find the employer, the employee's out of a job," Mar-Mar said, then leaned back in her chair and folded her arms.

"Well, you know, you all could be working on that, and Daphy and I can focus on catching Gage. Isn't that right, Daphy?" Benny asked, looking in my direction.

"Sounds like a plan," I said.

"Oh, yes," Ginny said, sighing. "That really would be perfect. Look, I have to get on that school bus before it leaves. Are you coming back with us?" she asked Benny and me.

"No," I answered. "I think we're going to talk a little longer. Then we'll burn the midnight oil and catch up with you tomorrow, okay?"

Ginny stood and pushed her chair back, waiting for something. *Oh, hugs,* I realized. I stood up and hugged her; so did Benny and Mar-Mar.

"And don't worry, Ginny, really," Mar-Mar said, all sweetness again. "The Protectors are on the case!"

As soon as Ginny was out of earshot, I growled at Mar-Mar, "The Protectors? We sound like a feminine hygiene product. And why the hell wasn't this cover story in our briefing?"

Smiling now, Mar-Mar had her good humor back. She liked to argue, and while I might simmer for hours afterward, she simply got revved up. "Because, *cara mia,* it's our little secret. The agency doesn't know, and they aren't going to know. That's why it wasn't in your case files."

I shook my head. "Okay, I suppose you have your reasons. So we're an all-woman security agency. What else do we need to know?"

"Well, here, take these." Mar-Mar fished some business cards out of her jacket pocket. They were bent at the corners from being carried around.

THE PROTECTORS
We Watch Over You
Surveillance ... Guard Service ... Investigation
Confidentiality Assured ... An All-Woman Agency

"Well, I guess that says it all," I stated flatly.

"Oh, this is just so cool," Benny said. "Now we're under-cover undercover."

"Exactly!" Mar-Mar affirmed. "But listen. I heard what you both said about somebody needing deep pockets to hire Gage. That's a given. Only we *do* have information that there's someone close to Daniel who's working with the deep pockets. You have to trust me on this."

"It would be a lot easier to trust you if you told us what you had instead of leaving us with our asses hanging out," I murmured. Benny rolled her eyes, figuring my mother and I were going to battle again. Wrong. Mar-Mar had switched from squabbling to a policy of appeasement.

"You're right, of course, Daphne. In this case there just wasn't time, so I do apologize. And dear, don't forget I'll be meeting you later for that little excursion I mentioned yesterday. Say around two thirty?"

"Where?" I said without enthusiasm.

"Why, the same place as last night. And, sweetie, do wear the same outfit. It looked so cute on you," she said, and stood on her toes to kiss me on the cheek. She's only five-three and I'm more like five-ten. I guess my father was tall. "Now I just have to boogie out of here."

"Well, go boogie," I said ungraciously, "but I need to have a word with you—in private, if you don't mind."

"Of course, dear. Why don't you walk me out?"

Mar-Mar and I got off the stage, and as we started across the empty room I said, "I need you to talk to some of your Italian friends so I can interview a hit man."

"I don't know what you're talking about," she said, not looking at me.

"Mother, I don't have time to play games. I would like you to call in a favor from some of your hoodlum friends. I would like to talk to a hit man, preferably somebody who's been around awhile."

Mar-Mar sighed. "I don't think you're going to find out much that way."

"As you've said to me, trust me on this. Can you do it or not?" I asked.

We had stopped in the middle of the room. She looked up at me, not speaking for a moment before saying, "I can do it. I'll make a few calls. Whatever you find out will be strictly off the record, you know—and I'll owe somebody a favor I'm not going to want to repay. You know that." She shook her head with disapproval.

"Look, I'd appreciate your making the contact for me. I'm just surprised you haven't already done it," I said, sarcasm seeping back into my voice.

"I am pursuing other avenues, Daphne. Personally, I don't think a Mafia hit man can tell you much about an international assassin. But who knows, maybe you're on to something. The agency hasn't found out anything more on Gage, I'm sorry to say. I'll be in touch with you on it. Look, I've got to run. Love you," she said, and hurried away, leaving me standing there.

By this time Benny was walking toward me. When she reached my side, she observed, "Girlfriend, your mother is just incredible."

"She's incredible, all right. Can we change the subject?"

"Sure. Look Daph," she said, glancing down at her watch. "It's not even ten yet. I want to run home and change before heading down to the club. We're supposed to meet Tallmadge at midnight, remember?"

"How could I forget?" When I thought about the evening ahead—a rendezvous at the vampire club, then breaking into Opus Dei with Cormac and my mother—I felt that I'd rather have a root canal. "Look, I'll head home too. I have to pick something up, and maybe I can take Jade out real quick. I'll see you in a couple of hours."

"I'll be waiting with bells on!" Benny sang out without a hint of sarcasm. "Oh, Daph, I still haven't told you about me and Tallmadge. Well, later, girlfriend. All I can say is . . . mmm-mmm, good." She kissed the air on either side of my cheeks and hurried off.

I stood there alone for a few minutes, feeling glum in that cave of a room. Twenty-four hours had passed, and we weren't any closer to finding Gage. I didn't know where Darius was. I didn't know how I felt about Fitz. And I didn't want to see Tallmadge again. He was mysterious, dangerous, and amoral. I felt a strong sexual pull toward him. I could picture sleeping with him and regretting it afterward. Then factor into that mess his affair with Benny, which I suspected she was taking much more seriously than he was. I thought about those blank areas on early maps labeled, HERE THERE BE DRAGONS. Those words aptly described the totally unknown territory of Tallmadge's heart, where I knew there was trouble. I could feel it.

When I walked through my apartment door, the phone was ringing. I nearly tripped over Jade as I dove to answer it. "Hello?" I gasped into the receiver.

"Hey, stranger, I can't believe I finally caught you," the voice said. My heart gave a hard squeeze. It was Darius. I didn't know what to say, really, and what I did say probably wasn't the most diplomatic choice of responses.

"I don't think you've tried very hard, Darius." My voice was harsh to cover up the hurt that was welling up in my chest.

"Believe what you want, Daphne," he said, his cheerful tone turning rough to match mine.

I let out a deep breath. I realized in a flash how much I had missed him and how good it was to hear his voice. "Okay, sorry. Let's not fight. I was feeling forgotten, that's all."

"I don't forget *anything*, Daphne. It was your decision not to come with me. But maybe that was a good thing. I'm not going to bullshit you; it's been bad over here. I can't talk about it, but . . . well, I've arranged to have somebody call you in case . . . in case . . . you know, something happens to me."

My hand tightened on the receiver. "What do you mean? Darius, it's damned hard to kill a vampire, and you've been a vampire hunter yourself. You have an advantage if they come after you."

"Yeah, I know that's what I said. But the band draws a lot of fans, and in the crowds . . . well, anything could happen. It's gotten hairy, that's all. Look, forget what I said. I'll be all right. And when I get back, we'll figure out what to do."

"Do? About what?" I said, purposely acting dense because I wanted him to spell out exactly what he meant.

"About us, Daphne. I mean that. We'll start over, if you're willing. It can be good between us. I really believe that. You know how it is when we're together. It feels good . . . it feels right." His voice grew lower and sexier. It got to me even if I didn't want it to.

"Darius, I'd like that; I really would." Hope started growing then, opening like a blossom in my heart. "When are you coming back?" I asked.

"I don't know," he said, hesitating. "Look, this is really confidential, but we're headed for Spain now. Then the Balkans, and probably on to Indonesia. It may be . . . well . . . it may be for as much as six months," he said.

Disappointment dropped on me hard, crushing the hope inside me. "Six months? A lot can happen in all that time, Darius." Sadness was filling my voice like a soft snow falling on a winter night.

"I'm asking you to wait, Daph," he said, not as a request but stopping just short of giving an order, "even if it is six months."

"I hear what you're asking *me*, but will *you* wait, Darius? You're with Julie every day, aren't you? Are you with her every night too?"

"Fuck! Can't you leave it alone, Daphne? Julie has nothing to do with us!" he exploded.

I guess the devil made me say what I said next. "Tell me you haven't slept with her already, Darius."

Where there should have been a quick denial, there was silence.

"Okay, I guess that answers my question," I said, and hung up. I'd like to say the pain I felt in that moment contributed to what happened later that night. Maybe it did, and maybe it's just that I'm bad.

I had stuffed my priest's disguise into a backpack and left my Guatemalan bag at the apartment. I hadn't bothered changing my clothes. I wasn't in the mood to dress up, and I wasn't trying to impress anyone at Tallmadge's club. I felt like shit. Disillusioned and disappointed, I wanted to believe that I didn't need anyone to share my life. I had managed on my own for centuries. Admittedly I had "managed" my life, but I hadn't enjoyed very much of it. I discovered instead how slowly time passes when life is meandering without direction, and how flavorless life is when experienced alone.

I blamed Darius for my sinking feelings. I had let myself care deeply for him, and I was angry about being hurt—angry at myself, and very angry at him. As that dark coal of rage in my stomach smoldered and grew hotter, I decided to show Darius that I didn't need him. I would do whatever I wanted to. I would sleep with whomever I damn well pleased. Blinded by the rage that covered up my hurt, I didn't see what was coming until it was too late.

I arrived at the club at eleven fifty-five and was greeted once more by Cathary. Ducasse appeared as well. He reached out with strong hands to take my down vest after I peeled it off. When I glanced up, I saw he was staring at me with eyes like pale silver moons. They were predatory eyes, and they seemed to hone in on my unhappiness. Suddenly Ducasse smiled and showed his teeth. They weren't pointed; he was no vampire, but my gut feeling was that something about him wasn't entirely human.

"Miss Urban," he said in a low, seductive voice. "We want to make you welcome here, for you to feel you belong here. Please do not hesitate to call for me if I can assist you in any way." His eyes glittered then, catching the candlelight, but a reddish glow seemed to illuminate them from behind the irises. They were strange eyes, and very cruel ones at that. "Any way, Miss Urban. Any way at all." He lowered his head and bowed before walking away so silently his feet made no sound on the marble floor.

Cathary broke into my observation of Ducasse. "I'll take you upstairs now, Miss Urban. Tallmadge and Miss Polycarp have already arrived."

He had started up the stairs when a noise from the sitting room to my right drew my attention. I hesitated at the first step. The light from the hallway didn't relieve the darkness within it, yet I could sense the room wasn't empty. Then I heard the noise again. It was a long, slow breath. A man stepped out of the utter darkness into the dim shadows where his form was visible, although still indistinct and wreathed in gloom. But it was clear that he was big. His heavily muscled torso was bare and cut like marble, and his head was covered by a leather hood. I shivered and began to mount the step. As I turned away the hooded man said in a voice just above a whisper, "I will be waiting . . . for you." It was Ducasse. I hurried to catch up with Cathary.

In the room at the top of the stairs, Tallmadge was positioned behind the silk brocade divan upon which Benny sat. A nice spread of steak tartare and rare slices of London broil sat on the coffee table, along with a plate of caramelized Brie, bruschetta, and crudités of asparagus, carrot, and haricot vert. Since none of us were big veggie eaters, I wondered if the latter were just for show. Some chocolate-dipped fresh strawberries sat in a silver bowl, and a bottle of white wine had been uncorked.

Benny held a glass of the wine in her hand, but I suspected she hadn't eaten anything. She looked like a porcelain doll, her skin ivory white and her hair pale as straw. She had pulled that hair severely back from her face, fastening it up in a chignon. A tight black leather jacket hugged her figure. When she stood to greet me, I could see that her pants were leather too, and she walked a bit unsteadily on very high heels when she came over to me. She hooked her arm through mine. Her eyes looked dazed and her smile was crooked. I could smell the wine and the sweet scent of marijuana clinging to her.

"Oh, Daphy," she said, "I'm so glad you're here. Come sit next to me." She tugged on my arm, and I followed her to the couch.

Frowning in disapproval at what had obviously been going on before my arrival, I glanced up at Tallmadge. He seemed entirely clearheaded, and he smiled. "I echo the lady's sentiments, Miss Urban. I too am glad you are here." With that he

leaned over from behind me and kissed my cheek. His lips
sent electricity dancing across my skin, and I pulled away as
if I had been burned. I warned myself to keep my distance
from this dangerously attractive vampire.

Cathary had slipped out of the room, and now he reap-
peared, bringing Cormac in behind him. Cormac gave me a
puzzled look. "Has the party started without me?" he said.

"There is no party," I snapped. "This is a business meeting, isn't it?"

"For now," Tallmadge said from behind me.

"Would you mind coming out where I can see you?" I
asked, feeling uneasy. "Frankly, Tallmadge, you're getting on
my nerves."

Cormac's eyebrows raised. I'm sometimes acerbic, but
I'm usually polite.

"Of course," Tallmadge answered, and moved around to a
chair on my left. Cormac sat across from me on the same sofa
he had occupied last night. Now he leaned forward and
grabbed a plate. He piled some of the steak tartare on a piece
of bruschetta, poked a fork into some slices of London broil,
and filled his plate. Then he proceeded to chow down. I
wasn't hungry and didn't touch a thing.

"What have you found out? Anything?" I asked. I felt unexpectedly angry at finding Benny thoroughly stoned and
blamed Tallmadge. I felt sure he had encouraged her to
smoke, and I had my suspicions that he enjoyed corrupting
her as much as possible. What would be next? Cocaine?
Heroin? I could handle someone like Tallmadge. Benny
couldn't. My anger started to build.

Tallmadge's silky voice broke into my thoughts. "I haven't
found out a lot, but something." He reached out and picked
up a manila file from the coffee table between the couches. "I
made you each a copy of my research, but I'll recap my find-

ings in brief, if that is okay with you?" He handed another folder to me, making sure his fingertips brushed mine. I stifled a gasp as electricity raced up my arm.

"Go ahead," I barked. "Let's get this over with. Cormac and I have someplace else to go." Suddenly I wanted to get away from Tallmadge.

Benny stirred then. "Oh, Daphy, please don't rush off. I was so hoping you'd stay awhile. And I want you to meet the countess." She put her hand on my arm, and I looked over at her. There was a naked pleading in her eyes. It occurred to me that, even in her dreamy state, she might be afraid.

My voice softened. "We have a little time, Benny. I guess we can stick around. Okay with you, Cormac? You're on break, aren't you?"

Cormac's face was unreadable. I don't know if he picked up on Benny's feelings. He looked at me and answered, "Yes, but I can't stay. I'm on my lunch hour—a half hour, really. I can stretch it out a little, but I should head back to Opus Dei in twenty minutes. Sorry. I was assured I wouldn't be working there much longer, right? This may be the last night I'll have to endure it. Isn't that true, Daphne?"

"I don't know any more than you do, Cormac. But I hope you can wind up your assignment tonight. I really do," I said without conviction. "Tallmadge, maybe you'd better get started."

Tallmadge sat up straighter. His words were crisp, his demeanor serious. He was all business when he started his report. "Okay now. To begin, the first assassination tied to Gage was the gunning down of the son of the president of Zambia; it occurred in 2000. Before that I can't find anything. Gage seems to have dropped out of nowhere. He left a calling card. The victim was shot next to his vehicle, and Gage wrote, 'Gage kills' in the guy's blood on the side of the car.

"The most recent assassination was of a peace activist in Somalia. That assassination was tied to al Qaeda, but Gage left a calling card, again writing on the victim's vehicle. This time he wrote only the initials GK.

"All the shootings confirmed to be committed by Gage took place outdoors. The shots came from above, although the exact location of the shooter was never pinpointed in any of the cases. Never. I thought that was significant. Also, no one has ever gotten a clear picture of Gage, even when the area of the assassination was being filmed on surveillance cameras. Outside of the grainy photo in the agency's file, the best they've got is the shadow of what seems to be a tall figure in a long coat. Why no pictures? I don't have any answers. And from the weapon used in the killing—an M107—I suspect Gage is ex-military, and very possibly American."

"I thought the same thing," I said quietly. The Special Forces link had been something I wanted to run by Darius. Well, that wasn't going to happen, I thought. Maybe I should go to J about it. And maybe I'd better not. He might think that Darius was linked to Gage, that Darius might even *be* Gage.

"Well, that's about it. I think anything else we get is going to be from humint. I have an idea I'm going to try to run down over the weekend. If I turn up any rocks with creepy crawlers underneath, I'll call everybody right away. Otherwise I feel as if we're up against a brick wall here. Any ideas?"

Cormac said, "Nothing here. But then, I'm out of the loop," he added bitterly.

Benny shook her head slowly and said, "Nothing here either. Daphne and I spent the evening with Daniel's people. We didn't learn anything, did we, Daphy?"

"No, nothing. Just a dead end there, as far as I'm concerned," I said. "I agree about the humint. Like Tallmadge, I'm toying with a crazy idea. Let me check it out. When we meet again we should pool anything we've got. Anything. We have one week and one day to find Gage. And frankly, my friends, right now it ain't looking good," I quipped.

"Well, if push comes to shove, we'll protect Daniel at the rally," Tallmadge said.

"Plan B," I agreed. "And we need it to be worked out to the minute. What do you think? If we don't have anything concrete on Gage by when, Wednesday? We get plan B set in stone. Okay?"

Cormac finally spoke up. "To tell the truth, I think plan B is going to be it. At least, I can see exactly what we'll have to do. There are four of us, and we're vampires. We have surprise on our side too. We can do this," he said with a confidence I wasn't used to hearing in his voice. All traces of whining were gone. I noticed he was wearing a red silk scarf along with his usual all-black attire. He looked bigger. I wondered if he was lifting weights. Well, good for old Cormac. "Look, guys, I have to run," he said, and stood up. "Daphne, later?" he said quietly to me.

"Yeah, later," I answered, and gave him a little salute. I was getting too warm sitting next to Benny in her leather, so I got up and took Cormac's place on the sofa, a decision I instantly regretted, because it put my back toward the door, making me feel vulnerable. At that moment Cathary entered, carrying a tray. On it was a bottle, four glasses, a perforated spoon, some sugar cubes, and a water decanter with a spigot.

"Ah, the refreshments have arrived," Tallmadge said as Cathary put down the tray, nodded at Tallmadge, and left.

"What is it?" Benny said with more life in her voice. Finally her marijuana high was dissipating, and I felt relieved.

"*La fée verte.* The Green Fairy, an original recipe, not the weak imitation that's legal today."

"Ohhhh, you mean it's illegal?" Benny said, sitting up straight and looking interested. "Why?"

"Because," I broke in, "it's absinthe with a high worm-wood content. In the eighteen hundreds it was said to drive drinkers mad. Vincent van Gogh drank it, so I guess it did."

"Rubbish!" Tallmadge said. "Oscar Wilde also drank it, along with many others. Perhaps absinthe occasionally in-duced hallucinations, but even that assertion is questionable. Absinthe is, however, not to be missed. I hope you will join me in experiencing the pleasure."

"Count me out," I replied. "I have work to do later."

"Oh, Daphne, I just don't understand you! Tallmadge is trying to be nice. You just bring me so down. Please don't be such a party pooper," Benny pleaded. "I'm going to try it. I'd feel so much better if you did."

I was coming off as a prude. I had no right to stop Benny from doing exactly the same things I had once done. My tone softened. "Benny, I have tried it. In Paris—long ago. If you want to do it . . . well, the Green Fairy is . . . interesting. I have to keep a clear head for later; that's all."

"Yes, absinthe is . . . 'interesting,'" Tallmadge echoed, and smiled a sly fox's smile. He leaned forward and poured some of the green fluid into the bottom of a glass. Then he put a sugar cube on the spoon, held the spoon over the glass, and ran the water over the sugar to sweeten the drink, because absinthe alone is bitter. As the water filled the glass, the green absinthe turned a milky white.

"Whoo! That is so cool," Benny said as Tallmadge handed her a glass. She took a little sip. "It tastes like licorice, and it's really good!" she exclaimed.

"Drink it slowly," I warned. "It's not lemonade."

Tallmadge raised an eyebrow at me and prepared a second glass.

"I've asked the countess to join us," he said.

Just then the door behind me opened. I quickly stood up in time to watch a tall woman stride in. The countess wasn't what I had expected. Her hair was completely white, although her face was young, unlined, and quite beautiful. Her lips were cherry red and sensual, but her long body was androgynous. She wore a white silk shirt open to her waist, showing no cleavage at all. A heavy gold collar holding a jeweled medallion encircled her neck. Her loose pants were a shimmering silver.

The countess strode over to me and said with a trace of a French accent in her voice, "Daphne Urban. Your reputation precedes you, as does that of your mother, Marozia. This is a rare pleasure." She extended her hand and I took it. It was extremely strong, more like a man's hand than a woman's, and I felt a surge of blackness course through me. The countess clearly had dark powers; she was a vampire to be reckoned with. Her eyes looked like a cat's and she suddenly appeared to me as a sleek silver beast who lay in the shadows, a predator waiting for prey.

"I don't know if I can say this is a pleasure," I responded.

"I hope you find it to be once we become better acquainted," she said, smiling without warmth. Then she moved toward Tallmadge, whom she kissed lightly on the lips before bending down and giving Benny an air kiss beside her cheeks. "And how are you tonight, little one?" she asked. As she straightened up I saw her hand stroke Benny's cheek.

"I'm jest fine, Countess," Benny said. "I'm glad you could join us. Don't mind my friend Daphy. She's in a bad mood tonight. I think she had a fight with her boyfriend. Am I right, Daphy?" Benny said mischievously.

I gave her a sour look, sat down again, and didn't answer. I was curious about the countess and what Tallmadge had in mind for Benny this evening. I hoped my presence would keep things from going too far, but I knew how most vampires were. They pushed the limits of every pleasure. Jaded to most things, they kept looking for new sensations. Seducing an innocent like Benny provided entertainment, maybe a good laugh, and some new sexual games as well. I feared for my friend, but I couldn't run her life. All I could do was hang around as long as I could.

Tallmadge handed the countess the second glass of milky-white absinthe and prepared a third. He offered it to me, but I waved it away. He put the glass down on the table in front of me. "You might change your mind, especially if you did try it in Paris."

"I did," I said.

"You will find this is very much the same drink you sampled back then, an original recipe. The effects will wear off quickly, I promise," he said seductively. "You might enjoy reliving the experience. It's not harmful, just delightfully relaxing, as you know."

I didn't answer, and Tallmadge turned his attention to preparing the last glass for himself. The countess lowered herself next to Benny on the sofa, sitting on her folded legs and staring at my friend. "You look lovely tonight, Benny," she said. "You are a beautiful woman," she added.

"I don't think another woman ever called me beautiful before. Most of the time I heard that from rednecks while we were doing it in the backseat of a car," Benny answered.

The countess laughed. "You are so unique, Benny. I just adore you."

"Why, thank you kindly," Benny said, gazing in something like awe at the countess. She was clearly starstruck. I hoped she kept her wits about her. I had a bad feeling where this was all headed.

"I know you don't have much time, Daphne," Tallmadge said. "I thought when we finished our drinks, I'd take you downstairs and show you the rest of the club. I showed Benny around last night, didn't I?"

Again I caught a frisson of something like fear passing quickly over Benny's face before it disappeared and was replaced by her smile. "You surely did. I never did see anything like that in my life. Especially that there party room. Are we gonna be partying again, Tal?" she asked as her voice dropped low and her eyes got smoky.

"If that's what you wish," Tallmadge said. "You deserve to get whatever you would like to have. Remember, you are a vampire. All you have to do is ask."

"Then I'm asking, Tal," she said in a whisper. "Let's go soon, okay?" She took a long drink of her absinthe, ignoring my warning about draining the glass too quickly. The countess leaned over and kissed the top of Benny's head. "You are such a sweet little one."

The whole scene was getting to me in conflicting ways. I was very uncomfortable about the obvious sexual dynamic between the three of them. But on a deep, subconscious level, the situation was stirring up some long-buried memories and turning me on. The candles in the wall holders had burned down, and some had gone out. The room was very warm and swathed in flickering shadows that seemed to undulate across the walls.

While my better sense told me I shouldn't, my hand, almost of its own accord, reached out and took the glass of absinthe and brought it to my lips. The licorice taste filled my mouth and slid down my throat like golden fire. Warmth filled me, and within seconds a pleasant tingle infused my veins. I drank again and drained the glass dry. Tallmadge watched me like a snake, and although he held his glass in his hand, I noticed he had not drunk a drop.

"Countess," he said. "Why don't you take Benny downstairs? I'll join you in a few minutes. I want to speak with Daphne for a second."

I inhaled sharply. I didn't want to be alone with him, especially after downing the powerful liquor.

"Of course, my dear," she said, and rose. She offered her hand to Benny, who got up on unsteady feet. Her breasts swayed beneath the leather jacket as she slipped her arm around the countess, who in turn encircled Benny's waist with a strong arm.

"Now, you all don't be too long." She giggled. "The countess and I are waitin' on you."

"We won't be a minute—promise," Tallmadge said. Linked arm in arm, Benny and the countess slipped out the door.

"Daphne," he said, walking over and hovering above me. He lowered a hand to help me up. I stood and swayed. He was too close. "Why do you fight this, my dear? It is the vampires' way. It hurts no one—in fact, it is one of the privileges of our race." He leaned close and touched my cheek with very soft lips. He moved his lips to my mouth, and although I willed myself not to respond, he kissed me.

The room tilted. Pleasure spread through my body. "Don't," I said.

Keeping his lips very close and putting his hands on my shoulders, he asked, "Why? Don't you like it?"

"Benny likes it. That's why, among other reasons," I answered.

His hands held me fast, like iron bands. He had a male vampire's immense strength. The knowledge that I could not

easily move aroused me. Tallmadge kept kissing me with ca-
resses that dropped like flower petals on my cheeks, on my
eyes, on my lips. Then he took little nibbles that became
sweet little bites. It felt wonderful, but I fought responding. I
had to resist him. "Don't," I said again.

He pushed his body against me. I could feel the stiffness
of his member press into me. It was large and hard. "Let me
pleasure you," he coaxed. "No one will know. Benny will
never know. Why shouldn't we enjoy each other, Daphne?
The chemistry is there. You can feel it. I know you can."

I could. I did. But I wasn't going to do this, not with this
vampire. I thought I had given up sex without an emotional
connection centuries ago. Yet I was being tempted. Perhaps if
Benny had not been my friend, I would have surrendered. I
can be weak, but I am loyal. I took my hands and pushed
against Tallmadge, moving him back. "No. Thank you, no.
You're an attractive vampire, Tallmadge. But this isn't my
scene; I told you that."

To his credit, Tallmadge took the refusal well. He smiled
at me. "Perhaps next time. Are you coming downstairs with
me?"

"I think I had better go. You go do whatever it is you do in
the 'party room.' I'll let myself out."

"As you wish," he said, and moved away so quietly I
didn't see him go. But my mind was becoming clouded with
dreams, and instead of leaving, I sank down on the sofa once
more. Images rushed into my mind. Wild colors swirled and
undulated. *It's the absinthe,* I thought. It was my last rational
thought.

CHAPTER 7

❧

The sky was a midnight-blue, like warm, deep, blue water, and the moon seemed to lie on it like a water-lily, floating forward with an invisible current.

—Willa Cather, *One of Ours*

Surrendering to the absinthe, I began to dream, and the face that swam into my mind belonged to Darius. Then his face became that of George Gordon, Lord Byron, that mad, bad boy I had once loved too much. I remembered all too well Byron's amorality and brilliance, understanding in a moment of clarity that I always lost my heart to the same type of man. And usually—no, make that always—I ended up destroying him.

I remembered first meeting Byron in England, and the wild, dark, and decadent affair that followed. Then I went too far, gave in to my needs, and bit him, draining him nearly dry of blood. After getting Byron to a physician, who managed to save his life, I felt ashamed of what I had done. I ran off to the continent determined never to see him again, troubled at losing both my control and my emotions to a human.

I remembered ending up back in Italy. That was in 1820, a time not so long ago when you are a vampire with nearly eternal life. Whenever I became deeply depressed, I always returned to my villa on the outskirts of Montespertoli, a hill-top town which was, at that time, a few hours by carriage ride to Florence. Now, by car, I could drive the distance in twenty minutes. Maybe, I thought as I began to confuse the past and the present in my drug-addled brain, I needed to go back there and straighten out my feelings, either to get Darius out of my system or to find a way to keep us together. A thought edged into my brain that if I always destroyed the man I loved, Darius would be next. I pushed that thought out of my mind and thought of Italy instead.

I remembered staring out into the soft gray dusk of Tuscany, feeling restless and utterly bored. In that state of ennui, I wandered though the great halls and beautifully ap-pointed rooms until I ended up in the kitchens, where I asked Dulcinea, the Spanish cook, for slices of wild boar to be served to me in the long, rustic dining hall that predated the rest of the building. As I tore into the pieces of raw meat on the plate put before me, I looked up at the battle-axes and armor hung on the walls. Some still held the rusty stains of the owner's blood. I knew what it was. I am a vampire; I am extremely sensitive to blood. I shook my head at the human penchant for war, so barbaric and cruel and so rarely neces-sary. The night crept into the room, and I sat in the dark, won-dering how I would pass the long hours stretching before me.

As the sadness that is still my constant companion again took its place in my heart, I cursed my immortality and mean-ingless existence. It would be nearly two more centuries be-fore I found a purpose in life, and in that dolorous state of mind, even a late-night visit from my mother was welcome. In truth, I thought she'd show up sooner or later.

Shortly after I had arrived at the villa, Marozia had writ-ten me to request that I give refuge to a man named Pietro Gamba. He arrived shortly before dawn a few days afterward, much exhausted and extremely nervous. I had sent my servants to settle him comfortably in the "yellow cottage," a charming stucco house near the olive groves that bordered my grounds. I paid him no more attention, for Gamba, if he left the yellow cottage at all, roamed by day, and I came out only at night.

"Mar-Mar," I said, not bothering to rise from a divan where I reclined, reading a small quarto of poetry. Little white slippers covered my feet; a thin, pink muslin gown clung to my body. "*Come stai?* How are you?"

"*Bene*, fine, as always," she replied tersely. My mother remained standing on the far side of the room, wrapped from head to toe in a silken black cloak so sheer it was almost like a veil. Golden earrings dangled from her ears, and a huge ruby ring sparkled on her slim white hand. "I have come for Pietro Gamba, and to thank you for hiding him here."

"So he is part of the Carboneria, like you? I don't know what you find so attractive in those secret societies. I find politics a bore," I said, letting the book drop onto the floor beside me and sitting up.

"Perhaps that is why you are so unhappy," she replied. "The fight for Italy's freedom consumes me."

"Time consumes me, and nothing else," I said. My mother gave me a long look, seeming to hesitate before she spoke again.

"Perhaps that will change when I tell you that your Lord Byron is in great danger," she said at last.

I was shocked into silence. Years ago I had told my mother about the affair and while she had not lectured me on my foolishness, she had emphasized that it was unwise to have revealed to Byron that I was a vampire and, having done so, to have let him live. I had resisted her urging to have him killed and made her promise not to do the deed herself.

In the intervening years since then, Byron had descended into debauchery. The man had no shame and certainly no morals. Perhaps that was why I had liked him so much. I had heard that Byron came to Italy a few years ago, and after nearly killing himself with drink in Venice, he had predictably become entangled with yet another woman. With Byron, there was always another woman who became his "great love." This time he began a scandalous affair with the pretty eighteen-year-old wife of the elderly Count Guiccioli. I still felt angry when I remembered his profligate ways, but in the ten years since we had parted I had put Byron out of my mind—and certainly out of my heart—long ago. Or so I thought.

"What do you mean?" I snapped, and rose to my feet quickly.

"You know of his liaison with the Countess Guiccioli?"

I nodded.

"You may not know that the countess is the sister of Pietro Gamba, your guest."

"And so?" I said, taking control of my emotions and feigning disinterest.

"As you guessed, Pietro Gamba is in the Carboneria. So is Byron. His affair with the countess is simply a fiction—"

"A fiction?" I broke in. "I had read that he was completely infatuated with her and that she had abandoned her home for him. The pope finally granted her cuckolded husband a separation."

Mar-Mar laughed without mirth. "Teresa, the young countess, had been kept under lock and key at their Ravenna estate, a virtual prisoner of her decrepit and insanely jealous husband. She had been pulled from her convent at sixteen and forced to marry that randy old goat. After her rape on her wedding night, she wanted nothing to do with love or men, including Byron, who quite frankly drinks too much and has grown fat. The countess, like her brother, wants nothing less than Italy's freedom and a constitutional government. Her 'love' for Byron is a smoke screen. That second-rate English poet is simply a friend, one with lots of wealthy friends of his own to help support their cause. You can't believe what you read in the newspapers," she added.

"I know that," I said sharply. "It is just that everyone has said that this Teresa is Byron's greatest passion." My words were hard, belying my rapidly beating heart, and Mar-Mar had my attention as she went on.

"Pietro escaped arrest, thanks to your allowing him to hide here. However, Byron has not been so lucky. He has been taken into custody and imprisoned in the Palazzo dei Cavalieri in Pisa. They say he is destined to lay his head on the executioner's block."

"When?" I said, shaken and seized with a terrible fear for him.

"I don't know. In a few days? Next week? His friends have been trying to buy his freedom, but I have heard they failed. Unfortunately, I have been identified as a conspirator with the Carboneria, and there is a price on my head here in the north. I am taking Pietro back to Naples in the south. Pietro's sister has begged for assistance, but neither he nor I can go to Pisa. Perhaps you wish to help?"

I was stunned that my mother was suggesting that I go to Byron's aid. If I thought about it more deeply, I would have seen that she viewed the request as helping the cause. If my heart were entangled in the process, it mattered nothing to her. When she was immersed in intrigue, she would manipulate anyone, even me, to achieve her ends.

Later that night I called for my carriage and started the journey to Pisa, about eighty kilometers away. Cold autumn rains had replaced the warm weather and turned the roads into quagmires. Two nights later I arrived in the city. My carriage pulled into the wide piazza around the famous Leaning Tower, and I slipped from the coach, instructing the driver to wait at a discreet inn right outside the thick city walls.

I had filled my purse with silver coins and brought some of my most ornate jewelry to use as barter. The Florentines and Pisans loved gold; I hoped Byron's jailers would be willing to trade him for these baubles. But if they refused, I had no compunction about making the terms of the barter be their very lives.

As rain drenched the ancient city, I pulled a heavy cape around me and walked quickly through the narrow streets to the Piazza dei Cavalieri, where a statue of Cosimo de' Medici looked down with a cruel eye upon all who came here. I made my way not to the main palace, but to the nearby Palazzo dell'Orologio, which had long been used as a jail. It was a forbidding place of ghosts and nearly unspeakable horrors. In times past, the mayor of this city, along with his sons and grandsons, had been accused of treason. Condemned to death by starvation, the mayor was said to have devoured his own children, one by one, until the entire family was exterminated. I shook my head, not doubting at least a kernel of truth to this old story. We vampires are called evil, yet humans deserve that epithet far more than we.

Inside the Palazzo four guards were hunkered down on the floor, engaged in a game of dice. They would have continued to ignore me if I had not kicked one with my wet and muddy boot. My haughty demeanor, my bejeweled hands, and my heavy cloak of the finest cloth marked me as a member of the aristocracy. "*Cane!* Dog!" I yelled sharply. "Get up. I wish to see Lord Byron."

A young, weasel-faced peasant looked at me insolently.

He didn't rise. "You and half the ladies in Pisa wish to see him. He is permitted no visitors. Go away."

I took a handful of silver coins and threw them down on the floor. The four guards scrambled to pocket them. "You filthy animals," I said in a voice filled with threats. "I should have you torn limb from limb. Say in your prayers a special thanks that I gave you money instead." The four faces turned toward me when I spoke, for my voice was not a lady's voice. It was the voice of death. As they looked at me, I smiled a terrible smile and hissed with a vampire's soul-chilling hiss. "I wish to see Byron now, you mangy curs."

One of the jailers quickly led me down a narrow flight of stairs to the dungeons below. With trembling hands, he unlocked a rusty iron door and swung it wide. It was dark within and smelled of filth. I saw the prone figure of a man lying on some dirty straw. He raised himself onto his elbow. If Byron had been fat, weeks without abundant food had restored his figure. If his looks had been ruined by drink, weeks without wine had renewed his health and handsome face. He was unkempt and bearded, but he was a gorgeous human being.

"Ah, a beautiful lady at my door," he said. "I'm afraid I'm not dressed for company, my dear, but do come in." He stood then, a lopsided grin lighting his grimy face. Clearly his spirit was unbroken.

I turned to the guards. "Leave us in private," I ordered. They hesitated, their fear of me fighting with the fact that they'd surely lose their heads if Byron escaped. "Wait at the end of the corridor if you must watch the door," I said dismissively, and turned to the prisoner, who now wore a puzzled look.

"Do I know you?" he asked. He stared at me blankly. Then recognition and a wide smile lit his fine features. "I must be dreaming. Or perhaps I am already dead if you are really the fair Daphne? I remember our last meeting, or at least part of it, the part before you drank my blood and damn near killed me."

"You have more lives than a cat, but you will be killed if I don't get you out of here," I replied. Although I didn't approach Byron, my pulse raced at the sight of him. He had an angel's countenance and the devil's own charm. "This is no time to rake up old memories. How much have your friends offered in bribes for your release?"

"A king's ransom. I fear that after my latest indiscretion only my head seems a high enough price for the authorities. Perhaps we should just kiss and bid farewell. Or better yet, let your bite offer me a sweet way to die, for in your arms I would gladly expire. You see, money can't buy my freedom this time," he said, and moved toward me into the dim corridor. "Forgive my lack of a bath, fair lady. My valet has been otherwise occupied," he said jokingly, then his voice turned serious. "I have never, ever forgotten you, Daphne," he whispered. "I have been bad since we parted. I'm sure you know. But I was driven out of my senses by wanting you and not ever being able to have you again."

That was a load of blarney. I did not believe him for a minute, but the very nearness of him aroused me. He was as rakish as ever and totally without fear, yet this was no time for games.

"I cannot believe that you would try to seduce me in a dungeon," I snapped. "As for your pretty words, they are just that. You have enjoyed every female from Italy to England who has been willing to spread her legs for you. I'm not here for a poke and a tickle. I'm here to save your worthless life."

"I'm cut to the quick. You have rejected a condemned man's final request," he mocked.

"Are you strong enough to fight?" I asked.

"I can't fight all four of them, if that's what you're asking," he said, glancing down the hall where the guards stood watching us.

I shielded what I was doing by turning my back and draping one hand around Byron's neck. With my free hand I pulled a dagger from my bodice and passed it to him. "I have a feeling you won't need this," I said. "Just try not to faint at what I am about to do. And oh, yes, would you please be sure to pick up my cloak and shoes? I'll need them later."

Byron shook his head, not comprehending my words, and then his eyes grew wide as I pulled off my boots and ripped the long cape from my body, letting it fall to the floor. I had nothing beneath it. I heard one of the guards call out, but what was about to happen was unstoppable: I began the terrible, magnificent change into my vampire self. I released the beast beneath my skin.

With a burst of energy, light swirled around me in sparkling waves. I grew bigger; wings sprang from my back. My nails became sharp talons, and my skin turned into a dark pelt that was not fur, but something finer and iridescent, its tiny prisms casting rainbow colors across its surface. My long hair wrapped around me like Medusa's snakes, and my eyes turned golden, the ebony pupils deep, unfathomable, and bottomless as the hell within me.

Now resembling a giant bat, I whirled around and flew at the four hapless guards. Two fled up the stairs, one passed out in terror, and one fool pulled a sword. I smashed into him with my massive bulk, breaking his ribs with a satisfying crunch and sending him to the ground.

With Byron somewhere to my rear, I soared up the staircase after the two running men. I grabbed one by the hair, yanking him off his feet. I slung him headfirst into a wall and he fell to the floor insensible as a stone. The insolent weasel-faced guard I had first encountered was trying desperately to reach the door. I descended on him, and he unsheathed his sword and sliced frantically at the air. I danced backward, dodging his flailing weapon. Then, like a lightning strike, I raked him with my sharp nails. He pulled back with a scream and one of my blows, aimed for his face, caught him in the throat. As a look of horror passed over his terror-struck features, a gaping red wound crossed his neck from ear to ear. His life's blood poured down across his jacket.

I hadn't meant to kill him, but I didn't care that I had.

With all four guards dispatched, I landed on the floor. In an eyeblink, a shining spiral of white light obscured me. When it was gone I stood there in the room, returned to human form and naked as a babe. Byron emerged from the stairwell to see me at that moment, and he leered at my bare white flesh. "This dream keeps getting better and better," he said.

"Just hand me my cloak and boots, " I demanded. "There is no time for a dalliance."

Covered again in the voluminous folds of the dark cape and with my feet shod, I took Byron's hand. We rushed into the dreary night. Rain soaked my hair and sent droplets running down my cheeks like tears. I led the way through the cobblestone streets, but we had gotten only a few hundred feet when Byron pulled me into a sheltered doorway. He put his arms around me and showered my face with kisses. Then he took my lips with his and kissed me deeply. I sighed and hungrily returned the caress. As I was naked beneath the cloak, he lost no time in finding my breasts with his hands, pinching my nipples as he greedily devoured my mouth.

Excitement surged through me. The proximity of danger heightened my desire. Byron pushed me against the wall as he fumbled with his pants and pulled out his stiff member.

"We shouldn't," I mumbled. "We should run—" I began to say before I felt his hand between my legs guiding his hardness inside me. Then all words failed me and I sighed.

With short, hard thrusts, Byron drove into me. My eyes closed, and I arched into him, tightening around his stiffness. My love for him exploded in my heart once more, a joy mixed with sadness because I knew he felt lust for me, but perhaps nothing more. The hard stones of the wall behind me jabbed into my back. Pain and pleasure, the twins of sexual arousal, made me breathless and left me wild with desire. A sweet tension built inside me as Byron pushed rhythmically in and out, slippery with my wetness. Right before I came, I opened my eyes to see Byron's face transfixed by ecstasy. His fingers dug into my bare shoulders. He plowed into me with all his strength, and then I couldn't stop the waves carrying me higher. I closed my eyes again and let sensations overwhelm me. I wanted to scream out, but I muffled my groans of delight by burying my face in his shoulder. That was a mistake. His neck was so close to my lips, I found my fangs growing longer, and a nearly irresistible urge emerged from somewhere deep within me.

My eyes snapped open. I pulled myself back, horrified at what I was a hairbreadth from doing. "My lord, your life is worth more than a lay," I said harshly, and pulled away from him, stopping him right before he spilled his seed.

"No!" he growled, and pushed to enter me once more. But my strength was far greater than his, and I held him back. " I promise we can resume this position later, once we reach my villa in Montespertoli. For now I must insist we go." I pulled my cloak around me and impatiently waited for Byron to fix his trousers. Then I grabbed his hand and yanked him back into the street. Shouts came from the direction of the Piazza dei Cavalieri. I assumed one of the guards had raised the alarm.

I remember that I ran, laughing, wet with rain and sex, toward the city walls by the Leaning Tower. Suddenly, irrevocably, George Gordon, Lord Byron, was back in my life, and I could not know that the consequences of our reunion would one day be tragic for us both.

Those sweet memories had been born of the absinthe, that I knew. Had the drink also contained an aphrodisiac? I wondered, because I found myself in the here and now sexually aroused so greatly that I hungered for release. *If I'm this badly off,* I thought, *what must Benny be feeling?* Deeply worried that she might be in a state where she could not resist anything the countess or Tallmadge thought to do, I jumped up and rushed from the room, intending to go in search of her as I cursed Tallmadge and the temptations of his world.

Dizzy and disoriented, I nearly tumbled down the stairs in my frantic haste. Once on the first floor, I started running down the long hall leading to the back of the mansion, where I could hear music playing. Suddenly, from the shadows of a doorway, a strong hand reached out and grabbed my wrist, halting me in my tracks. Adrenaline poured through me. Another instant and I would have begun to transform into bat form. I looked at the figure that held me in an iron grip. It was the half-naked man, his face obscured by a black hood, a zipper closing its mouth, narrow slits allowing the wearer to see out but no one to see in.

"Now," he said quietly.

"Let go of me," I responded through clenched teeth.

"Make me," he said with a laugh, and released my arm.

I looked at him and shivered. Everything about this figure

was sexual—and cruel. I was about to flee but suddenly felt myself held in the grip of a force much stronger than his hand.

"I am here for you," he breathed in a soft, seductive voice. "Come with me," he said as he unzipped the black leather hood with one hand and pulled it off. Blond hair and a face with silver eyes emerged. As I suspected, it was Ducasse. His eyes bored into me. They were hypnotic, mesmerizing, irresistible. They were doing something to me, robbing my will and making me see only those eyes, those strange, glittering orbs. Ducasse continued speaking in a voice so smooth it caressed me like silk. "Come. I will be prey for you."

With the dreams of Byron so close, with the wormwood working its magic in my brain, I lost my reason. Suddenly I had to have blood. Ducasse took my wrist again and pulled me toward him. I hesitated a moment, and then, in a trance-like manner, I followed.

Ducasse led me into the interior of a large room that was lit softly with the yellow glow of candles and filled with flickering shadows and dark corners. As he moved, Ducasse never took his eyes from me. Then he stopped and smiled. "Goddess. Vampire, look at me," he ordered. "Look at all I am for you."

Ducasse was indeed a magnificent male: The muscles of his arms and chest were hard and well defined; he had perfect six-pack abs; his skin was flawless and glistening with a light sheen of oil. As I devoured him with my eyes, I stretched out my hand and with one finger I traced a line from his navel to his neck, to the vein that throbbed there. He shivered. Then he reached behind him and moved a heavy curtain aside to reveal a huge, wide altar draped in soft red velvet. Above it hung an iron pentacle, not a cross.

"Let me help you take off your clothes, dear lady vampire," he coaxed, and, feeling helpless to resist, I allowed him to pull my sweater over my head, leaving my breasts bare. Standing there transfixed, I watched him crouch down and slip off my clogs. Then he stood up very close to me, close enough so I could feel the warmth of his flesh on mine. He unbuttoned my jeans and pulled them down my legs. I stepped out of them and stood like a marble statue before him.

Ducasse climbed up and lay upon his back across the profane altar bed. Reaching out his arms and taking my hands in his, he drew me to him. When I began to mount the platform, he turned his head to fully expose the white of his neck.

"Take me," he whispered. "Bite me now," he pleaded, pulling me to him with his powerful grip.

I wish I could say my morals stopped me. They did not. I was driven by ancient hungers that raged with such force that I began to shake from head to foot. I leaped upon Ducasse with a terrible hiss. On all fours above him, I bared my sharp white teeth. I lowered my face to his strong neck and found the sweet spot, the pulsing vein of his hot, thick blood. I bit him then, my teeth sinking brutally into his skin. I drank, quenching my thirst with no thoughts and no guilt as the euphoria of blood whirled me toward madness.

Beneath me Ducasse was writhing and groaning in pleasure, and I was growling, intent upon the animal lust of my feeding. I was so lost in ecstasy that I did not perceive that he had loosened his trousers. Then he touched me between my thighs with his hard, rigid pole and I knew what was about to begin.

"Ohhhhh," I breathed, wanting to resist but soon conscious of nothing except the thrill of taking this forbidden joining to the next level. Without releasing his neck with my teeth, I stretched out upon him, the ghostly white of me touching him stomach to stomach, thigh to thigh. I slowly spread my legs, languidly, seductively. I moaned as the tip of Ducasse's member touched me in that hidden place and began to push into me, forcing my nether lips apart. With exquisite slowness he inched his way into the dark space within. And as he did, I gasped. His male rod was huge, well over ten inches long but even more impressive in girth, thicker than a fist, bigger than any man I had ever experienced.

Stunned, I widened my legs farther apart, as far as I could spread them. I received him then, and as I did he grasped my waist with hands of steel. He pushed my body down onto him, forcing me to permit him complete entry. An ache of sweet pain heightened the pleasure while his immense size possessed me, filled me, and made me wild.

I squirmed and wiggled. I tightened around him. Ducasse thrust his member up with all his might, brutally taking me with his entire length. I screamed as a quick surge of pain coursed through me. I tried to escape but I remained impaled. My teeth pulled free of his neck, letting a stream of blood trickle down his flesh. I cried out, "Ducasse! Ducasse! No, oh, no!" I was filled with him, stretched and engorged. The sensation made me crazed, insane for more, and my nos became, "Yes, yes," as I screamed again when he pulled back and slammed into me over and over, sliding deep inside me as far as he could go.

Yet I craved more. I needed more. I was swooning and swaying, breathing hard and slick with sweat. "Harder," I demanded. "Go harder." As I slipped across the boundaries into the dark land of hungers and pain, my voice became a plea, and I begged, "Harder, oh, please, oh, please, harder." Still yearning for something I could not understand, driven by instincts I didn't control, I frantically sat up with him inside me, an act that pushed his member even deeper. Another stab of pain shot through me. The pain did not in any way lessen my pleasure, but only intensified it. "Oh, God," I screamed, my head tilted, my back arched, and my eyes closed. "Oh, God," I screamed again as Ducasse pushed cruelly down on my waist again, shoving me tight and hard upon him as he cried out with a low moan that excited me even more.

He looked at me above him. "Ride me," he demanded. "Ride me hard," he ordered, loosening his grip on my waist and reaching up to pinch my nipples. I gasped again. Crying, groaning loudly, I was somewhere in a faraway place, my feelings on fire, a spiraling wave became an orgasm that took me, shook me, and set me free as Ducasse grabbed my ass and squeezed.

Ducasse's own blood dripped in thin rivulets from my red mouth and dropped like rose petals on his chest. My body was slick with sweat. My legs had begun to quiver. I slipped somewhere between awareness and oblivion, unconscious of everything except a need to come again and again. I glanced downward at my captor. His silver eyes were closed now and his face in bliss, his mouth open in ecstasy as he suddenly groaned louder. I felt him pulse once, twice, and then a third time as he shot his seed hot and warm inside me, sending me over the edge of pleasure with an orgasm. This one continued unabated for nearly a minute as I rocked back and forth upon him, blind with excitement, moaning as I was flooded with his fluid and a heat that radiated a continuing stream of ecstasy through my core.

Then it was done. I felt limp, weak, and unable to move. But Ducasse lifted me up, and with a heavy groan he pulled out of me, leaving me empty and bereft. I could not bear to end this yet. One last time I spread my body on top of him and pushed my teeth into his neck. I felt the skin break and tasted the saltiness of his blood. I had to be careful not to drink too much with this second feeding, not to kill him with my thirst. So I sucked for just a few minutes, pulling his hot fluid into my mouth as he took his hands and cradled my head until I lifted my lips, feeling sated and gorged with his life's stream. I kissed him then. "Ducasse," I murmured. "Oh, Ducasse, what are you?"

His eyes opened and his strong, handsome face looked at me in adoration. "My mistress," he said. "What I am is yours. Your slave. Your creature, now and forever." And somewhere deep within my still-addled mind, a revulsion grew at what I had just done.

CHAPTER 8

When lovely woman stoops to folly,
And finds too late that men betray,
What charm can soothe her melancholy,
What art can wash her guilt away?

—Oliver Goldsmith, *She Stoops to Conquer*

Despite my inner turmoil I had the presence of mind to ask Ducasse to retrieve my vest and backpack. I wish it had been so simple to retrieve my dignity. Since I couldn't bear to look at him, I ordered him to leave me, and I dressed quickly in the priest's costume I had picked up earlier at my apartment.

I left Tallmadge's club determined that I was closing its door behind me forever. That I departed dressed as *SNL*'s Father Guido Sarducci gave the whole episode a touch of absurdity. Despite the late hour, I planned to walk from the club to Opus Dei headquarters, hoping that the fresh air would revive me. I stopped at a Korean deli to grab a cup of coffee in an attempt to chase the last of the wormwood's visions from my brain.

I took a gulp of the scalding-hot coffee. It burned my mouth, and the sensation snapped me out of my funk. I had been beating myself up from the moment I had finished with Ducasse, and I was already getting tired of it. I acknowledged to myself that I had been drugged, but no one had forced me to drink the absinthe. I had put the glass to my lips myself. I had probably been hypnotized, yet I had known in advance that I should be wary. Around vampires, one must always be on guard. They will stop at nothing to get what they want, and Tallmadge, who obviously believed I had strayed from the ways of my own kind, wanted my capitulation and return to the fold.

Rather than agree with his conclusion that I had departed from my essence as a vampire, I preferred to think that I had evolved from a creature forever in pursuit of pleasure to an entity of principle. But I had had a slip, and I had fallen hard. What happened tonight had been a serious mistake. Over my four hundred years on this earth, life had taught me many lessons, most of them cruel, but one rock-sure thing I knew—behavior matters. As Sir Isaac Newton had observed, "For every action, there is an equal and opposite reaction." In other words, everything I chose to do had a consequence. Now I was being eaten up from the inside out with the knowledge that my licentious encounter with Ducasse was going to come back and bite me in the ass.

Mulling this over, I kept sipping the black, bitter coffee as I walked. I was nearly alone on the streets. An occasional taxi drove by, sometimes slowing down as it passed in case I might decide to ride. A full moon floated like a great white spotlight above the buildings, which were not especially tall this far from Midtown Manhattan. The air was crisp and clear. The New York night held a promise of springtime. I was free and answered to no one. However, I had to deal with this mess or one of two things would happen. I could make myself sick with self-recrimination. Or I could surrender to temptation and become what Tallmadge wanted, something like the Queen of the Damned.

Being that queen would have its benefits. Ensconced in the vampire underworld, backed by all my mother's influence and wealth, I could wield formidable power. If I wished to, I could intensify the primal fear in humans already engendered by the undead. I suppose, ultimately, I could further the goal of some vampires to rule the world, as if we needed more bloodsuckers to try to do that. But most likely I could live a purposeless, self-indulgent life where I daily satisfied my basest needs. I could hunt humans. I could drink my fill of warm, fresh blood. I could be the slave master for Ducasse and his ilk. I could become my dark side and forget about the light, the bright, good parts of me I had worked so hard to nurture and embrace.

As soon as I realized that, I decided on the course to best deal with it. The worst thing I could do was to hide or deny what I had done. The only way to live with it, to fight it and to conquer it, was to acknowledge it. I was going to sing like a canary to everyone who would listen. The first person I intended to tell was Fitz—the person who thought more highly of me than anyone else I knew. I *intended* to tell him, but when push came to shove, would I have the courage to go through with it? I steeled my resolve and planned to return to his hospital room as soon as I could.

I finished off the coffee, flattened the container in my hand, and threw it into a trash container on a street corner. Along with the empty cup, I tossed out my guilt. I put the events of the night behind me and went on.

I was a block from Opus Dei headquarters when I saw another priest on Thirty-Fourth Street, pacing back and forth and looking at his watch. The figure was too big to be Mar-Mar in disguise—I wondered who it was. I didn't wonder long. The priest turned and walked toward me. It was J.

Oh, shit. I wasn't in the mood for J and the mixed signals he always sent. Sometimes he made me feel as if he loathed me; other times he acted as if he respected me; and then, every once in a while, he let me see that he desired me. My feelings toward the entire male gender were negative in the extreme at the moment. J stepped into the line of fire. I was frowning when he reached me.

"What the hell are you doing here?" I demanded. He was wearing a black shirt with a priest's collar, black pants, and a black suit jacket. Over his shoulder he had slung the strap to a case that was about three feet long, similar to those that hold folding director's chairs for tailgate parties. I assumed J wasn't carrying portable seating around. I figured he had brought tools or a weapon.

"Nice to see you too," he said. "You're running late. We need to talk before we go in."

"Where's my mother?" I responded. "She's the one who needs to do the talking. This burglary is her project, isn't it?"

J was looking at me as if he were trying to figure out where I was coming from. "It's her project, yes. She asked me to help. She's not coming, by the way," he answered in a calm, even voice.

"What! In that case I don't want to be here either. I never did see why Cormac couldn't handle it himself. Okay, I'm out of here. I'm going home," I said, and turned to leave, thankful that I could skip this whole adventure.

"Hold up, Agent Urban," J said, pulling rank, and putting his hand on my shoulder to stop me in my tracks. He turned me around and looked right into my face. "You need to be here. It's a three-man job. From what I understand, Cormac can't get all the files out of there himself. There are several cartons."

"Files about what? Cartons of what?" I said, spitting out my words. "Who the hell cares about files right now?"

"Quite frankly, I don't know. These are some kind of records that were originally in the Vatican. That's all your mother told me about them. She also said this was an easy-in, easy-out operation that would take us just a few minutes. So let's do it."

I looked over at the hulking mass of Opus Dei headquarters. Suddenly I was overcome by a bad feeling about entering that building. My instincts started screaming at me to walk away. I didn't want to die inside that forbidding structure, and I had the sinking feeling my extermination was all too real a possibility. I stood unmoving on the pavement, fighting with emotions that were jangling like a fire alarm. I took a deep breath and said urgently, "Look, J, I don't get this at all. We've got an assassin out there getting ready to gun down Joe Daniel, and time is running out to stop him. Mar-Mar has had Cormac planted in Opus Dei from the day the Darkwings started, so she must have been planning to get these files for months now. You know the timing is all wrong on this. Let's put it off. Let's get out of here, okay?"

J's face registered surprise, then concern. "You're really bothered by this, aren't you?"

"I am way past bothered, J. I think we need to abort this mission and abort it now. Listen to me, please," I said, a plea entering my voice as I grabbed his sleeve. "This is *not* going to be a piece of cake."

J was listening to me intently. He was silent for a few seconds; then he said matter-of-factly, "Daphne, I can't disobey a direct order. Your mother put me on this mission because of my Special Forces training and, she explained, because I am a human, and you're not. She suspects I might be able to penetrate places you can't—and I might have to blow up a safe as well."

"And maybe she doesn't want three vampires to be killed at one time, J. She's smart and she's a survivor. For my mother the end always justifies the means. I hope to hell you're armed." I tasted bitterness in my mouth.

"I am, but I'm not about to shoot a priest tonight, Daphne. If anybody gets killed here—"

"Besides us, you mean," I broke in.

"Yeah, that's what I do mean. If a member of Opus Dei dies, the press and the cops are going to be all over this, and we can't afford that."

"And if you or I or Cormac dies, we'll disappear with no mess and no fuss. Isn't that right?"

J's face was adamantine. "We're soldiers, Daphne. That's the risk. Now, are we going to keep talking about something we can't change or get rolling?"

"Fuck it," I said, realizing that all my arguments weren't going to change the inevitability of my fate. "Let's roll."

Cormac was waiting for us. He opened the front door as we approached the building and motioned us to come in quickly. He wasn't surprised to see J. I soon discovered that behind my back—or at least that was how it felt—the two of them had talked earlier this evening while Benny and I were with Joe Daniel's campaign. J and Cormac had a plan, and I hadn't been told about it. I was seriously pissed off. I felt as if I couldn't trust anybody to be straight with me. Everybody had a secret agenda. My life was at stake here, no pun intended, and I had a right to be given all the facts.

I balked. I stopped right there in the entrance hall and said in a low voice, "Just a goddamned minute, you two. Fill me in, and fill me in right now, or I'm walking back out the door and to hell with both of you. And start with how we're going to get these files out of here without being observed. Cameras are everywhere."

"I rigged the surveillance system to keep playing the same tape loop," Cormac said impatiently. "They're not going to record anything. I worked on the system earlier tonight, but we've got to move quickly. Some security company watches them. I don't think they're paying much attention at three a.m., but if they observe me reading the same book and drinking the same cup of coffee for too long, they're going to get suspicious."

"Okay," I agreed. "But where are these files? How hard are they to get to?"

"Well, that's the strange thing," Cormac said. "They are in a subbasement, but they're in an ordinary room. The door's locked, but it's just a regular Yale lock. I didn't have any trouble getting inside last night. I counted six sealed cartons, all clearly marked VLM, as your mother told me they would be. Yeah, I spoke with her, Daphne. Don't get that look on your face. Basically, we need to go down there, break in again, and carry the cartons out. It's going to be easy. Let's just get it over with."

"It sounds too easy, Cormac. For one thing, why didn't you take the cartons out already? There must be some other kind of security protecting them. A silent alarm? Laser protection? Something?" My suspicions were growing. Opus Dei didn't do things half-assed, and if these files were as important as Mar-Mar believed, they should be in a vault like Fort Knox, not stored like janitorial supplies in a vacant room.

"I swear to you, Daphne, they are stacked up in an empty room. There's absolutely nothing else in it and no security whatsoever."

"What about when the boxes are moved? Will that trip some kind of system?"

A look of concern washed over Cormac's face. "That was the one possibility I couldn't dispense with. That's why I didn't move them and why J's been brought into this. He's going to take a look before we get them."

"That's a little late in the game, Cormac," I said.

"We don't have a choice. Now let's get this over with, please." Some of the all-too-familiar whine was returning to his voice. J had already gone into an adjoining hall and was motioning us to hurry.

"All right," I said. "But there's something not sitting right with me about this."

We slipped into a hall and proceeded to a freight elevator. I felt overwhelmed with claustrophobia as we stepped inside the car and started the descent to the basement levels. The light in the dimly lit elevator blinked on and off a few times as the car passed by two subbasements before stopping at B3. I figured we were fifty or sixty feet below ground level. Despite having a bat's natural affinity for caves, I felt suffocated and buried alive.

The three of us started half walking, half running down a long corridor between two walls of concrete blocks. A string of bare lightbulbs lined the low ceiling, which I could have touched if I had stretched my hand above my head. I heard water dripping and a low hum of some kind of machinery; maybe it was the heating-cooling system. My nerves sensed a low energy field around us. I felt as if something was observing us, even if the cameras weren't operating. I glanced behind me at J, who was covering our backs. He had drawn his weapon, and I recognized the dull dark gray of a Glock .45. It is a deadly gun that will more likely kill, not disable, its target. J had said he wasn't going to use it, but if he did, whoever was on the receiving end would be dead.

The farther we went from the elevator, the heavier my legs seemed to become, and I had to force myself to move forward. Every fiber of my being told me not to go, that we were walking into a trap. But Cormac was the point man, leading the way, and he wasn't wasting any time. The machinery hum obscured our footsteps, so we rushed forward unconcerned with stealth. Finally Cormac stopped in front of a stout metal door. He pulled out a set of lock picks and had it open in seconds. That bothered me. The standard Yale lock was too flimsy for that secure an entrance. Cormac flipped on an overhead light and I saw a room that was at least twenty by twenty feet in size. The walls were painted a pale tan. The floor was cement; it appeared unpainted and very clean. Absolutely nothing occupied the room except six small white cartons sitting three cartons wide and two high against the back wall. Each carton bore a bloodred Vatican wax seal, each was numbered from one through six, and each was marked clearly in black letters: VLM.

"Wait," J said from behind me. Cormac and I had entered the room, but we stopped in our tracks. "Let me take a look before you touch anything." He put down the rectangular pack he was carrying and took out a device that looked like a voltage meter or a radiation detector. He scanned each of the cartons. He inspected the floor around the cartons. I supposed he was looking for a booby trap or an alarm sensor. He walked over to the walls and did a visual inspection as well as scanning them with his handheld device. My heart was beating hard. I wanted to get out of there, and get out of there fast.

"Looks clean, but be prepared for anything," he said. "Let

me start; then each of you grab two boxes and let's get this over with."

J picked up two cartons, one stacked on top of the other. I held my breath. Nothing happened. The room was silent. Outside in the corridor I could still hear the hum of machinery, but there was no alarm. J waited while Cormac and I bent over and grabbed our two boxes apiece. I had no sooner straightened up than the shit hit the fan.

First of all the door swung shut of its own accord, and I clearly heard a bolt slide into place. Then the hum of machinery got louder, much louder.

"Crap," said J. "Look at the fucking walls."

I did. The two opposing side walls were slowly moving toward us. And as I watched, hundreds of round apertures, each maybe two inches wide, opened up in the two flat surfaces. From these holes, sharp-pointed wooden stakes pushed out with a terrible finality. I could see that even if we lay on the floor or got close to the ceiling we would not be able to escape them. I figured I had maybe three minutes before Cormac and I would be dust and J a bloody mass of pulverized flesh. That I was going to leave this world dressed as a *Saturday Night Live* bogus priest added insult to the injury.

J and I looked upward at the same time. I had never even considered the door as a way out; it was solid steel and bolted. But I did know that wiring was going into that light fixture, and if we were lucky, above the ceiling were rafters and enough space to save our lives. It was our only chance. I made the first move. I could take getting zapped by a live wire, whereas J couldn't. I put down my boxes and stepped on them. J set his two boxes next to mine to give me a better platform. Then he nudged Cormac, who stood frozen, staring at the moving walls like a deer caught in a car's headlights, rousing him from his stupor. Cormac quickly put his boxes down as well. After I climbed up on them, J handed me a screwdriver from his kit. I unscrewed the flange around the light and pulled the fixture down. It hung by its wires but didn't go out. J handed me a crowbar. The walls with their cruel spikes were closer now. Panic inched up in my own throat. I started smashing through the Sheetrock of the ceiling until I cleared a space wider than my shoulders. I could see horizontal two-by-fours on either side of the light and an empty space above it, maybe two feet of clearing, not a lot but enough. I stood on my toes and was able to see above the ceiling a narrow crawl space running between fat aluminum air ducts.

"Boost me up!" I called to Cormac. By this time the distance between the crushing walls had narrowed to about eight feet. Time was running out. "Wait!" J yelled. He handed me a flashlight. Then, as if I were a prima ballerina, Cormac deftly grabbed my legs and threw me upward. His dancer's training probably saved my life. I scraped my head on the low clearance, but I threw myself lengthwise into the darkness. I clicked on the flashlight and could see a long, narrow catwalk running along the ducts. Before I knew what was happening, a carton pushed against my feet.

"What the shit?" I cried out.

"We need to take these. We can handle three of them." I heard J's voice arguing with Cormac, who was saying, "Forget the damned boxes, man. We need to get up there— the walls!"

"Go! Go!" J screamed as two more cartons hit my feet. I wriggled ahead in the tunnel. Then I heard shuffling.

"I'm in!" Cormac called from behind me.

"Where's J?" I yelled, frantic and unable to see anything behind me.

"He stopped the walls with the crowbar. It's not going to

hold them, though," Cormac answered. "Move up! Move up! I need to get out of his way."

On my elbows and my knees I squirmed forward as fast as I could, cursing the damned priest's cassock, which was bunching up around my butt by this time and leaving my legs unprotected from the rough boards of the catwalk. Just then I heard a sickening crunch from the room below.

"The crowbar's collapsed!" Cormac called out. "J! J!" he screamed.

"Pipe down!" J's gruff voice answered. "I'm in."

"Are you okay?" I called back.

"Yeah," he said in a strained voice.

"You're hurt. How bad?" I smelled the blood.

"Forget it. It's not life threatening. Just get moving. Go ahead as far as you can," he ordered.

I started crawling as fast as possible down the long, dark tunnel made by the floor two feet above me and the catwalk of rough wood. The beam of my flashlight revealed no openings or exits. The crowbar was gone, and I had no idea how we were going to get out of this. I pushed away the thought that we could die like rats caught in a maze that went nowhere. I knew only that we were all still alive. For now.

CHAPTER 9

But at my back I always hear
Time's winged chariot, hurrying near.

— Andrew Marvell, "To His Coy Mistress"

I crawled ahead, my flashlight cutting a beam through what seemed like black ink. Suddenly I stopped and switched it off.

"What are you doing?" J called from behind.

"I can see in the dark," I said in an urgent whisper. "And I need to watch for a crack where light is leaking in. There must be a trapdoor out of here. The workmen get in somewhere. Can you keep up?"

"Don't worry about me. Just keep moving. Somebody's going to be looking for us soon." I pictured men in monk's robes holding crucifixes in one hand and wooden stakes in another. J was probably envisioning guards brandishing submachine guns. We all have our own private visions of what the bogeyman looks like.

Cormac broke in, talking more to J than to me. "We need to leave these cartons. Pushing them along is slowing us down."

"No!" J said.

"Do what *you* have to," I snapped, "but *I* have to find a way out of here. Wait! Shut up," I whispered. I listened intently. Above the pervasive hum of machinery I could hear the bell of the elevator somewhere ahead. I guessed Opus Dei personnel were responding to our invasion. I hoped they thought we were dead. Until the walls returned to their original position and they spotted our escape route through the ceiling, we should be okay. How long did we have? I thought. I guessed maybe ten minutes tops—if nobody heard us moving through the ceiling.

Crawling as quietly as I could, I went forward into an unrelenting darkness. I came to a T in the catwalk. Should I go left or right? One way could lead to nowhere; the other to an exit. Sweat beaded on my forehead. Life and death might rest on which way I turned. I went right. My hair brushed against the floor above me, a strand catching on something rough. I put my hand up to free it and panic took me. A shiver ran through my body. I imagined the tons of brick and concrete above me and irrationally thought of it crashing down. Fear is the enemy, and it was squeezing its bony hands around my throat.

I pushed the thought away and took a deep breath. Then I sniffed the air again. It was stale and had a chemical smell, but I sensed something, a faint current. There had to be an exit, but would I find it fast enough? I mentally prepared myself to fight our way out of the basement after busting through the ceiling, but I couldn't transform into bat form where I was. The space was too tight. My nerves stretched like a rubber band about to go *boing*. And what time was it? Four a.m. or so? *Shit*. The night was almost over. We had to hurry.

I forced myself to be calm, forced myself to believe that a trapdoor lay ahead. I crawled forward, feeling the plywood beneath me scrape my bare knees and abrade my palms. I twisted my body between a wall and a bend in the aluminum duct. Then I saw a faint silver line of light. My heart thudded hard as adrenaline surged through my veins. I threw my body forward and ran my hands along the catwalk. I found a latch. I prayed it wasn't bolted on the outside. A box bumped into my feet, and I felt Cormac right behind me. "I found a door," I whispered. "Quiet now."

The latch turned. I started to push the door outward with agonizing slowness, while all my instincts urged me to somersault out of there no matter what I might encounter. I put my head through the opening and discovered I was maybe eight feet off the floor overlooking a utility room filled with switch boxes, gauges, and meters. A ladder with metal rungs was fixed to the wall below and provided access to the floor. An open doorway leading into the dim corridor lit the room with a murky gray. There was enough light for Cormac and me to see clearly with our vampire eyes. J might need some help, though. I pulled myself through the trapdoor and went down the ladder. Cormac's head popped out of the hatch. Silently he handed me down one white box, then two more before he emerged and swung down, barely bothering with the ladder. J came next, and when he was on the floor I saw that he was avoiding putting his weight on one foot.

"Can you walk?" I asked as he stooped over to pick up a box. I grabbed it from him. "We don't have time for macho heroics," I whispered. "Can you fucking walk?"

"Yes, I can fucking walk," he said through gritted teeth. "Cormac," he ordered. "Take the other two boxes. I need to draw my gun." I could smell J's blood. He would leave a trail when he walked—*if* he could actually walk—and there wasn't anything I could do about it.

Holding the damned carton in one arm, I sneaked a look into the corridor. It was empty. Cormac joined me and whispered, "The elevator is to the right, I think." His two cartons were balanced on his shoulders.

"Let's go!" I urged, and we started running down the long

hall. But J didn't. I looked back. One of his shoes was missing, and I could see his foot was bloody. He was using the wall as a crutch, but he couldn't move fast. I doubled back and put my shoulder under his armpit and my free hand around his waist. He didn't resist. With him hopping on one foot, we hurried after Cormac.

When we got to the elevators, I knew we'd have to risk using them because J would never make it up three flights of stairs with any kind of speed, if he could make it at all. His face had become pasty white, and sweat beaded his forehead. A trail of blood stretched down the corridor as far as I could see. Cormac hit the elevator's UP button while I looked around nervously, my head swiveling back and forth.

When the elevator doors slid open, a thin, gray-haired man in a plaid bathrobe and slippers was standing there. J aimed his Glock at the guy. "Don't shoot," the man yelped.

"Get out of the car," J growled, and extended the gun at him. "Move it!" The man started to walk out, and J gave him a shove into the corridor while we piled into the elevator. The bathrobed guy's eyes were round as pie plates, and his mouth was hanging open. He just stared at the gun and didn't make a sound. Cormac kept jabbing the CLOSE button until the doors snapped shut and I couldn't see the man anymore.

"Get ready," J said. "Chances are we're going to have to fight our way to the front door."

"You're not in any shape to fight," I said. "Let the Glock do the talking. People seem to listen to it real well."

The doors slid open on the street floor. Three men stood between us and the front door.

"Freeze!" J yelled in a voice that could turn blood to ice. "Nobody move and nobody gets hurt!"

"We're priests," one man squeaked. "We're not armed."

"Back up to the wall, turn around to face it, and put your hands above your head."

Two of the men complied, but one just stood there staring at us. Then he started saying, "Hail Mary, full of grace, blessed are thou . . ."

"Do what I told you to, Father," J snarled. "Now!" With the gun, J motioned for Cormac to head for the door. Using me as a crutch, J started hopping in that direction. Cormac got the door open. We were almost out.

Uh-uh, I thought. *It's not going to be that easy.* Out of nowhere another man, a young and very foolish supernumerary, I guessed, came flying at J and me. I aimed a kick at his throat, but the damned skirt of my priest's disguise hampered my extension and I caught him in the balls, which was a lucky break. I let go of J and, using two hands, I smashed our attacker in the face with the carton. I heard his nose snap, and blood ran down his face as he slowly, almost gracefully, slid down a wall to sit dazed on the floor.

I ducked under J's arm again and, still hanging on to that frigging box, he and I made it out the front door into the night. Cormac had run over to Thirty-fourth Street looking for a cab, but at a little after four a.m. the street was empty except for a sanitation truck a block away.

We need to find a cab? Piss-poor planning for our get-away, I thought.

"Cormac!" J called, his voice a lot weaker. "I've got my vehicle. On Thirty-fifth."

I expected a Hummer. I got a black Chevy Silverado with an extended cab. THE INTIMIDATOR, 2-18-01 in homage to the late NASCAR driver Dale Earnhardt, was tastefully stenciled in gold above the right fender.

"I can drive," J said, and I helped him hop over to the driver's side door. He pulled himself up behind the wheel, and I threw myself through the back door into the interior of the pickup. Cormac jumped in the passenger side after dumping his two cartons beside me in the backseat as J screeched away from the curb, turned onto the avenue, and raced uptown, running red lights and weaving all over the road.

Nobody came after us. No sirens wailed in the distance. "Their security stinks," J said, shaking his head and slowing down.

Cormac wasn't talking. He seemed lost in thought as he stared out the window at the quiet city—and all the while he was smiling.

"Oh, yeah," I said. "Those damned priests just don't know when to break out the rifles or go to the mattresses. But you see, J, they don't *need* security when they've rigged a booby trap that will personally be giving me nightmares for the rest of my life. We're supposed to be dead, and we damned near were."

"Point taken. Look, get your mother on my cell and pass it back to me," he ordered as he pulled his phone out of his jacket pocket and lobbed it into the backseat. I hit the buttons and handed it back to him before she picked up. I wasn't in the mood to talk with her, that was for sure.

J drove through the quiet streets while he talked, heading uptown toward my place, I guessed. "M? J. We're out. Yeah. Look, we had a problem. We only got three boxes. The others? Probably destroyed. Which did we get? Four, five, and six. Yeah. Okay, I'll tell her. Roger." He snapped the phone shut and said to me, "She'll come down to your place to pick up the cartons."

"I can hardly wait," I replied, and leaned back in the seat. "Don't you think we should be going to a hospital? Your foot looks like dog meat, and you're driving like you're drunk."

"I'll drop you off; then if need be, Cormac can drive me

downtown. I'll be okay," he said, but his voice was strained, and I knew he had lost a lot of blood. I leaned forward and tapped Cormac on the shoulder. "Do you know how to drive?"

Cormac twisted his head toward me and shot me a hurt look. "Yes, I can drive. I used to own a car. When I was in *Cats* I drove up to Martha's Vineyard every summer. The garage fees in the city got too expensive, though."

"Cormac, that was twenty years ago. Can you handle this truck?"

"He'll do fine, Daphne," J broke in. "It's not a stick shift. Now leave him alone."

A thought occurred to me. "Is this your truck, J? I mean your personal vehicle?" I asked.

"Yeah," J said, wincing when he braked for a red light.

"Well, now, isn't that interesting," I said. And it was. Outside of my knowing that J was a former army Ranger—something Darius had told me about him—this truck was the first glimpse I ever had of J as a person. I didn't even know his name. I had never seen him outside of a work context. I didn't know his age, his background, his marital status, or his address. But now I knew he had a truck. I looked around. There was a gun rack mounted in front of the back window. It might mean he was a hunter—of game, that is.

"So do you have a dog?" I asked.

"Why?" he asked, keeping his eyes on the road as he got to Central Park at Seventy-second Street and took the crossing to the West Side.

"Because you have a pickup," I answered. The logic of my deduction was perfectly clear to me. I guess the adrenaline was wearing off, since I was starting to feel tired. Sadness washed over me. Here was this guy I had kissed on, what, two occasions? And I didn't know diddly-squat about him. The situation reminded me of my relationship with Darius, whose past and present remained a mystery to me. Darius was my lover, in fact one of the great loves of my life, or so I had believed. But he had never been open about himself with me. I had discovered only by accident that he owned a car and where his apartment was located. He kept the basic facts about himself a secret. Right now, from where I sat, falling for a spy looked like a lose-lose situation. I needed to remember that epiphany if Darius wanted to patch things up—or J ever came on to me again.

I shook away my ruminations and turned my attention back to the here and now. I started talking to J again while I absentmindedly rubbed my fingers against the velour fabric of the seat. "If you have a pickup, you might very well have a dog. Come to think of it, I can see you with a black Lab or a golden retriever. I bet you wear camouflage pants on the weekends. And you have a country place. Hey, J, you might even have a wife. Do you?"

"Do I what? Have a dog, a country place, or a wife?" he asked me back.

"Oh, who gives a shit," I said, suddenly pissed off at having to play Twenty Questions to get a straight answer from him. I turned my head to stare out the window. "It's none of my business," I said, and strengthened my resolve to straighten out my act: No more relationships with secrets— on either side—and no more basing relationships on good sex and sizzling chemistry, which I obviously tended to do. What did I want from a man, anyway?

To be completed, was the answer that came into my mind. *Hey, girl,* I said to myself, *the only person who can complete you is you. Forget your romantic notions of "oneness," two halves reunited, the sum greater than the parts, and all that romantic bullshit. Figure out what you want* besides *sex and you might have a shot at love—real love, not infatuation.*

That mental shakeup brought my thoughts back to Fitz. From the first he had been honest with me about who he was. He introduced me to his family. He told me about his past. True, he had hidden his work in the Secret Service, but an e-mail before he was shot indicated that he was about to tell me that too. In fact, Fitz acted like a pretty normal guy, not one who was tormented by inner demons or pursued by his own nightmares. Considering that I was an accomplished liar, a clever thief, and a bloodsucking vampire to boot, he was probably too good for me.

I sniffed and stared out the window at the darkened storefronts, the empty sidewalks, the shadow-filled doorways, as my thoughts moved back to my decision of earlier tonight. I didn't know how Fitz was going to take my planned session of True Confessions, but I still felt driven to tell him everything. In the murky world of shadows, fog, and mirrors that I roamed, I suddenly craved honesty with a hunger greater than my thirst for blood. And I wanted acceptance as the vampire I truly was. *Now, that revelation would be the ultimate test of love,* I thought.

I turned my gaze back into the interior of the Silverado and fixated on the back of J's head. His hair was in a buzz cut and his neck was thick and muscular. He was an attractive guy, but what did we have in common? I had no idea, but it might be nothing but our job as spies. Period, end of list. I wasn't a pickup-truck kind of girl. I can't imagine a vampire like me at a NASCAR race, but maybe Benny had gone to one.

Oh, shit, Benny. I sat up with a jolt. Crawling through a ceiling in mortal fear of losing my life, I had forgotten about her. I needed to call and make sure she got home safely. She was into something way over her head, and I didn't know if I could pull her out of it . . . or if she wanted me to.

Cormac helped me carry the three cartons up to my apartment while J sat in front of my building in his truck with the motor running. Cormac grinned like a fool all the way up in the elevator, and he was humming "Memory" from *Cats*. As we walked into my apartment, I asked, "And just what are you so damned happy about, Cormac? This has been one hell of a night."

He looked at me and smiled even wider. "You know what, Daphne? All I can think about is that I never have to set foot inside Opus Dei headquarters again. I'm out of that fucking place forever."

Then his face got more serious. "Shit, Daphne, in the end the building itself tried to kill me, kill all of us, but God knows it was slowly grinding me down and eating me up before that. I can't tell you how cold I felt sitting there night after night. I felt as if the bricks themselves crushed the life out of everybody who walked in there. Look, I know that building is supposed to be a place of God, but all I saw was oppression and pain—and people who got off on pain in the guise of being devout Catholics."

His voice had turned hard. "Daphne, I cannot believe that suffering is necessary to be a spiritual person. I don't think a loving deity would demand that of anyone." Anger took the place of his former joy. "So you know what, Daphne? Bottom line? I think they're full of shit."

Then he shook his head and smiled again. "Oh, hell, who cares anymore? I'm done!" Grinning widely, he actually pirouetted right there in my vestibule. "Whooeee," he yelled. "We beat it! Beat them! Opus Dei didn't get me. I'm still here. I'm still here!"

With that Cormac hugged me. I sort of hugged him back, but he had taken me by surprise. And as he went out the front door, he hesitated and popped his head back in.

"Daphne? I know you're going to go through those boxes before your mother shows up. I just risked my neck to get them, and I expect you to share." Then he sent me an air kiss and closed the door.

The hours were inexorably marching toward dawn, and my dog needed to be walked. I had been dead tired, but I felt so damned relieved to be home, I got a second wind. I left the cartons unopened on my dining room table and headed into the waning night once more.

I became hyperalert. As soon as we hit the sidewalk I was watching every shadow. I didn't relish the prospect of another confrontation with dognappers. I needed to get to the bottom of what had been going on the other night—why that man had been murdered and why somebody wanted my dog really, really badly. It might even be tied to this mission on the Joe Daniel assassination, or it might not. I'd just be careful with Jade for now, but if anybody tried anything, I was ready to trash some ass.

Despite my bravado, out in the street that night I was grateful we were left alone. Jade did her thing and I did mine with the pooper-scooper. We got back upstairs without incident in minutes. As soon as I unhooked Jade's leash, I looked up. Those three white cartons seemed to glow where they sat on my dining room table. Suddenly I wanted nothing more than to open them and find out why going into the bowels of the earth to get them was so important. Did they hold information about my father and his death? Although I desperately wanted that to be the case, I had my doubts that they had anything to do with him at all. Did they contain some sort of priceless treasure or evidence about Jesus, Mary, or the Church that could change history? Did they contain secrets, suppressed for decades and passed from the Vatican to Opus Dei? Would their contents ruin lives or save them?

I grabbed a knife from the kitchen and hacked my way through the Vatican's wax seal on the box labeled #4. Under the white wrapping paper was a lid that lifted off. Inside I found file folders. I did the same thing with boxes five and six with the same results. Nothing looked earth-shaking. I would have to go through the files themselves to get any answers.

I started with the last box, number six, packed tightly with plain-looking manila files. I pulled out a handful. Each file was labeled with a country's or city's name. I chose one at random. It happened to be France. Inside were dossiers of men and women of all races and all walks of life. Some dossiers had photos clipped to them. Then my heart started speeding up like a locomotive pulling out of a station, racing faster and faster, louder and louder as I realized what I was looking at: the dossiers of people who were secretly vampires, hundreds of them, vampires who were still walking the earth. I had no doubt each of them was targeted for extermination by the Church. I pawed through the box of files. There it was, the file on New York City. It was bulging with papers. I put it down on the table and started leafing through it as fast as I could. I found what I was looking for: DAPHNE URBAN. My dossier. *Oh, shit, shit, shit, shit, shit.*

What could be worse than this? I turned to box five. Part of the box held files of more countries and more cities, all of them filled with vampire dossiers. But half the box held black files. I pulled out one of them and thumbed through it. These files were chronological by year, going back to the 1950s, and in each year were black-edged dossiers of vampires who had been staked by the Vatican's vampire hunters. All the details were there—who died, when, where, and how, along with code names for the hunters. *Damn,* I thought. *Who are these hunters? I need their names. I need to identify them and stop them before they find me and mine.*

So keyed up that my hands were shaking, I turned to box four. It too had files, but I quickly found out these files didn't contain dossiers. They held historical records of some sort. I went back and removed the very first file in the box. It was labeled LIBER MAGNUS. I mentally translated the Latin: *The Great Book.* I sank down onto a dining room chair with the file in my hands, beginning to understand that what this box held was the recorded history of my kind. I opened the file with a trembling hand and began to read.

CHAPTER 10

Weary with toil, I haste me to my bed
The dear repose for limbs with travel tired;
But then begins a journey in my head . . .
—William Shakespeare, Sonnet 27

On top of a thick stack of handwritten pages was this title: *Liber Magnus 1: Der Dunkelflügel Erzählungen* [*The Great Book, Volume I: The Darkwing Chronicles*] by Baron Wolfgang Ungern Sternberg, translated by Brother Timothy Finnegan. Evidently I was not holding the original document, but a monk's translation. The second page of the stack was dated December 14, 1937, and marked, VIENNA, AUSTRIA. By that time in 1937 it was after the *Anschloss*, when Hitler made his homeland part of the Third Reich.

Having no idea what I held in my hands, I began to read:

I, Baron Wolfgang Ungern Sternberg, as one of those entrusted with the ancient wisdom of the Darkwings and their history, have taken it upon myself and my damned soul to write down this knowledge which had been preserved, heretofore, only by the spoken word. With Hitler strangling Austria in his demonic grip and my days numbered, I fear that what I know may be forever lost if I do not.

I alone of all the vampires who once lived in Vienna remain alive. Hitler and his sadistic minions have already rounded up the Gypsies of Germany and Russo-Poland, Czech/Slovakia and Hungary, and, here in the south, in Austria. The SS death squads have massacred the people who have sheltered us for centuries—men, women, and children on the spot, along with their ponies and dogs. A few survivors have turned up in concentration camps, but most are rotting in mass graves that make the earth cry out in sorrow.

The Darkwings are a proud, fierce race. We do not run. We avenge.

Yet for now, here in Austria, we are beaten, and before I am killed I feel compelled to record in this great book of wisdom what we know to be true about this earth, the vampires upon it, and the history that has transpired since before recorded time.

Here in my modest hotel on the Schulerstrasse, I can hear the harsh steps of jackboots on the cobblestones. Nazi bastards. From in this room I can watch the street and see them before they come for me. I have sent hundreds of those death's-head brutes to hell, and I hope to send hundreds more before I am killed.

I digress. My anger overwhelms my intellect, and time is too short for such indulgences. I must write down what I know. I have lived on this earth since ancient days—well over three thousand years—seeing much of which humans are ignorant, but which Darkwings must remember. More than what I myself have witnessed has been entrusted to me by the Old Ones, who were here before me. Now let me commence my record.

*   *   *

I thumbed through the remaining manuscript. It was far too long for me to read tonight, but I had never before encountered a history of my own kind and couldn't resist reading a few pages, beginning with the first chapter.

How Vampires Originated

The Old Ones instructed that there is no beginning and no end. Vampires did not become; they always were. Neither human nor divine, vampires exist in a netherworld somewhere betwixt the two, and they have always done so.

The Old Ones also taught that in the early days vampires were nomadic creatures, living in small tribes or clans and seeking shelter in caves or trees, unclothed, uncultured, unlettered, and undead. Sometime during the first millennium they joined with bands of wandering Rom, whose culture embraced magic and did not reject demons. From that time forward, vampires and Rom have intermarried and intermixed.

But before that alliance, many millennia before—some accounts say four, some say six thousand years before—the first vampire was created. She was a female, a human, not a demon, and so beautiful it is said stones wept to behold her. . . .

One day, while the woman walked on the slopes of a high mountain, she was seen by an immortal, a minor deity such as the Christians call angels, and the Greeks called gods. Although the god was comely and filled with charm, he was a dark divinity, quick to anger and unkind, as excited by war as by lust. From his first glimpse of the woman he was overcome by lust, aroused by her beauty, and determined to possess her.

Dropping from the starry night sky and landing before her on the grass, he approached Lilith and boldly asked her to be his consort. He promised her pleasures and great riches. He offered her immortality. But this woman loved a poor shepherd and resisted the god's advances. When he persisted, she did a foolish thing. She ridiculed him. This enraged the god, and in his great anger he pulled forth a sword and stabbed her so deeply that her life's blood poured out and ran onto the earth. She cried out and fell insensible to the ground as her spirit waned.

The moon god, passing at that time, heard her cry. He took pity on the woman and raised her up to save her life. The lesser deity could not undo the resurrection. Instead he cursed her who had spurned him, and his curse turned the dying woman into a vampire bat, a creature forever bound to the moon and unable to bear the sun. A woman without, a beast within, she became in that fateful moment eternally driven to hunt the humans whose blood could replace that precious fluid drained from her body that night. And her adored young shepherd became her first victim to bite.

Interesting, but of no immediate help to me. I skipped forward.

Chapter Two: Things Seen and Unseen—Vampires, the Divine, and other Spirits

What do vampires know of the divine? We do not embrace any organized human religions, although ritual and acknowledgment of the spirit life are part of the very

*fiber of our being. Why? Because we know that every-
thing with mass and weight—the rocks, the stars, the
oceans, the air—is alive. We know that which has neither
mass nor weight—the spirit life—is animate, and we
perceive it in abundance in the universe. Souls, ghosts,
minor gods, powerful gods, demons, monsters, dragons,
witches, wizards, and angels act and interact with all
other life. Who are they? They have already revealed
themselves innumerable times. Look to the myths and
histories of humankind; all has been recorded there.*

*Yet more powerful than all seen and unseen things is
the divine, the life force of the universe, the mother
goddess, the great goddess, She who breathes out life,
benevolence, and beauty. More than all else, She is in-
finite, omnipresent, and omniscient—She simply is.*

Chapter Three: The Earth we rest upon and Stellgedächtnis [translator's note: Place Memory]

*Nomad. Wanderer. Whatever the language, the very
word for people who move from place to place, change
homes often, or have no permanent domicile is always
tinged with sadness or wistfulness. Why does the mere
utterance of a word evoke sadness? That happens because an ancient racial memory is touched and awakened. Deep within the mind's unconscious lies a
memory of and a homesickness for the place of one's
own birth—as well as the place of one's forefathers'
birth, even if its name is lost and its location but vaguely
known. "My grandfather came from Lithuania," so
many humans might say, but Lithuania might as well be
Neverland, for he or she has been told nothing more.*

*Despite what the conscious mind does not know, hu-
mans and vampires retain a "genetic memory" of the*

*homeland, even the village, where centuries of ances-
tors lived and died. We vampires so need to retain contact with this birthplace that we sleep upon the soil of
Transylvania, whether a handful or much more, which
we place in the coffins we call our beds. As for humans,
most are ignorant of this need to touch the very earth
where their forefathers dwelled. They do not understand the melancholy which overwhelms them. Yet if
they return by accident or design to that English town,
Austrian village, Russian hamlet, or Mediterranean
city, they will know they have been there before. They
will be overcome by a feeling of acceptance and peace.
They will have come home.*

*Vampires "come home" each time they slumber.
Humans would sleep better if they did so too.*

I rubbed my eyes and continued.

Chapter Four: Nothing Dies; It Changes and Goes On

*This truth is so self-evident I wonder if I need to record
it, but I shall. The life force, what is usually called the
spirit, is inextinguishable. It may change form, it may
leave one body and inhabit another, but it cannot disappear. Energy is eternal. Spirit is energy. Spirit is
therefore eternal.*

*So what does happen when a plant, an animal, a
human, or a vampire dies? For one thing, it is the physical form or the body that stops functioning and decays,
but that is all. The spirit is set free. The spirit may become what is commonly called a ghost, which is simply
a spirit being. If not, the life force might return in an
unborn child or inhabit the nearest living entity it finds.*

I skipped forward again.

Chapter Five: The Vendetta of the Roman Catholic Church against the Vampire Race—and the Expunging of the Bible

Vampires have a mortal enemy on this earth: the Church of Rome. Unlike the current persecution of Hitler's SS, which I know shall not last once the dictator is overthrown, the Roman Catholic Church's persecution of vampires has been relentless and vindictive since the time of Constantine the Great.

Why?

I can only reason that the Christian God is a jealous God. After all, He keeps His own angels as servants and insists on the rejection of all other divinities. Angels who have refused to obey Him have been cast out and called demons.

Vampires are no fallen angels, but we are neither invisible nor subservient. Who is to say that humans one day would not worship us? It is a danger the Church dare not risk.

As a precaution the Church fathers have expunged all references to us from the gospels and sacred Christian tests. This was done at the Council of Nicea. At that historic meeting, it was decreed to deny our existence publicly while secretly seeking to exterminate us from the earth.

The records of this lie in the Vatican along with a compilation of vampire names. Every parish priest in every village in every Christian land is told to be watchful for signs of us. Dossiers have been compiled over the centuries. A religious order consisting of vampire hunters was created, installed, and financed. Its members were trained in the ways to murder us and have been regularly dispatched to do so.

I'm not saying the Roman Church is wrong in this. Vampires hunt humans. Perhaps it is only just that we are hunted too. It is the denial of our very existence I find so hard to bear. That, too, one day will change. . . .

CHAPTER 11

Something wicked this way comes.

—Shakespeare, *Macbeth*

Many more chapters written by the Austrian vampire followed, but fatigue overtook me as the night slid into dawn. My eyes were heavy, and the words before me on the page began to blur. I put down the great book and headed for the shower, hoping to scrub away more than the grime of crawling through Opus Dei's headquarters. I hoped to send the memory of the night and the tears I still had not shed for Darius and for my own fallen self down the drain.

Once I was physically clean, I was even wearier. My palms burned where I had scraped them, and my knees looked like somebody had gone at them with a cheese grater. I walked naked into my secret chamber, crawled into bed, and, without knowing when sleep overtook me, I tumbled down into darkness.

I don't know how many hours had passed before I was possessed by a great feeling of anxiety. I began to dream of hitting a white ceiling with a huge crowbar, hearing in my slumber the repeated thud of the iron on the drywall. Again and again I struck the ceiling, but it would not break. Then J appeared in my dream, telling me to hurry as blood spread in a pool below him. As I watched, a rivulet of red began to rush toward my feet, and Jade wandered into my dream. She lapped at the stream of blood; then she began barking loudly at some creature she had chased up a tree that had appeared from nowhere.

However, when both the barking and the god-awful banging continued without ceasing, my sleeping self figured out the noise wasn't in my head at all. Someone was pounding at my front door like a hammer on my skull, and Jade was barking, doing her watchdog thing.

I groaned and sat up, realizing I had no choice but to climb out of my cozy crypt and see who was rapping at my front door. And, remembering Poe, my next thought was, *"'Tis some visitor,"* I muttered, *"tapping on my chamber door. Only this and nothing more."*

I threw on a worn terry-cloth bathrobe and made my way into the hall. I put my bloodshot eye to the peephole in the front door. I wasn't surprised in the least to see my mother standing there along with one of her helpers, an aging hippie whom I had met before. I grabbed Jade by her collar and flung the door open. The huge dog stiffened, and hackles went up on her spine.

"It's okay," I said to Jade, and marched her toward the kitchen, where I told her to lie down on her bed. She did, but cast a baleful gaze in my direction, as if to say, *I know what I'm doing. Do you?*

My mother, followed by her assistant, a middle-aged hipster with a gray ponytail, went straight to the boxes on the dining room table. "So. You looked at them," she said.

"If you didn't want me to look at them, you should have stolen them yourself."

My sarcasm earned me a disapproving look. "I suppose you realize how important they are," she responded, then turned her back to me as she quickly scanned through the contents of each box.

"These files don't have anything to do with my father. You lied to me," I said.

"I most certainly did not," she replied. "That information was in one of the first three boxes."

Yeah, right, I thought.

"Do you believe those boxes have been destroyed?" she asked.

"They're confetti," I said. "But if someone wants to reconstruct them and has a few hundred years to do it, it can probably be done."

"Then we may still find out who killed him," she said.

"What difference can that make now?" I shot back at her, not bothering to hide my irritation. "It was over four hundred years ago. And stop pretending about this. Investigating my father's death was not your motive for getting your hands on these files. I don't understand why you had to mislead me. I would have wanted to get my own dossier out of the Church's possession. And yours. A few weeks ago you promised you were going to be honest with me, Mother."

"This had nothing to do with honesty," she said. "It wasn't safe for you, or anyone else, to know what was in these boxes. Other entities besides the Church want us all dead and desperately want these files. The files' whereabouts has to be kept as secretive as possible. I didn't tell you for your own good."

I stiffened. There might be a grain of truth in what she said, but I didn't buy it. In her defense, Mar-Mar had survived by keeping secrets. Telling anyone, even me, what she was doing was probably a habit too ingrained to break. But it made me feel used and devalued. Worst of all, I felt rejected and unloved. I wanted my own mother to feel that she could trust me, and she didn't. A sulky, "Yeah, right," was the only response I could make.

Mar-Mar's voice softened. "You did a great and wonderful thing by getting these files, Daphne. I don't know if I could have done it, or if I would have displayed such courage had I been there. I knew I could depend on you. I felt you above all others had the best chance to succeed. No one can stop you when you make up your mind to do something. I've seen that. And I didn't believe anyone else would succeed in getting these boxes out."

"So you did know I could be killed in there?" I said, the hurt welling up in me despite her praise.

"Yes. Don't think it is easy for me to live with knowing the risk you took." Her voice shook a little when she said that. I took it all with a grain of salt. My mother could have been an accomplished actress. She paused for a moment, and when she spoke again her voice was devoid of emotion. "I need to hurry and get these out of here." She put two of the boxes into the arms of her helper and carried the third, which was number six, herself.

"How is J doing? Do you know?" I asked.

"He's going to be okay. He's out of surgery. I'll be in touch, sweetheart," she said as she headed for the door. "And you'd better get dressed. You have company coming. He's called Fudd. He's the person you wanted to talk to. He'll be here any minute."

Mar-Mar's helper carried his two boxes without any effort, and as he passed, I noticed how big his hands were and that he was missing part of his index finger. Seeing me staring at him, he nodded at me and said, "Nice dog."

"Thanks," I said.

"Still practicing kabbalah?" he asked.

"No, I'm into Wicca now," I answered. Mar-Mar raised an eyebrow at this exchange, but I just shut the door on them both.

*   *   *

Before I dressed, I tried to reach Benny by phone. No answer. I was connected to her voice mail. I left a message: "Benny, it's Daphne. Please call me back ASAP." I made a mental note to call her again in an hour. If I still didn't reach her, I'd try another way to track her down. A small flame of uneasiness began to flicker into life in my gut. I didn't feel good about not reaching her. In fact, I felt something was very, very wrong.

Then I turned my attention to preparing for my expected visitor. I have a passion for fashion—I don't deny it—but picking appropriate clothes to meet with a hit man wasn't an easy task. I figured he was going to be paranoid about me being wired or armed, or his being set up somehow. Answering the door naked would probably be the most convincing thing I could do, but that would lead to other problems. I wasn't going there. Instead I decided to wear a close-fitting white pullover, one with latex in the fabric, and a reasonably formfitting pair of camel-colored gabardine slacks.

On my feet I wore my Manolo Blahnik leopard-print suede boots, currently my favorite footwear, and they would probably stay my favorite until my next round of shopping therapy. The way my love life was going this March, I'd be flying back to the Galleria in Houston to do major damage to my bank account before April showers came my way.

Ever since I slipped into my first formal gowns in Renaissance Italy, I have liked pretty clothes. No, it is more accurate to say I have loved them with a fidelity I have never given to a man. No fine silk or well-spun wool has ever hurt my feelings. Even a fit of buyer's remorse never left me as devastated as hearing the voice of Darius's ex-girlfriend in the background when he called me. I have lived through four hundred years of being a smart woman making stupid choices when it came to lovers, but I possess a true genius, if I do say so myself, for buying clothes. It helps to have a Swiss bank account filled with lots of spending loot. Being a vampire, and Mar-Mar's daughter, has a couple of benefits, and money is one of them.

I suppose that getting entrée to a hit man is another.

Mickey, the doorman, buzzed the intercom around six thirty and announced that I had a visitor named Fudd. I told him to send Fudd up. Mickey hesitated and added, "Are you sure?"

"Just let the guy in," I replied.

A minute later I opened the door and was face-to-face with a stocky man in his late sixties or early seventies whose face looked as if he had gone one round too many against George Foreman.

"Fudd?" I asked.

The guy nodded and looked nervously back toward the elevator, which had started back down to the lobby. He was wearing a leather jacket, a blue sweater, and a pair of Dockers. He had a complexion the color of sand, which could be a fading Florida tan or a symptom of liver trouble. His eyes were deep-set in a mass of wrinkles. And as he came through the door, something about the way he carried himself warned others to back off and leave him alone. His attitude might be connected to the gun I guessed he was carrying in an ankle holster or stuck in the back of his pants.

I had locked Jade in the kitchen before I invited him to take a seat. As Fudd's eyes darted around my apartment, I asked him if I could take his jacket. He declined. Then I asked him if I could get him a drink.

"You got Diet Coke? I got suhga, you know, diabetes," he said, and sat down in a chair that gave him a view of the door.

"Sure," I answered. "I won't be a minute."

I put the Coke in one of my Waterford tumblers, added a slice of lime, and took it out to the guy, who, except for the cauliflower ear and busted nose, looked more like a retiree from Florida than a professional hit man.

I handed him the glass.

"Tanks," he said.

I sat down on a chair opposite Fudd and started the conversation. "My name is Daphne. I want to thank you for agreeing to speak with me. Please be assured I don't want to know anything about you or . . . or . . . your business associates. I'm looking for information about a particular individual. And if you don't mind, I am hoping to use your expertise to help protect a client of mine."

"I don't want to be mean," he said. "I just don't know what I can tell you. I am a man of few wahds. I was told to coopah-waite with you as a favah. But don't get too pawsonal, you know."

I tried not to get distracted by his speech impediment. It dawned on me that Fudd was his nickname for obvious reasons. I leaned forward and said in a quiet voice, "I understand your time is valuable, Mr.—"

"Just Fudd," he said.

"Right. Fudd, let me get straight to the point. I'm looking for a professional in your line of work who goes by the name of Gage. Have you ever heard of him?"

"I hoid of Gage. But he ain't one of ow guys. And we ain't nevah used him." Fudd did a neck roll, as if he were trying to loosen up before a workout. He looked really uncomfortable.

"Do you know who he works for?" I pressed.

"Woid is he's an independent contwactah." Fudd began cracking his knuckles.

"Is he an American?"

"Nevah hoid he wasn't," Fudd said.

"Do you know where he's located? A city?"

"Lot of button men come from Detwoit. But nah, don't know about this Gage chawachtah. Nobody evah hoid of him five yee-ahs ago. He came outa noweah. I wed about him in the papahs. I asked awound. Evewybody bet he was ex-militawy. Guy outta the south looking to make a buck."

"How could I contact him? If I had a job for him?"

"Don't know. Not my depawment. Best I can do is put woid out on the stweet."

"Would you do that?"

"Yeah, I guess."

"I'd appreciate it," I said, and pushed an envelope containing a thousand dollars in cash across the coffee table. Fudd picked it up, discreetly looked inside, and stuck it inside his jacket.

"Now, if you don't mind, I have a problem with a client and need your advice."

"Suwah. Shoot."

"Well, somebody wants to assassinate him. I have information that this is going to happen in public, in front of a lot of people. Why make the hit in front of an audience? Isn't it riskier?"

"Yeah, it's wiskier. But it's a message, see. Whatevah this guy's doin', it's gonna send the woid that nobody else bettah stawt doing it. It's not a revenge thing. This client of yous. He's stepping on somebody's toes. Pushing into somebody else's business. You know?"

"I see. One more thing. How often is the shooter going to look over the place he's making the hit? And when is he going to do that? What's your opinion?"

"I'd say two times. Once to do measaments. Positioning. Figa out the hit. The second time a week or maybe a few days before the hit. Just to see if anything's changed." This line of questioning was obviously making Fudd nervous. While he talked, he kept shrugging his shoulders, rolling his eyes back, and acting punchy. It was hot in my apartment, too, and sweat had beaded on his forehead. "Nice meeting ya and all, but I gotta be someplace." Fudd got to his feet and started for the door. I jumped up to open it for him.

"Thank you for your help," I said to the back of his head as he left.

"Don't mention it," he said as he started stabbing his finger into the elevator button. He didn't look back.

Once Fudd had left, I started thinking about what he said. I went over to my computer and decided to take another look at the files on Daniel's closest associates. I did, and didn't learn anything new.

Then I Googled each of them—Ginny, Chip, and LaDonna. The only new information that popped up was that LaDonna Chavez had gone to Pepperdine—a fundamentalist Christian university—for both her undergraduate degree and her law degree. It was a good school, but I found her choice of a college . . . well, interesting. She had also served an internship straight out of law school with a conservative Republican California Congressman. Then the Exxon *Valdez* drenched the Alaskan coast in oil and ruined the ecosystem for the next couple of hundred years and she walked away from the job. Like Daniel, maybe LaDonna had her own conversion on the road to Damascus. Or maybe not.

I thought about that awhile. Then I called Benny again. Still no answer. I found the card with Tallmadge's number and punched it into my cell phone. It rang and he picked up.

"Is Benny there?" I demanded.

"Daphne?" he asked.

"Yeah. Look, I can't get in touch with Benny. Is she with you?"

"No, she's not," he said.

"When did she leave the club last night? Did you take her home?"

"I'm not much help there, I'm afraid," he said. "I left before she did. Around three, I think. She was with the countess. I'm sure she's fine. Maybe they went somewhere together."

"She's on a mission. I don't see her just taking off."

"I didn't mean that she took off anywhere. I was thinking maybe Benny stayed with the countess for the day if it got too close to dawn or something. Or maybe she just fell asleep in the club."

"Yeah, that's probably it. But she's not checking her messages, and that bothers me. Would you contact the club? If she's not there, get hold of the countess, okay? I'll go by Benny's apartment and check it out. Then I'm going back to Joe Daniel's headquarters. It's on Twenty-ninth Street. I'm not trying to be an alarmist, but Tallmadge, she'd better be all right or you're going to be answering to me," I said, my feelings of unease rapidly increasing.

"Calm down, Daphne. I think you're jumping to the wrong conclusion here. If Benny's out of touch, it's because she wants to be. Nobody's kidnapped her."

"How about drugging her? That's not exactly far-fetched, now, is it?" My voice had a steel edge and my fingers were tight on the phone.

"We were only having some harmless fun last night. I heard you had fun too, Daphne. Why deny your friend the same pleasures?" His voice was smug. In that moment I hated him, and I hated that he knew what I had done.

"Fuck you, Tallmadge. And fuck your fucking club. Just find her." I hung up, shaking with rage.

I grabbed my backpack, threw on a leather jacket, and took a cab up to Benny's place, which was maybe fifteen blocks from mine. I had the doorman of her building buzz her apartment, but she didn't answer. He hadn't seen her, and when I said I was concerned, he mentioned that she hadn't picked up either her mail or a dry-cleaning delivery that had come in that afternoon. My rational mind told me that Tallmadge was right: Benny was at the club or with the countess. I wasn't happy about either possibility, but it was the most likely explanation. So why were my instincts jumping up and down and waving a red flag? In my gut I felt that wherever Benny was, she was not okay. Right now, however, there wasn't anything I could do except hope she called me back.

My next stop was supposed to be Twenty-ninth Street, but once I got in the cab and headed downtown, I changed my mind. Suddenly I wanted to see Fitz more than anything else in the world, and I wanted to see him now.

I hadn't set up a visit beforehand. I was going to try to talk myself in, but I didn't have to. When I spoke to the security people, I found out that Fitz had left a pass for me to be admitted any time of the day or night if I showed up again. I breathed a sigh of relief and hurried through the halls to his room. He was sitting up in a chair.

"Hi! How are you feeling?" I said. His cheeks were pink and his eyes were bright and alert.

"Much better now that you're here," he said, smiling.

"Seriously, Fitz," I said as I walked over and gave him a light kiss on the cheek. "How are you doing?"

"Seriously, Daphne," he teased. "I really am feeling better. I should be out of here next week. The doc says I'll be recu-

perating for six or eight weeks after that. The bullet nicked
my stomach and I lost my spleen. I was lucky. But enough of
that. I'm glad to see you," he said, reaching out and taking my
hand. "The other night did a lot for my recovery. It motivated
me to get out of here as fast as I can."

"It did a lot for me too," I said, and smiled. "It also gave
me a lot to think about. Do you feel well enough to hear some
really shitty things I want to tell you?"

"If you're going to break my heart, I warn you, you'll send
me into a relapse," he said, only half kidding. His eyes were
soft when they looked at me. He was an incredible guy, and I
hoped I wasn't about to drive him away from me forever.

I squeezed his hand. "I absolutely have no intention of
breaking your heart, Fitz. But I have some things to get off
my chest. I don't want our relationship to go any farther without you knowing what you're getting yourself into. I need
you to know that I understand if you can't handle it, me, what
I am. But if you meant what you said last time about wanting
a relationship, I have to be fair to you. We won't have a
chance if I'm not. I'm sick of secrets, Fitz. Really sick of
them."

"Daphne, I told you: I care about you, the woman I know,
who is smart, brave, and good. There's nothing that's going
to scare me away. I have some things I need to tell you too."

"Fitz, believe me, whatever you have to tell me is going to
be a molehill next to my mountain. Let's start with that fact
that I'm not a woman, exactly."

Fitz jerked in his chair, his eyes got huge, and his mouth
dropped open. "Holy Mother of God, Daphne. Don't tell me
you're a transsexual. They did one hell of a job on your sex-
change operation! Look, I can deal with that, I think. I think
I can deal with it."

I couldn't help it; I started laughing. "No, no! I didn't

mean that I'm not a woman physically." I took a deep breath and sobered up fairly quickly, because I knew what I was about to say wasn't the least bit funny. "Fitz. I meant I'm not a *human* woman. I'm a vampire."

He just sat there looking at me without understanding; then he said, "I don't get what you're telling me."

"Just that. I'm a vampire. As in Transylvania and Dracula. You know, I can't go out in sunlight, I sleep in a coffin, I turn into a giant bat, I drink blood, and, oh, yes—I'm immortal."

"Daphne," he said, his voice filled with sympathy. "Are you on meds? Did you stop taking them?"

"Fitz, I'm *not* crazy. I'm a vampire," I said, disengaging my hand from his and starting to pace back and forth. "Look, I don't want to prove it to you right here by turning into a bat, but trust me—I could."

"Daphne," Fitz said, starting to sound upset. "Vampires aren't real. They don't exist. You're hallucinating. Thinking you are a vampire is a delusion. It just seems real."

"Oh, my God," I said. "Fitz, please. I'm not hallucinating. I was born in the sixteenth century. In Italy. My father was a frigging pope in the Roman Catholic Church. I'm over four hundred years old. A few months ago I was tracked down by some U.S. security agency—I think it was probably the CIA, but it could have been the NSA. I was recruited to be a spy. If I didn't do what they asked, they threatened to put a stake through my heart. I'm serious! Don't look at me that way. I am not nuts! Oh, shit, I guess I'll have to show you."

I stripped off my clothes, which got Fitz's undivided attention, and then I transformed, giving him the whole show—the flashing lights, the whirling vortex of wind, the transmogrification of woman into monster. Within seconds I stood before him in all my vampire glory—a giant batlike creature with iridescent wings and golden eyes, clearly not human and definitely not socially acceptable. For added effect I took a short flight around the room.

"Holy shit!" he said, looking poleaxed. "I haven't had a drink in a week. I must have the DT's." He sat there and just stared at me. I had to give it to him: He wasn't scared. He just figured I wasn't real. *Oh, great!* I thought.

"Fitz!" I hissed, and showed him my teeth. "I'm real. I'm a vampire. This is not a dream." I moved close to him. "Touch me. I'm fur, not flesh."

He did, then looked, astonished, down at his fingers. Then I saw emotions pass over his face as if I were watching a movie—shock, fear, confusion. Then he seemed to disappear somewhere inside himself, his eyes lowered and staring at the IV line running into the back of his hand. He didn't move or speak or look at me. I wondered when he'd look up, and if he did, how he would look at me. I prepared myself to face his revulsion, disgust, or anger.

Seconds dragged into minutes. "Dammit, Fitz," I finally said. "So what do you think? Do you want me to leave? I know you didn't expect to be dating a vampire, now, did you?"

He raised his head. I held my breath.

"You know, Daphne, it would have been a lot easier if you were a banshee or a selkie. At least you'd be Irish. But I can handle a vampire. You wouldn't happen to be Catholic, would you? It would make things easier with my mother."

I rolled my bat eyes. "Fitz. Be serious. Can you ever envision yourself loving *this*?"

"I don't know. I had an Irish wolfhound once. I guess if I could love a dog, I could love a giant bat." He had the audacity to grin at me.

I picked up a pillow off the bed and lobbed it at him. There was no point in staying in bat form except to give some inquisitive nurse a heart attack if she walked in, so I changed back.

After the minitornado had passed, I stood there naked as a jaybird and feeling perplexed, stared at Fitz, not knowing what to do next.

"Hey, this is definitely the good part," Fitz said, raking my body up and down with his eyes.

"You're an impossible man," I said crossly. I picked up my clothes and got dressed. "Can't you see why this relationship won't work?"

"I can see that we are going to have to make some accommodations for each of our, shall we say, *problems.* Look, Daphne, in case you haven't noticed, I drink. I'm an alcoholic. I go to AA when I feel my drinking gets out of control, but I'm still not serious about stopping. Frankly, my dear, loving an Irish drunk might be far worse a bargain than loving a vampire. Whiskey is the curse of my race. So let's it call it even. We're both imperfect in a major way. Maybe love can conquer all, and maybe not. But I'm willing to give it a go if you are."

I walked over to him then and stooped down in front of him. "You are a pretty amazing guy," I said. "It isn't going to be easy. I've done a lot of things I'm ashamed of."

"So have I," Fitz said. "I don't think we have to compare war stories."

"There is at least one thing I have to tell you before we go any farther."

"Is it about Darius?" he asked.

"No, not at all. That's over. I guess it is, anyway. This isn't about him; it's about me and something that happened last night."

"Do you feel you have to tell me?" Fitz asked. "You don't,

you know. We haven't made a commitment to each other. You don't owe me an explanation."

"I know that, Fitz. It's just that I'm disappointed in myself and concerned that I don't know myself as well as I thought I did. Let me explain. It might help you to understand me better, and really, I need you to know who I am inside. I can't keep secrets anymore from somebody I care about, from somebody I very much want to care about me."

"Is this your way of telling me that you *do* care about me, Daphne? Because I'm crazy about you. I've been thinking of you and dreaming of you since that first night at the Kevin St. James, when you walked over to me at the bar. You knocked me out; you really did. I couldn't believe how lucky I was to meet you," he said.

What he was telling me made it even harder to go ahead with what I was going to reveal. I felt as if I were swimming in the ocean and suddenly realized I had gone out too far. If Fitz turned away from me, I might never get back to shore. I might be lost in a vast sea of loneliness forever. I took a deep, shaking breath and began.

"Fitz, listen—I drink human blood. I need it like you need food—"

"Or whiskey," he broke in.

"Fitz, this is hard enough for me to get through without you interrupting!" I cried, tears welling up in my eyes.

"Sorry. I'll be good and shut up," he said, but he reached out and took my hand and brought it to his lips. I left my hand in his and sat on the floor next to his chair, my head on his knees, unable to meet his eyes as I went on with my story.

"Fitz, the blood need, it's a bloodlust. It's an irresistible desire," I said, and let out a deep sigh. "Be patient and let me explain. Some vampires hunt humans and take them by force.

The vampires think it's exciting and fun. The humans don't get to think anything. They usually die.

"Other vampires prefer to seduce humans and enter into a opportunist relationship with a man or a woman, making the blood donor their slave. It's a very cruel situation because the human is powerless and completely in thrall to the vampire. Most of the time the vampire doesn't give a damn about the human. It's just a relationship of convenience for him—and a power trip.

"And some vampires bribe humans into giving up their blood for cash or other goods. Wealthy vampires usually do that."

"Is that what you do?" Fitz asked.

"No! I mean, I used to, but for decades I've been able to purchase human blood from a private blood bank. It's more ethical. I don't have to abuse anybody. And I thought it was the ideal way to deal with . . . with my 'problem.' But something happened last night that showed me I might be just fooling myself, that I might be denying that I really am a blood-drinking monster who can't control my base hungers."

"Daphne," Fitz said, stroking my hair. "You aren't a monster. I am convinced of that."

"Well, I drank a human's blood last night, and it wasn't from a blood bank," I said, and sat up straighter, turning my eyes away from Fitz and staring at the light above his hospital bed. I really hated remembering what I had done, and I was considering how much of what happened with Ducasse I could bear to tell Fitz. I was getting cold feet about confessing everything. I took a deep breath and began.

"This young guy offered himself to me, and . . . well, I took the offer. It's a long story. I had been drinking absinthe. Have you ever drunk that?" I asked, and looked at him.

"No. I admit to once resorting to NyQuil, but I usually stick to Jameson."

"Well, don't *ever* drink absinthe. It not only has alcohol in it; it contains wormwood, a hallucinogenic. I drank it last night. I knew better, but I did it anyway. Then this . . . this *opportunity* presented itself and I couldn't resist. That's what bothers me. I thought I could. And I didn't. I just wanted to have this guy's blood, and nothing else mattered."

"I understand it. It's not all that different from needing a drink. You hate yourself afterward, but at the time, having that drink is all that matters."

"Yeah, that's true. But whiskey isn't blood and another person isn't involved. Drinking blood is sexual too. That's part of it. Sex and biting, it's euphoric. It's beyond ecstasy. It's dark and it's wild. And maybe it's evil. I don't know, but the experience is very pleasurable. It's why I'm really worried about intimacy between you and me."

"You mean you are worried about having sex with me?" Fitz said, sounding puzzled for a split second; then he got it. "Are you afraid you'll bite me?"

"Yes. I have to face the truth. I've fallen hard for only two guys in hundreds of years, and I bit them both. I killed one of them by biting him. The other I turned into a vampire, and the upshot was that I made him hate me. Fitz, you have to be aware that in a moment of passion, I might want to bite you."

"And in a moment of passion, I might not care," he said. He took his hand and gently turned my face toward his. "Look at me. I understand your concern for me, and for yourself. But I'm not those other guys. And I'm willing to take my chances."

"Fitz, it's a very big risk to take," I said, looking up at him, looking into his kind gray eyes.

He pulled me up from my knees then and sat me on his

lap. He put his arms around me. "Daphne, let me tell you a story. In Celtic myth, the selkie folk are magical shape-shifters who live in the sea as seals. But a selkie female can shed her skin and come ashore as a beautiful woman to dance under the light of the moon—or to make a human fall in love with her. I feel as if I have found my own selkie, and it's not a curse. It's a blessing. The other men you loved, they weren't Irish, now, were they?"

"No," I said, putting my cheek against his.

"Then they didn't understand you. Their culture didn't prepare them for magic or what others would fear and run from. We Irish know the world is made up of many marvelous things and many magical creatures—who aren't all good, you know. Fairies play terrible tricks on humans, and leprechauns do steal babies. Did you know that, girlie?" he said with his lips muffled in my hair.

"Don't tease me. People hate vampires. Maybe you'll hate me too," I said, and a tear ran unbidden down my cheek.

"People hate what they don't understand. I won't hate you, I promise," he said. And deep in my heart, I wanted to believe that promise.

CHAPTER 12

Everyone wants to change humanity, but no one is willing to change themselves.

—Leo Tolstoy

We spoke of love, and that was all we did. For one thing, Fitz wasn't in any shape to fool around, although, if I'd let him, he would have tried to please me like he had before. But I was too emotionally overwrought to have sex. I felt cherished, not all hot and bothered.

We ending up talking for quite a while. I told Fitz I was headed for Joe Daniel's headquarters and gave him a quick rundown of the assassination threat. I promised to come back when I could, and he made sure to give me his home address before I left. He said he'd call me the minute they discharged him. I kissed him and said good night. My heart felt lighter than it had a few hours ago, but as soon as I hit the street I thought about Benny, and a wave of cold anxiety hit me hard.

I checked my cell phone for messages. Tallmadge hadn't called. I was seriously annoyed. I called him, but he didn't pick up. I figured that was on purpose. I didn't know what to do. I didn't want to return to the vampire club, but we don't always get what we want. If I had to, I'd go down there after I touched base at Daniel's storefront.

*   *   *

Daniel's headquarters was wall-to-wall people. I showed my ID to get in and shouldered my way through the crush into the back room. I spotted Ginny answering telephones and made my way over to her.

"Hey! Ginny!" I called out.

She raised her head and covered the mouthpiece of the phone. "I'll be off in a sec. Did you see this?" she said with a huge smile, and handed me a fax of an AP bulletin. Then she gave me a thumbs-up sign before going back to her call.

I looked at the AP wire and realized why Ginny was so up. The polls gave Daniel a growing approval rate. He was nearly neck and neck with the president on issues relating to the war and the economy. Then came the bombshell. The liberal Democrats had announced they wanted Daniel to run in the primaries—as their candidate. Daniel could go into the presidential election, not as a Green, not as a third-party candidate, not as another Ralph Nader—but as the pick of the Democratic party.

As far as the assassination threat went, this news bite just upped the ante.

I looked around. I spotted Moses Johnson standing by the watercooler. He nodded at me. I gave him a Boy Scout salute, and he scowled.

So much for trying to be friendly, I thought.

While I waited for Ginny to finish the call, I started running through the possible suspects behind this assassination plot. Least likely was some crazy right-winger, like Godse, the man who'd shot Gandhi. This was a highly organized hit, not the work of a lone gunman. More likely the assassin was being sent by some racial extremist or fringe group, like whoever sent James Earl Ray to kill Martin Luther King Jr. It was no big stretch of the imagination to see that white supremacists would love to gun down Daniel, especially if they believed he had a chance of getting elected. Individuals didn't think like governments. Discrediting Daniel would never be enough for those who hated him.

But what Fudd told me pushed me to think outside the box too. Because Gage was an independent contractor doing the hit for money, and not a member of some fringe organization, I was positive that whoever was behind the assassination wasn't an individual, but a group. But who felt Daniel was getting in the way of their "business"?

This line of thought opened up a lot of possibilities. For one thing, Daniel, with his Green position, threatened anybody with oil interests in the United States. He had called for complete independence from foreign oil within ten years, and he had a plan to do it. That meant OPEC or one of the big oil states went down on my list. Daniel had also gone after industries tied to global warming, chemical companies who dumped toxic waste, and coal-burning electrical plants still contributing to acid rain. He had pissed off a lot of very powerful people.

And despite Mar-Mar's insistence to the contrary, I did believe some element in the American military establishment or in the security services could be using Gage. Hell, they could have him on their payroll. I was certain there was a nest of true believers in the government who thought war was the answer to America's troubles. Need oil? Invade a country and take it. Want to stop terrorists? Blow them, and any innocent civilians around them, to kingdom come. It wouldn't matter that killing Daniel was murder. Some people didn't care if they broke the law: They felt they were above it.

And what about the alliance of powerful men in the government and on the courts with Opus Dei? Daniel had openly attacked the religious right. He wanted a clear division of church and state. I could see him cleaning house of the guys with ties to extreme religious groups. Could that figure in somehow? I didn't know. Dammit, I just didn't know.

Ginny's voice jarred me out of my ruminations.

"Daphne? Do you need me for something?" She was clearly busy, so I made it brief.

"Can I get an updated schedule for Daniel, everything he's doing between now and next Friday? And I'd like to talk to him for a couple of minutes."

"The schedule I can get. I'll ask a volunteer to copy one for you. Getting you time to talk to him? Not so easy. I'll tell him you need to see him, but your best bet is to hang out and watch for an opportunity."

"Where is he now?" I asked, looking around.

"He's here somewhere. At least, he was a few minutes ago."

"I didn't see him when I walked in."

"He's probably in a conference with Chip or LaDonna. Ask around, okay?" she said, clearly ending the conversation. The phone was ringing, and she reached over to answer it. "Joe Daniel for president. This is Ginny. Can I help you?" she said into the phone. I made a beeline for Moses Johnson. I knew he'd be thrilled.

"Detective," I said as I walked up to him.

"Miss Urban." Johnson was chewing on a toothpick and not looking glad to see me.

"You know where Daniel is?" I asked.

"Out front somewhere, I guess," he answered.

"So what's up with security? I would think you'd want to know exactly where Daniel was every second."

"I do want to know, but it's not my choice. It's Daniel's." Johnson spit the toothpick into the waste container next to the watercooler. "He's insisting on everything staying low-key. He doesn't want uniforms all over the place. He says it sends the wrong message to his supporters. Scares people away. The only concession he's made is to wear a Kevlar vest. Otherwise, he comes, he goes. Tells us to take a walk."

"I can see his point."

Johnson gave me a disgusted look.

"Hey, I didn't say I agreed with him. I just see his point; that's all. I think I'll take a look-see and try to find him. Nice talking with you, Detective," I said. Johnson didn't echo my sentiments. He didn't say good-bye at all.

I did need to find Daniel, and I thought I should talk to Chip and LaDonna. They were the two people closest to their boss—and maybe one of them was a wolf in sheep's clothing. They both watched him closely. Either one of them could be reporting back to someone else. Okay, I didn't want to believe it. I wanted to believe that these were good people; unselfish people, people with ideals. Salt-of-the-earth types, not the elite who got power along with the silver spoon in their mouths. I didn't know if OP and Daniel were one hundred percent right. I didn't know if they were fifty percent right. But they weren't wrong. They deeply wanted to change the world for the better, and their positions made a lot more sense to me than trying to shoot the world straight.

A volunteer came up and handed me a copy of Daniel's schedule. I stuck it in my backpack, then walked around the storefront trying to spot Daniel in the sardine can of a room. Somebody had turned on a ceiling fan, but I was wearing a leather coat, and it felt hot as Hades. The storefront was Spartan and the walls were bare, but the fluorescent lights ratcheted up the nervous energy in the crowd, the cocktails and wine coolers were flowing, and the noise level was high. The mood was optimistic: People were laughing, debating issues, and looked to be having a good time.

Near the back wall, a white teenager wearing baggy Levi's

and hip-hop chains was attempting to set up a portable screen. I asked him what it was for. He said they were having a showing of *An Inconvenient Truth* in a couple of minutes. I made my way around the edges of the room and looked carefully, but Daniel wasn't there. Chip wasn't around either.

I did notice LaDonna talking to a group of college students, and walked over. I caught her eye, and she reluctantly broke away from her audience. I asked if she had time to talk. She said no. I insisted it was important. She looked annoyed and said she'd give me some time on Monday. Tonight was definitely out, and the weekend was going to be crazy, she said. She also told me that Chip and Daniel had gone outside for some fresh air.

I went out into the street and didn't see them. I decided to head east down the block toward Fifth Avenue. I didn't spot Daniel and Chip until I actually got to the corner. I looked over at the church and saw them standing up on the steps near the front entrance to the church. I had reached the end of the metal fence that was festooned with yellow ribbons, and I could hear their raised voices.

I turned the corner and walked by the church, keeping my face averted toward the street in case they looked up. I wanted to find a place within earshot where I could eavesdrop on what was going on. I stopped slightly to the right of the church and stooped down, just out of their view. I couldn't catch every word; the traffic starting up when the light changed sometimes drowned them out. But I heard enough.

Chip was saying, "I know you're in pain, but the pills are a political hot potato."

Daniel responded fast, his angry words like steel bullets ricocheting off the stone walls of the church. "*You* know I'm in pain? You don't know. You don't have a fucking idea about being in pain. Those pills are the only thing keeping me from blowing my head off."

"Can't you have the back surgery that doctor told you about?" Chip asked.

"No! I told you before—no motherfucking surgery. I already lost a leg. I'm not ending up in a fucking wheelchair for the rest of my life."

"You're just looking at the worst that can happen," Chip muttered.

Daniel's voice got loud. "You don't have to take the risk. I do. And I'm not taking that risk." Then it sounded as if Daniel clenched his teeth and ground out his words between them. *"Now get me the goddamn pills."*

"I don't know—" Chip started to say when Daniel cut him off.

"They're prescription drugs. They're fucking OxyContin from a pharmacy. I'm not asking you to buy smack on the goddamn street."

Then Chip was talking, his voice pleading. "Yeah, I know that. But you're taking so many, the doctor couldn't give you any more. You're taking three times what the doctor prescribed for you."

"Not every day. Not every day. Only when I have to drive or sit in a plane for hours." Then Daniel's voice got softer. "I give you my word: As soon as this campaign is over, I'll go into detox and get off of them. I'll try an epidural. Another drug. But right now the only way I can handle the pain is with these damned pills."

"If the media finds out—"

"Don't give me a hard time about this. I'm not a fucking drug addict." The emotion in Daniel's voice had jagged edges. This was a man close to losing it.

Chip's voice grew softer. "I know that. But the pills make you edgy. Your temper's on a hair trigger all the time."

Daniel's anger shot out at him again. "Jack Kennedy was on fucking speed. He had his Dr. Feel Good shooting up him *and* Jackie with methamphetamines. I'm just trying to fucking function. So don't put this guilt trip on me. I've got enough to deal with. Goddamn it, there's an assassin out there coming for me."

Chip's voice was muffled and I couldn't hear it. All I caught was, "I'm sorry, okay. I'm sorry. I'm here for you. I'm just worried. We're so close. We can win this, Joe."

"Only if I can stay alive."

I heard them start down the steps of the church toward the street. I scurried along the sidewalk before I straightened up and walked away, up Fifth Avenue toward Thirtieth Street. The night was mild, but I felt colder than ever. I now had information that could discredit Daniel, information I knew J would want. But would I give it to him? I really had to think about it. And I wondered who else knew about Daniel's pill popping. With that kind of explosive secret just waiting to detonate, Daniel might be more valuable to the others in his political party as a dead martyr than as a live presidential candidate. After all, Daniel was sure to lose if the truth leaked to the media. It certainly was a reason for someone in the Daniel camp—a fanatic—to want their guy dead and a martyr before a scandal broke.

No way was I going back to Daniel's headquarters now. I turned my attention to finding Benny. I checked my cell. No messages. I called my home phone. No messages left there either. I called Benny on her cell phone again. She still wasn't answering. I called Tallmadge. He still wasn't picking up.

The whole phone thing was taking me down a dead end. If

Benny could answer, she would. Obviously she couldn't. I didn't know if she was drugged or just lost, the kind of lost when the rational part of one's brain doesn't operate and a person has on mental blinders, following somebody who's stronger. Or more clever.

I'd have to go back to the club. It was something I didn't want to do. And I didn't want to see Ducasse. I knew what he would want to give me. As Fitz said, it was like offering an alcoholic a drink, and my shaky control over my thirst for blood was a part of me I wasn't ready to test.

But wherever Benny was or why, I was convinced she couldn't get away on her own. I had to find her. I had vowed with my team, "I will never leave a fallen comrade to fall into the hands of the enemy." More important than that, Benny was my friend. She was in trouble, and I needed to bring her home.

I got to the club right at the witching hour. Just standing on the front steps brought on a cold sweat that made my flesh clammy. I wanted to make this visit all business. Maybe I'd get lucky and Ducasse would have the night off.

Cathary let me in.

"Listen," I said. "This is important. Is Miss Polycarp here?"

"No," he said politely. "She hasn't been in yet this evening."

"Did she stay here last night?" I pressed.

"Do you mean, did she reserve one of the guest rooms? I don't believe so. I think she left before dawn." He wasn't offering up a word more than he had to.

"Cathary, I don't have time for games. Did she leave alone? Who was she with?"

"Miss Urban, she had been with the countess. To the best

of my knowledge they both left shortly before daybreak. I didn't see them go, however, and I don't know where they went."

"Shit. Look, is Tallmadge here?" I was getting really antsy about standing there. I wanted out of this place as soon as possible.

"He's upstairs. Would you like me to call him for you?"

"Yes, dammit," I said. I figured any minute Ducasse was going to come walking into the hall, and I really didn't want to be there when he did.

Cathary made the call. "He says you can go up there, if you wish."

"Right. Don't bother taking me. I know the way," I said even as I hurried over to the stairs and took them two at a time.

Tallmadge was sitting on the sofa smoking a cigar. He blew out a cloud of smoke in my direction and saluted me with a glass of wine. His long legs in pin-striped trousers were stretched out on the coffee table. "Please sit down and join me. It's an unexpected pleasure to see you this evening."

"I'll stand. I'm not staying. You didn't call me back," I said accusingly.

He looked at the tips of his polished black dress shoes, not at me. "I haven't found out anything useful. I've been waiting for a call back from the countess," he said, then leaned forward and tapped ashes into a glass ashtray. "I think you're overreacting, you know."

"And I think you're wrong. Even if Benny had stayed with the countess during the daylight hours, she would have gone back to her apartment by now. She would have contacted me. Where can I find the countess? I need to talk with her." I walked closer to Tallmadge and glared down at him.

"I told you, Daphne. I haven't been able to reach her. But

look, I was going to invite you to join us anyway," he said, putting his feet on the floor and sitting up straight. "We're having a hunt tomorrow night at the countess's country estate. She's sure to be there. She's probably busy preparing for it now, and that's why she hasn't returned my call."

"A hunt?" I asked. "What kind of hunt?"

Tallmadge's handsome face broke into a warm smile. "A manhunt, Daphne. Of course, there will be women, too. It's going to be very special. The countess has been setting this one up for weeks. These hunts are her specialty. People rave about them for weeks afterward. This time she says she's found the most beautiful humans to be the quarry. Everyone in the club is so excited about it. We don't get this opportunity very often."

"You're talking about a planned hunt to capture humans to bite them?" My voice was disapproving and my face had gotten rigid. "What happens—the humans run for their lives trying to escape us?"

"No, of course not. That would be too crude. Too much like a paintball war. The club's hunt is very elegant. It's strictly black-tie and by invitation only. My dear, don't look so disapproving. This is a fun game, with rules. The young people who audition to do this are highly trained and very well paid. Every one of them is a top athlete, and tremendously attractive."

I didn't know what to think, really. I stood there next to Tallmadge and he took my hand, stroking it with his thumb. I wished his touch didn't feel so good. "I don't think it's my cup of tea," I said, disengaging my hand from his.

"But it is!" Tallmadge said, his eyes alive with excitement. "These are superb young people. Don't get the wrong impression. They compete fiercely for a spot in the hunt, and they are thrilled if they get chosen to take the part of the prey.

There is no coercion involved. The countess has created a giant maze with all sorts of surprises scattered throughout it. The humans get led to the center of the maze and try to get out. If they do it without being stopped by one of us, they get a huge bonus. We all go into the maze after them, and it's great fun. Very challenging and very exciting. You shouldn't miss the experience. I'm sure Benny will be there. She said she would."

"What do you mean?" I asked.

"I told Benny about it before I left last night. She was as excited as a child on Christmas morning when the countess invited her. She'll be there; I'm sure of it. In fact, I'd bet she's out in New Jersey at the countess's estate near Peapack already. That's probably what happened. She and the countess went out there right after the sun set, and she probably didn't get your message."

"Maybe. It's possible, I guess."

"Come with me and see for yourself. You really have to come. We can ride out together." He looked at me like the wolf eyeing Little Red Riding Hood.

I stood there without answering. I didn't like this at all. I had the feeling there was a hell of a lot about this hunt that Tallmadge wasn't telling me. But I didn't know how else I was going to find Benny. "Yeah, sure. Sounds good," I said without enthusiasm. And as soon as I said those words, I saw something gleaming on the coffee table, half-hidden by a book and out of Tallmadge's view. It was Bubba's West Point ring. I kept talking and sat down on a chair, dragging it so close to the sofa that my knees practically touched Tallmadge's.

"It's very sweet of you to ask me," I said, changing my tone and seeming to get flirtatious with the handsome vampire who looked ready to jump my bones. I leaned over toward him, idly moving the books on the coffee table, and palmed the ring while I did so. "It will give us a chance to get better acquainted, and I would so like that," I lied, and smiled brightly. In truth, being alone with Tallmadge again was the last thing I wanted.

"That's wonderful!" Tallmadge smiled and moved toward me. My body involuntarily stiffened as he took my hand, the one not holding the ring, and brought it to his lips. "You've been away from your own kind too long, my dear. I'm glad you're coming back to us. We're vampires, Daphne. We must never forget that."

He pushed my dark hair back from my face and traced his finger down my cheek. I shivered. "We would make a great team, you know," he said, and brought my hand to his lips once more. I sat there mesmerized, like a mouse watching a cobra getting ready to strike.

Tallmadge kissed my fingers one by one, then unexpectedly he took my index finger gently into his mouth and sucked. Sensation shot up my arm. I gasped and closed my eyes. He stretched out my arm and his tongue licked inside my wrist. He kissed behind my elbow, leaving a burning trail with every touch of his mouth. Then his arm slipped around my waist and brought me to him. Suddenly he was kissing me.

I wanted to hate it, to hate him. I didn't. Instead I was drowning in sensation. Part of my mind realized that it must be this club that took away my inhibitions. I seemed to have no will to resist any temptation here. I didn't want to surrender to Tallmadge, but I couldn't seem to stop myself.

"No," I said, but my voice lacked conviction.

His tongue slipped between my lips into my mouth. My head went back against the soft chair. His lips ground against mine. It felt wonderful. I couldn't remember why I was resisting. We kissed long and hard, hungry and devouring each other. Again and again his tongue entered my mouth. Before long I was hot and panting. While we kissed I felt Tallmadge's fingers at my waist. I realized he was deftly unbuttoning my slacks. After they were loosened, he slipped his hand down my pants.

"No," I said again. This was so wrong, yet I couldn't seem to stop it. My body was betraying me, and I knew that betrayal would haunt me. My knees went weak as I felt Tallmadge's index finger slip between my legs and find my sweet spot. He put his forehead against mine, groaning as he pushed his finger into me, first one, then the middle finger, using his thumb to stroke me in just the right place. As he did so, I sagged into his arms. I opened my eyes and looked into his. His gaze pierced my soul, and all I saw was blackness.

"No," I said once more.

"Relax," he instructed, and kissed me softly. "Let me pleasure you."

"Ohhhh, ohhhh, no." I sighed. I was rapidly losing all control and letting the bonds of pleasure take me prisoner. I could smell the wool of his jacket and the musky man-scent of him. I closed my eyes and spread my legs wider. A third finger slipped into me, and he pushed his hand deep within me as his thumb circled where I wanted it to. I made little moaning sounds with each circle. I gripped Tallmadge's arms hard, my nails digging into them through the sleeves of his coat. Suddenly I tensed and tightened my muscles around his fingers that were slipping in and out of my wet center. My body went rigid and I went flying high, ecstasy building and taking me into a white rush upward, then a quick sliding down as I screamed out loud. The release was electrifying and deliciously satisfying. I went limp.

But then my eyes snapped open. What had I done? Once

again I had fallen to temptation and perhaps committed the worst sin of all.

"I have to go," I said, roughly pushing Tallmadge's arm away. He sat up and wiped his fingers on a damask napkin.

"You sound upset. Don't be. We're vampires. This is what we can do together. Don't forget that."

"I can hardly forget that I'm a vampire, Tallmadge. You have reminded me in an unforgettable way just how much of a vampire I am. I am forever in your debt." Still tucked into my palm, Bubba's ring was biting into my flesh as I spoke. "I'd better go."

I stood up and straightened my clothing. I couldn't look at Tallmadge. My cheeks burned with shame. "What time should I expect you tomorrow?"

"My car will pick you up at your apartment around eight. The hunt itself will begin around ten, but we have a cocktail party beforehand," he explained.

"Fine." I was about to say good-bye; then something occurred to me. I looked squarely into his glittering eyes. "One more thing, Tallmadge."

"Yes, sweet girl?" I cringed at his use of the endearment.

"Countess what? What is her full name?"

"I thought you knew. Countess Giulietta Ariadne Giuseppina de Ericé. We call her the Countess of Darkness for short."

My face registered my shock.

"I'm kidding about that part, of course," he said, and laughed.

"Okay. Giulietta de Ericé, thanks," I said repeating that mouthful so I wouldn't forget it.

I stood unmoving as Tallmadge kissed me on both cheeks before I exited the room and rushed frantically down the stairs. I almost reached the front door.

*   *   *

As I hit the bottom step and started across the hall, a strong hand grabbed me by the shoulder and spun me around.

"Ducasse!" I cried out loud as I beheld the beautiful, god-like face of my nemesis. His shining silver eyes sought mine. I looked down quickly to escape them and instead ended up staring at his shirtless chest and low-riding pants. His abs were as sharply defined as if Michelangelo had carved them from marble. Tendrils of silky hair made a dark shadow from his navel down to his belt, where his pants molded like a second skin to his hips and muscular legs. My breath caught. *Not again, not now,* I thought frantically.

I had descended into hell once this night already. I had to escape. I looked around desperately, but as I did, I glanced into Ducasse's face. It was a mistake. He was not human. His powers captured me as surely as if chains encircled my body. I tried to move my feet. They would not budge. It was like a terrible dream. I wanted to turn and run, but felt rooted to the spot. Then Ducasse smiled.

"Mistress. You were leaving without seeing me?" he said in a soft voice.

"Ummmm, yes. I'm working tonight, actually, and I'm looking for my friend Benny. Have you seen her?" I asked, and tried to force my feet to turn, my hands to open the door, and my being to escape this place of forbidden temptations.

I could not. Panic surged through me. I had lost my will. This club controlled me—or Ducasse controlled me. It didn't matter which. I was slipping away into a place where I would be a damned creature and become everything I had fought against so long.

Ducasse was speaking again, and his voice was leading me deeper and deeper into a velvet prison of dreams and desires. "I have not seen your friend tonight, dear mistress," he said. "I believe she left with the countess before dawn. They spent the previous hours in the game room with a number of other club members." His hand was still on my shoulder, and all the time he spoke, he was staring intently into my face with his hypnotic silver eyes. I was completely still now, my arms falling uselessly to my sides, my mind no longer willing my feet to move toward the door. Ducasse's voice was saying, "Why don't you come with me and we can look for her."

"No," I said with a dreamy slowness. "I don't think I should."

"But why not, mistress? It will take only a few minutes. You haven't seen the game room yet." Ducasse slid my backpack from my shoulder and unzipped my leather jacket. He moved close. His breath fluttered lightly, like butterflies across my skin. I shut my eyes. He kissed my eyelids, and I flinched as his hand slipped inside my jacket and brushed my breast.

"You must be too warm with this coat on. Aren't you too warm, mistress?" he said in his soft, soothing voice.

"Yes, too warm," I murmured.

He lifted the coat from my shoulders and pushed it down my arms until it dropped to the floor of the vestibule. Then, putting one of his strong arms back around my shoulders, he guided me toward the interior of the club. We reached a pair of tall double doors standing open. Beyond them a room was lit by a red glow and inhabited by at least a dozen vampires. Some of them, male and female both, stood by a roulette wheel, although there was something extraordinary about this wheel. Instead of numbers, the spinning ball landed on some sort of pictures; I thought I could discern figures of men and women, or both, in different sexual positions.

Slightly off to the side of the wheel, two male club

members were talking to each other while a beautiful young woman stood nearby. She was entirely naked. As Ducasse and I paused in the doorway, I watched one member nod and the other smile. The male who nodded walked back to the roulette table; the other embraced the woman, and her knees seemed to buckle from beneath her. He lifted her up in his arms and her head fell back, her golden hair so long it touched the floor. She didn't resist; instead she made a sound that was something between a moan and a purr. Her new companion carried her deeper into the room, out of my view.

"I don't want to go in," I said to Ducasse as I watched this, my heart thudding in my chest. His arm remained firmly around my shoulders. I tried to rouse myself from the lethargy that seemed to envelop me, but I still felt dreamy and unfocused.

"Some other time," Ducasse murmured into my ear. "You are tired, aren't you, mistress?" he suggested.

I did feel tired. I was getting sleepy. "I think I'd like to lie down for a minute," I admitted.

"Let's go in here," Ducasse said, and steered me through another doorway. The room we entered, like all the others, was dimly lit. A fire burned behind a grate at one end. A soft, thick rug was spread before it, lined with soft velvet pillows. Ducasse led me over and knelt down on the rug. He pulled me down beside him. He kissed me then, uncaring if I returned the caress, which I did not. He stroked my face and pushed my hair back from it. He lifted my sweater over my head and ran his hands over my body, while I knelt there as if in a trance.

He was whispering all the while, telling me how good he could make me feel, how happy I would be. And then he murmured, "And you must be so thirsty. In the game room they will all drink their fill of blood. It is a treat you would enjoy.

But you have a more delicious meal in me, my mistress. My blood is warm and rich. My mistress is thirsty, isn't she?" he coaxed, his silver eyes holding mine.

Suddenly I was starving for blood. I needed blood. An urgency passed over me that blinded me to all other thought. I must drink. A dark presence as snarling and bestial as a lion in pursuit of a deer consumed me. My mouth opened. My teeth grew long and sharp. A hiss escaped my throat. A darkness emanating from deep in my soul leaped forth.

Ducasse pressed his body against mine then, his naked chest skin to skin against my breasts and stomach, his arms encircling me and becoming bonds from which I couldn't escape. With one hand he reached up and took the back of my head, pushing it forward until my lips touched his neck, in that sweet spot where the vein pulsed just beneath the skin. A shiver of anticipation ran through my body; my breath became a pant.

Ducasse sank down before the fire until he was prone on the rug, pulling me with him. As I stretched upon him, he groaned loudly as my hands grabbed the sides of his face, possessing him and tipping his head back until I exposed his white, inviting throat. I growled then as my mouth descended, and when my lips touched his flesh, my pointed teeth broke his skin and I bit deep.

After it was done between us, my disgust returned. My mouth was still filled with blood, and a red stream now spilled over and ran down my chin. The same red stream flowed from the puncture in Ducasse's white throat. I pulled myself away from him, recoiling in horror, realizing that he had entranced me, and knowing all too well that I had not been able to resist. Beneath my conscious mind, a cruel, irresistible hunger had begun to emerge. It had swept me away to do the deed I resisted, and now I was sated.

Suddenly a terrible realization washed over me: My appetite for blood was growing. Where once I could drink a single time a day, sipping a glass filled from my blood bank supply, I now had a raging thirst. Refrigerated blood could not slake it. The urge to take my fill from prey was releasing the monster I tried so hard to tame. I hated Ducasse, but I wanted him. I loathed his very existence, but I looked at him with lust and desire. I didn't want to want him, but I did, driven wild by the sight of his flesh.

I looked down at his body beneath me. His eyes were glazed and his color waxen, but he breathed long, steady breaths. I was relieved to see that I had not killed him. Instead I was taking Ducasse into that twilight state of existence where he was no longer human—although I suspected more strongly than ever that he was not entirely human to begin with. But I had not yet made him a vampire. He was still my creature, my slave who would gladly die to feed me as I drained him dry. If I did not bleed him out, he would transform soon, to become one of us. And behind his handsome countenance, beneath his perfect skin, I sensed a corrupt and evil mind. I believed he was not a vampire to set loose upon the world without setting evil free as well.

CHAPTER 13

*If I had to choose between betraying my
country and betraying my friend, I hope I
should have the guts to betray my country.*

—E. M. Forster

I made my way back to my apartment, sorely troubled in mind and spirit. I was changing in ways I didn't like, in ways I feared. But when I pushed through my front door into familiar surroundings, I immediately felt stronger. Back in my own space I was quickly gaining more control. Perhaps Jade and Gunther, with their animal goodness and innocence, acted as a counterweight to the vampires pulling me down.

So, as Jade leaned against my leg and Gunther came out of his cage to perch on my shoulder, I took stock of my situation. I needed to stay away from the decadent ways of these New York vampires and the destructive forces they called forth. But Benny was somewhere among them. After tonight I was no closer to finding her, and now I was committed to attending the hunt tomorrow. If she were in thrall emotionally to the countess and Tallmadge, or even being held against her will, it might be my only opportunity to bring her back from that shadowy path that leads to an abyss of mindless pleasure and personal corruption.

But the risk I faced was of being pulled down into the

depths myself and lost. If I entered that maze tomorrow night, would I follow a twisted way toward a point of no return? Would bloodlust became my raison d'être; would hunting prey became a compulsion; and would power over others— for that was the erotic basis for it all—became an obsession?

I needed to prepare myself, although I didn't yet know what to do. However, knowledge is power, so I called my mother.

I didn't bother with small talk. "Mar-Mar, I need some information. A dossier. I'm hoping it's among the files we retrieved from Opus Dei."

She picked up in the urgency in my voice and responded quickly. She didn't even ask why. "Whose dossier?" she replied.

"A female named Countess Giulietta Ariadne Giuseppina de Ericé. And I need a copy of the dossier fast, before tomorrow night."

There was silence at the other end of the line.

"Mar-Mar? Are you still there?"

"Yes. Why do you want the file?"

"Huh?" I said. "She's up to something; I'm sure of it."

"Yes, I think so too," she agreed. "She needs to be watched. Carefully."

That surprised me. I didn't think my mother knew about Benny being missing, since I hadn't told J. Maybe she had talked with Tallmadge. Nothing about Mar-Mar ever surprised me. "After what has been happening, I thought it was obvious," I added.

"Not really," she said. "I know you don't have a fax, and the hours are turning toward morning. I'll have one of my people run a copy down to you. He'll put it under your front door. I don't need to tell you this dossier is highly confidential. Don't discuss anything—and I do mean anything—with your team quite yet. Do you agree?"

"Yeah, sure," I said. The request for absolute secrecy was typically Mar-Mar. I was just relieved she was willing to share the dossier with me.

I hung up and stood there for a moment staring at the phone. I should make another call and tell J what I had found out about Joe Daniel. It would solve our problems, because if the information about his addiction to prescription drugs was leaked to the press—and I assumed it would be—he'd be out of the presidential race. He would no longer be giving a speech at the John Lennon memorial in Central Park. He would no longer be a threat to anyone. That meant he'd be out of the assassin's line of fire. I'd be saving his life.

And ruining it. Daniel would be alive, but would he have any reason left to live? But there was something bothering me a great deal about telling J. Beyond the devastating blow I'd be dealing to Daniel, I had to admit I now believed that this country needed Joe Daniel—or at least needed to have Joe Daniel as a political choice. I stared at the phone for another moment. Finally I punched in J's number.

"Hello, J? Daphne here," I said. "How are you?"

"I'm on crutches, but otherwise mending. Not a problem," he said, his voice steady and familiar. I felt an immense sense of relief that J was still a rock. He might be a son of a bitch, but he was a man to rely on.

"Are you back at work?" I asked.

"I never wasn't at work," he groused. "I told you I was okay."

I let out a deep breath. "Okay, then, we need to meet. I have some new information, and the team may have a potential problem."

"Why not tell me now?"

"I'd rather we talk in person. How's Sunday night? I have something urgent to do tomorrow night. Something personal."

"Are you sure this can wait until Sunday, Agent Urban? You don't sound like yourself. Do you need backup?"

"No, seriously. Sunday is fine. I had a long night, that's all. I'm exhausted. Just need some rest," I said, being careful to keep my voice free of emotion.

"Okay, Sunday it is. I was planning to call in the entire team anyway. You and I can meet before the team meeting. Six thirty?" he asked.

I still hadn't made up my mind how much I was going to tell him about Daniel, about Benny, or even about Tallmadge, who might be working with the countess for all I knew. And Tallmadge was now a personal problem that I had to deal with. Outside of the physical attraction, I didn't know if I even liked him. I certainly didn't trust him. But a lot could happen between now and Sunday. I tried not to let my apprehensions color my voice. "Yes, six thirty is good."

"Agent Urban?"

"What?"

"Whatever you're doing, if you need help, just ask. You hear me? Don't take any unnecessary risks on your own."

"I hear you, and thanks. I'm fine. I'll see you Sunday," I said firmly.

"Roger," he said, and broke the connection.

With my ethics and my very identity under assault, I discovered that in moments of crisis, the mundane tasks of life gave me stability. I walked Jade, fed her and Gunther, went to bed at dawn, got up around five p.m., and made coffee. As I did these things, I held fast to the realization that I liked my life. And most of the time I liked myself. Despite what had happened with Ducasse and Tallmadge, I believed I had the inner strength to remain true to the person I was striving to be. I took solace from Hemingway's famous line in *A Farewell to Arms*: "The world breaks everyone, and afterward, many are strong in the broken places." I steeled my resolve to face the temptations ahead and not to give in to my hidden wild and very dangerous urges.

I hoped that what I found out about the countess could help me do that. When I awoke early Saturday evening, I saw that Mar-Mar was as good as her word; a manila envelope had been pushed under my front door. The dossier on the countess was inside. I took it into my breakfast bar in the kitchen and sat down at the counter with my mug. The coffee was hot and strong when it hit my tongue. I pushed my hair behind my ears, put my chin in one hand, and with the other flipped up the photo clipped to the first page and began to read.

The countess had been born into a noble Sicilian family on the western side of that strange and mysterious island during the kingdom of Roger II, whose consort she became in the early years of his reign around 1132. That made the countess roughly Mar-Mar's contemporary. At this point, as they say, the plot thickened.

I soon deduced that the countess was not, and never had been, a girlie girl. While the dossier skipped many centuries of her life when she had managed to drop below the Church's radar, she did surface in France in 1425 in Domrémy. At the same time in the same village a young girl named Jeanne d'Arc had begun seeing visions and hearing voices, accompanied by a great flash of light. The local clergy had dropped a dime not only on Joan, but on the countess. The "great lady" from Sicily had come to town and ensconced herself in a grand château. She refused to attend Mass, tossed the priest out when he attempted to visit, and maintained an entourage of sinister-looking servants and retainers. Strangest of all, people of the village and neighboring regions, all young and beautiful men and women, began to disappear.

Interesting in another way, since disappearances were a regular occurrence whenever a vampire came to town, the countess seemed to hold a special antipathy against the English, and like Joan, she put on armor to ride forth against the Duke of Burgundy, an ally of England's king. And the countess was damned good with a sword, if the reported number of Burgundians she beheaded with a mighty swipe was accurate.

The countess managed to fly in the face of the Catholic Church again in the seventeenth century, when she raised an army for the Protestants in Germany during the Thirty Years' War. Along with allegations of kidnapping of local peasants, the compiler of her dossier noted that, again taking on the guise of a man, she rode into battle herself. She had a taste for blood in any form, it seemed.

Then I came to a paragraph that gave me chills. The countess appeared in the American colonies shortly before the Revolutionary War. Her hatred of the British was unabated, and she soon joined the patriot cause, donating jewelry and gold bullion to George Washington and the Continental Army. At that time, the dossier noted, she had been seen in the company of the head of Washington's newly formed espionage unit, an officer named Benjamin Tallmadge, and the countess joined his Culper Ring of spies. Sweat broke out on my forehead. I now knew that Tallmadge had been a spymaster and the countess one of his spies. No wonder he chafed at taking orders from J.

How were they both connected to my mother? I was sure they were. I sensed her hand in this at every turn.

I stopped reading and remained lost in thought for a while.

Then I glanced over at the clock. It was getting late. I'd have to begin dressing soon for the evening ahead. I quickly scanned the rest of the dossier. The countess never lost her taste for war, participating in every one fought by the United States between the Revolution and Afghanistan. She had a string of aliases, and she disguised herself as a man as often as she took on a new female identity. She seemed to relish causes, and she definitely liked to kill.

Why had she latched onto Benny, and what did she want with my friend? True, Benny was a stunningly beautiful woman, but as far as I knew she was firmly heterosexual, even if the countess was not. Of course, drugged and perhaps corrupted by the degenerate pleasures of the game room, Benny may have become involved in a ménage à trois.

I quickly looked over the file again, feeling I was missing something, a flicker of an idea that flashed across my mind too fast for me to fully grasp it. But I was already feeling pressured to prepare myself for Tallmadge's arrival, and I was worried about how I could best protect myself from both mind-altering drugs and hypnosis tonight.

I doubted that Ducasse would be present at the hunt to turn his silver eyes on me—unless he was on the wait staff, since this was a members-only formal affair—but I couldn't trust Tallmadge. He might try to break down my inhibitions in any way he could, including slipping a drug into my food or drink. In fact, the prehunt party might be aimed at lowering every participant's inhibitions so that the hunt that followed could be as brutal and bloody as the worst instincts in all of us allowed.

With these disturbing thoughts running through my mind, I took the dossier into my secret room, where it would be safe during my absence. I then went back into the apartment and, despite the growing lateness of the hour, I put on Beethoven's

Eroica Symphony. It was a deliberate choice of music. The great composer had hated war and had a great sensitivity to suffering, and that was brilliantly conveyed in this work. I went to my meditation corner and sat in the lotus position, emptying my mind and letting the lush music overwhelm me.

Then I prayed for divine help and guidance, not to the jealous God of the Jews or the Christians, but to the Great Divine and all the lesser deities whose life force moves the winds and gives fertility to the Earth. I asked all that was good in the cosmos to strengthen me and save me from the forces of darkness, and to save me, in the end, from myself. Finally I called upon the spirits of Damon and Pythias to be with me tonight and to let Benny know I was coming, and I would get there before it was too late.

When I rose from those prayers to begin my ablutions, I already felt cleansed.

Tallmadge had said the hunt was a black-tie affair, and now I faced that age-old question, what to wear? Rummaging through my closet, I found a mauve stretch-taffeta cocktail dress by Nicole Miller, bought on sale during my last trip to Houston and the Galleria. It was a crinkled style with spaghetti straps, the perfect one-piece outfit that I could shed quickly if I had to transform. My shoes were dainty silver mules, and although the temperature had moderated, I looked at them and wondered how I, or any of the club members, could wander through a maze in March in such skimpy apparel.

I assumed the labyrinth or maze that Tallmadge talked about was exposed to the elements, although I might be wrong. The palace at Knossos on Crete was a big old building with a brutal Minotaur waiting in the middle, but I suspected this maze was more the English kind, a garden made of hedges and walls. I didn't plan on wandering through it in any event, so I pushed my worries aside. Then I chose a black, mink-lined coat as outerwear. It was understated, but immensely warm. The crowning touch was a choker of diamonds—paste, not real. I colored my lips very red and let my dark hair hang down straight and shimmering.

I had barely finished getting ready when the phone rang. It was Fudd.

"I got somethin' for you," he said.

"About the independent contractor?" I asked.

"Yeah," he said as he exhaled hard.

"What?" This could be a break in the case. My hopes climbed.

"He's not available. He's signed on pohmanently with somebody. He's on thew paywoll."

"Who?"

"Dat I don't know. Not foweners. Some U.S. outfit. You want me to hook you up with somebody else?"

"No, thanks," I said, disappointed.

"Something else you should know," Fudd added. "This contwactor. He's wee-ud. Weal wee-ud."

"In what way weird?" I asked.

"Like not human wee-ud. A scawee dude."

"Can you be more specific?" I asked.

"Nah. The guy I talked to, he was scawud. Wouldn't say more. Said youah contwactor is a weal monstah. Bad news. Weal bad news. I gotta go," Fudd said, and hung up, leaving me wondering if I had found out anything significant, because if I had, I wasn't sure what it was.

Just then Mickey buzzed and announced that Tallmadge had arrived. My heart beat wildly as adrenaline surged through my veins. *Let the games begin.*

*   *   *

Tallmadge picked me up in a black Lincoln Town Car. No surprise there. In an Armani tux, he looked sophisticated and drop-dead gorgeous. No surprise there either. He didn't put a move on me. Now, that *was* a surprise, and a great relief.

It took us less than an hour to get to Somerset County, New Jersey, an area of rolling hills, secluded wooded estates, and the subtleties of old money. Small, tasteful roadside signs announced hunt clubs, equestrian schools, and one of Richard Branson's exclusive spas. The countess's white Colonial-style house appeared large and understated at the end of an isolated private road. I saw a name plaque in front of open iron gates at the bottom of the driveway that said, FANTAZIUS, BUILT 1823. Yet as the asphalt drive wound through a lane of still-leafless sycamores up to the front door, I noted the absence of guards and security lights.

Inside the house a wide stairway swept upward in the boxy hall, where the furnishings were antique, of dark, well-worn woods; nothing was trendy. The countess had class and wealth; she didn't have to prove anything to anybody. A Thomas Eakins painting of nineteenth-century surgeons in an operating theater made a grisly presence on one wall of the entranceway; on another a large oil by eighteenth-century artist John Trumbull, of a Revolutionary War scene, spoke volumes about her tastes. I called the paintings to Tallmadge's attention.

"Hmmm, yes. She bought the Trumbull from the artist himself. She also knew Washington, who was headquartered nearby in Morristown," he responded after we left our coats with a maid. Then we entered an airy, high-ceilinged ballroom that ran the length of the countess's country place. It was a space for receptions and parties that we might now call a great room, but it contained little furniture, just some chairs and library tables around the perimeter. Except for staff, it was virtually empty. We seemed to be the first club members to arrive. The countess was absent as well. Tallmadge plucked a glass of champagne from a waiter passing with a tray. He offered it to me. I shook my head no.

"Were you here during that time? During the Revolution, I mean?" I asked disingenuously as we waited for more guests to arrive.

"I was. I was a patriot and a spy," he said crisply. "I still am."

My eyebrows rose. I was surprised at his candor. "Then why were you so reluctant to be a Darkwing?"

"Because I think my handler and his bureaucrat bosses are idiots, although your mother may be excepted. Let's change the subject. You look beautiful tonight," he noted, and toasted me.

"Thank you. And that reminds me of a question I had about the hunt. How can you play the game in a tux? I certainly can't run through the maze in these shoes."

He looked at me oddly. "Of course you can't. Why would you? We'll all have transformed."

"Into bat shape?" I was visibly surprised.

"Why not? We have absolute privacy on the estate. There's no danger of being seen by outsiders. Some of us rarely get to fly at any other time." Tallmadge smiled and looked pleased. "It's a wonderful treat to revert."

"But how can the humans possibly escape us? It doesn't seem fair."

"I never said the hunt was fair. I said it was fun," he answered, knocking back the champagne and getting himself another. "The quarry doesn't know about our transformation. It's quite a kick the first time one of them sees us coming."

"I bet it is. Terror is so fun," I said with sarcasm.

"Daphne, you are a prude. You also underestimate the

power of your instincts. Like any beast, when the chase begins, we lose any patina of morality that society has foisted on us. We become the predators that we truly are. It's very elemental. No civilized bullshit. I find the experience exceptionally liberating." His color heightened; his energy level soared. Excitement at the thought of what lay ahead put him in a state of readiness, and I could see he was clearly aroused. I wondered where the sex came in, because along with the blood and the biting, it surely would.

I wasn't excited. I was worried. Even though I was sober and forewarned about what to expect, I feared something inside me would crack and make me lose control. Plus, since I no longer thought it was going to be possible to wriggle out of going along with the activities, at least for a while, I would be transformed into the beast inside me, into the monster within. Keeping a check on my hungers would be difficult. I hoped it wouldn't be impossible. The sooner I found Benny and got us both the hell out of here, the better.

While Tallmadge and I waited around, a band set up at one end of the room, taking out drums, electric guitars, and a keyboard. They clearly weren't about to play Mozart. A couple of the guys had long hair; the others had shaved heads. They all had tattoos and leather vests or jackets over bare chests. One of them definitely looked like Tommy Lee. My first thought was that this was a tribute band for Mötley Crüe, and when they powered up and launched into "Shout at the Devil," I knew I had guessed right.

While the music blasted out over the sound system, other club members started to filter into the party—female vampires in their finery, males in classic evening wear. They were the beautiful people, physically superior and well-off. I wondered how many of them held positions of power in industry as well as in the government. I soon spotted the popular mayor of a large city, the young governor of a Southern state, and the playboy son of a real estate mogul.

Finally the countess appeared. Instead of an evening gown, she was wearing a costume, a formal English foxhunting outfit from the Regency era. I knew the style well. I had once worn it too, in the days when I first took Lord Byron into my bed. She greeted her guests and finally made her way over to Tallmadge and me. She air-kissed us both, and I tried to smile.

But I wasn't diplomatic. I launched right into the purpose of my attendance. "Where's Benny?" I asked.

The countess just laughed at my concern. "Your friend is fine. Did you think otherwise? She is still getting ready for the evening. She wanted to make an entrance. She'll be down soon. Please have some refreshments. I'll see you both later—when the fun begins."

As soon as she left us, I intended to search the house for Benny. Maybe I could slip us both out of here within the next few minutes. The thought occurred to me that Benny might not want to leave. I'd have to try to convince her. If I had to, I'd carry her away by force.

As it turned out, Benny's reluctance to leave was not the problem. The stake poised over her heart was. Had I known what was going on, I might have been more discreet with my entrance. As it was, I nearly blew everything to shit.

I had excused myself from Tallmadge's side by saying I wanted to find a bathroom. He was chatting up some other club members by that time and gave me a little wave as I walked away. I sneaked through the kitchen to the back of the house, figuring there would be a set of servants' stairs to take me to the second floor. I received some odd glances from the hired help, but no one stopped me.

I found the narrow, dark stairs without difficulty. I slipped

off my shoes and climbed upward. On its second level, the
house had a large open hall surrounded by doors. I opened
them one at a time. Behind one appeared to be the countess's
bedroom: An equestrian hat and riding crop lay on the simple white coverlet of the bed. Two of the other rooms, also
bedrooms, were empty. It was in the fourth and last that I
found her.

Benny was bound to the wall by chains, her mouth
gagged. With her extraordinary vampire strength, she could
have quickly freed herself—if a sharply pointed stake had not
been set up on a spring-loaded contraption. Any movement
would trigger a mechanism, and the stake would pierce her
heart. I opened my mouth. "Benny—" I started to say, and
stepped into the room to free her when her eyes stopped me.
She looked frantically toward a door that led into an adjoining room, where I heard a television playing. I got the message and stopped in my tracks. I silently backed out, but
before I did, I mouthed, *I'll be back.*

I had barely shrunk behind the door when a burly guy
emerged from the other room. I heard him stomping around,
but he didn't check out the hall. Fortunately his brains were
as dense as his hearing was bad.

The thoughts in my head were whirling around like a
category-five hurricane. Why was the countess keeping
Benny captive? Was she obsessed with Benny, but Benny
hadn't returned her passion? That was possible, but I have a
suspicious mind, and an idea was growing in my gut. Was
Benny the Judas goat to lure me out here? How much did
Tallmadge know—and what did the countess want from me?

I needed answers, but I needed to get Benny out of here
first—without walking into a trap myself. I planned to wait
until the hunt began. Then, with everyone caught up in the
game, I'd come back here, beat the crap out of Benny's guard,

and turn her loose. I noticed that the room I had entered had
several windows and was on the north side of the house, and
I hoped there was a window in the adjoining one as well. I
quietly made my way down the back stairs and returned to
the party as discreetly as I had left it. The difference between
then and now was the anger alive and growing in my gut.

I faked a smile and hung out near Tallmadge. I didn't
touch any of the refreshments. Everybody was acting a little
drunk, and when a vampire stopped to say hello to me, I was
sure his eyes looked glassy and the pupils were contracted.
The band stopped playing right at ten o'clock. The players
put down their instruments and headed for the kitchen. Once
they had gone, the countess went to the microphone and
began to speak.

She had a rough cigarettes-and-whiskey voice and a leath-
ery, tough demeanor that all her money couldn't smooth off.
But there was no denying she was beautiful, with her ivory
skin and rose-petal cheeks. She smiled and said, "I would like
to welcome you all to a very special occasion, a club anniver-
sary hunt."

The members all clapped politely.

"Some of you have participated before, but I have
arranged some new challenges for both you—the hunters—
and the prey. For the first time, we will be using the maze. It
covers twenty acres and has over four miles of cleverly con-
structed alleys. The hunters can fly above it if they wish, but
be warned: There are many sections not visible from the air.
In fact—now, I don't think I'm really giving away any surprises—part of the maze consists of a tunnel. I'm not telling
you what lies in the tunnel! That would be too naughty of me.
You'll have great fun finding out for yourselves.

"So while there is no rule against flying, we expect most
of you will prefer to stay on the ground. And since it has been

several years since our last extravaganza, and since there are some new members participating for the first time, here are the simple rules of the hunt."

She unfolded a sheet of typing paper and began to read:

" 'One. Members are limited to capturing one prey apiece. We have just enough participants for everyone, so don't get greedy!

" 'Two. You may use your prey where you capture them, or, for more comfort, you will find bowers throughout the maze. They are heated, whereas the alleys of the maze are not, so many members prefer taking their trophies there.

" 'Three. What happens in the maze, stays in the maze. In other words, do what you wish, but just as you agreed to keep the activities of the club strictly confidential, you should do the same about the hunt.

" 'Four. There is a transforming station set up behind the pool with lockers for your clothes and shoes. The maze entrance is directly on the other side of the station. You may enter the maze and begin the game as soon as you've transformed. You may quit the game and return for your clothes anytime you wish.'

"I think that covers it. Are there any questions?"

I raised my hand. "What is the time allotted for pursuit? At what point do the prey win if they elude us but don't find the exit?"

At first there was silence, and then there were titters from the crowd. I wondered what was so funny. The countess looked at me with derision. "My dear," she said. "The hunt is over when it's over, when all the vampires have had their fill. The prey don't *leave*. Of course, you can take your trophy home with you if you wish. You can even set your captive free if you want to reward a particularly good run. But most of us prefer for my staff to shall we say, *clean up* when the party's done."

"Oh, I thought . . . I mean . . . The prey think this is just a game, don't they?" I asked.

"It *is* a game. They can escape if they're clever enough. Most of the time, though, we win; they lose." With that the countess smiled a terrible smile. "Well, it is time! Let's go!"

A cheer went up from the crowd. French doors leading from the great room to the pool area were flung open, and everyone rushed out, including me. We all pushed into the transforming station. There was so much electrical activity generated from the transforming, it looked as if a fireworks show were going on in there. I stashed my clothes in a locker and let myself go—go to the monster within, go to the animal inside. All went as it always did, except for the diamonds. I had forgotten to take them off, and I felt slightly ridiculous that the glittering collar remained around my throat and the earrings hung sparkling from my large bat ears. I also wore Bubba's West Point ring on one of my taloned hands—as a talisman and for luck.

I sniffed the air and smelled both fear and excitement. I detected no prey nearby as yet. I was relieved at that, for I was anxious that my growing hunger for blood would blindside my reason and send me off into the maze. I shouldn't have worried. I was so furious at what the countess had done to Benny, the only driving force within me was a killer instinct to tear Benny's captor limb from limb. Like a mother bear whose cub was in danger, I looked around and saw the world through a red haze of rage.

Shaking my wings out and flexing my muscles, I moved stealthily to the outside of the twelve-foot-high wall that encased the maze. I ducked into its shadows and leaped into the night sky. I flew around to the north side of the house and hovered outside of the windows, seeing within one of them Benny bound and booby-trapped. Through another I spotted her guard watching a reality-TV show in the adjoining room.

Without hesitation I crashed through the glass and bowled into the guard, grabbing his throat and squeezing hard until he collapsed. He fell into unconsciousness without lifting a hand to fight back. I didn't think I had killed him, but I wouldn't mourn if I had. I rushed into the bedroom. Benny stood there unmoving, her eyes wide, but without fear.

I gripped the deadly stake carefully, not letting it move a fraction of an inch, and held it firm as I ripped it from its spring-loaded casing. My rage was so great that I broke it into splinters. Then I pulled the gag from Benny's mouth.

"Jeepers-creepers, girlfriend, I knew you all'd come looking for me. But you sure did take your time getting here," she quipped, and smiled. "And I jest love your jewelry."

"Save the sweet talk. We have to get you out of those chains and out of this place. There are sixty zillion vampires out there, all hungry for blood and probably out of their right minds by this time."

"I know, sugar. I heard them planning it. Okay, on three. One, two, three." Benny pushed her arms outward with a mighty thrust as I pulled the chains apart until the weakest link snapped. Within seconds she was free.

"Okay," I said, "let's get downstairs. We'll sneak out and retrieve my clothes. I saw where Tallmadge put his. I'll swipe his car keys and we can take off. And here, I brought you this." I took off Bubba's ring and gave it to her.

She felt its weight for a moment on her palm. Then she slipped it on her thumb. "Thank you, Daphy. Now let's get this show rolling," she said with a laugh, acting incredibly upbeat and amazingly cheerful for someone who had been a millimeter from being staked for God knew how many hours.

"The daring duo are back in action—now let's execute your plan!"

Yes, I had a plan, but I was about to see it tossed into the best-laid-ones-gang-aft-agley department. For one thing, I misjudged Benny's emotions. She wasn't cheerful. She was high on the prospect of getting even.

I exited through the window and Benny took the stairs. We both got out of the house into the transforming room without a problem. As I swooped toward the lockers, I was beginning to relax. I figured we were going to make it out of there more easily than I anticipated.

Yeah, right. Things started to go to hell the minute I opened Tallmadge's locker. His car keys weren't there—nothing was. His clothes were gone. While I stood there nonplussed, trying to figure out how we were going to get back to the city, I saw in my peripheral vision that Benny had stripped down completely, naked from her head to her toes. "What the hell are you doing?" I yelped.

"This Southern lady intends to rip somebody a new asshole," she said as the whirling energy surrounded her and she went from a diminutive country girl to a sleek, golden-pelted vampire bat, her wings unfurled and her claws out.

"Benny!" I argued. "We don't have time for this."

"You all don't have time. I'm gonna teach one highfalutin countess that you don't mess with a Missouri tiger," she said, and was out the door. I flew out behind her, and we went airborne.

Benny may have wanted to beat the shit out of the countess, but we soon learned that neither the countess nor Tallmadge was anywhere in sight. We flew over the maze, and I wish I could forget the things I saw and heard. Panicked prey, dead bodies, and pools of blood were everywhere. As we watched, one huge male vampire chased down a slight, red-haired girl. He threw her to the ground. At first she pleaded with him to stop; then she struck at him with her fists. He just laughed. He took her in his arms and we watched as she surrendered, unable to resist. She lifted up her neck to be his sacrifice, and he leaned over and bit her, drinking so hard and so deep I knew she would not survive.

From other places in the maze the screams were deafening. Benny looked over at me. "Can we stop this?" she called, her face set with anger.

"No," I yelled back over the wind. "There are too many of them."

"Well, let's do a little damage," she said, and before I could deter her, she was diving down at a hundred miles an hour after another vampire, who was in pursuit of a good-looking young man. Benny went in like a kamikaze, sending the vampire sprawling.

"Hey!" he said, struggling to his knees. "Get your own prey. This one's mine!"

"All that's yours, sucker," she yelled, "is this." She hauled off and punched the surprised bat hard in the face. Then she gave him an elbow to the temple and a kick to the groin. Meanwhile I flew over to the terrified runner. "I'll get you out of here," I said. "I'm not going to hurt you. Climb on my back."

The boy hesitated.

"Either get on or you'll die in here," I said gruffly. "Now hurry!" He climbed on, and while he did I yelled out, "Benny! Come on!"

"Nah! I still got a hankering to be hitting somebody. I'm gonna get me one more. See you by the pool," she called out happily, and went racing down the alley toward a skinny female vampire who had a muscular young woman in her claws.

Using all my strength to get airborne with my burden, I rose up over the top of the maze and landed by the pool. I let the boy off my back, saying, "Run out of here. The highway's not far. Go before somebody comes!"

Terrified out of his wits, the boy didn't even answer me. He just started running down the driveway toward the main road. Just then Benny descended with the strong-limbed young woman hanging on to her neck for dear life. Benny set the girl down. I pointed out the running boy. She took off after him. I hoped they made it.

"Now what?" Benny asked.

I shrugged. "No car."

"All of God's chillun' got wings," she said, grinning like a fool. "Let's fly away."

"Yeah, at least we don't have to walk," I agreed as we took a mighty hop and soared into the night sky. It was about a fifty-mile drive to New York City, and probably closer than that, since we were going as the crow flies. The flight was still going to be a challenge, but we could drop down and hang from a tree if we got tired. It wasn't even midnight and the whole night stretched before us. We were going to be fine.

I flew over close to Benny so we could talk as we traveled. "What the hell was going on?" I asked. "Why did the countess kidnap you?"

"Well, you can butter my butt and call me a biscuit," Benny said. "But I don't know. All I can tell you is that she kept calling me her insurance."

"Maybe she's just crazy jealous or totally nuts," I suggested. "I got her dossier; she's really old." I knew Mar-Mar had told me to keep the information about the countess confidential, but I felt no loyalties to the anonymous organization that recruited me. Although I rarely ignored my mother's instructions, my first loyalty was to my friends. The way I saw it, Benny had a right to know whatever I did about the vampire who nearly killed her.

"She might be a psycho, but she's not wacko," Benny said. "She's cunning and she's up to something. I just don't know what she's into. I didn't have a chance to poke around none."

"How does Tallmadge fit in? Do you know?" I said, and watched sadness lower over Benny's bright eyes like a veil.

"He's a skunk, Daphy. He's just a damned skunk. He and me, we were having a good time, you know. I'm not saying we had a relationship, but we were having some mighty nice times in bed. Then he introduced me to the countess, and things got a little strange."

"I noticed," I said as we flitted high and low, looking for the highway lights.

"I'm usually real good about holding my liquor. But they were giving me some different kinds of drinks, and I jest couldn't keep my head straight nohow. At first I liked it. That there club was something else. I met some really cute guys too. I heard something about you and that hunk Ducasse. Is it true?"

"I don't really want to talk about it," I said.

"Oh, honey, I'm sorry if he upset you. Didn't anybody tell you about him?"

"What about him?" I said, holding my breath.

"Well, he is a real cutie, and he calls himself a poet, but he's what they call a satyr. He just can't keep that thing of his in his pants. He's okay to fool around with, you know? They say he can just keep doing it and doing it. Now, that's my kind of date." She giggled, then looked at me with concern. "Honey, you didn't care none about him, did you?"

"No. I didn't even like him," I said. We started following a ribbon of paved road east toward New York. The night was clear, and I felt as if the rushing air were clearing the cobwebs out of my head. "Tell me what happened to you," I said to Benny.

She gave a deep sigh. "After we fooled around, Tal left me alone in the club both times we were there. I didn't mind. I was having a lot of fun with the games—and they really were games, Daphy. A lot of silly sex, but nobody got hurt, and it felt really good. The countess always seemed to be there, just a-watching me. She was always real sweet, though. Then Tal came back after a couple of hours—I think it was two nights ago; I sort of lost track of time. He whispered to me that the countess wanted to do this here ménage à trois, you know, a threesome. I threw a little hissy fit and told him I wasn't into girls. I said if he wanted to ask one of those young studs to join us, hey, I was up for it. He didn't want to, and told me no hard feelings and all. He promised that he and I would go off alone later. Then he brought me over something to drink.

"After that I stopped being able to remember much. Things started getting fuzzy, and I don't know what I did. I have to tell you, girlfriend, I surely don't. I don't remember leaving the club. How I got out to Jersey I don't know. It's all a blackout until I woke up in that there room. I felt as if I had been rode hard and put away wet. And before I got my head together, the countess and her thugs grabbed me and wrapped me in chains."

"I'm sorry that happened to you," I said. "I shouldn't have left you at the club alone."

"Ah, now, Daphy, you ain't my ma. I'm a big girl. And when I woke up with that stake just touching its point right on my skin, I knew you'd come git me. So if'n I didn't say thanks before, thank you, my friend."

"You'd do the same for me," I murmured, my face getting red.

"I surely would," she said.

After that we stopped talking and just flew along in silence. We saw Route 78 below us, and I knew it would lead us to Newark airport, with Staten Island and lower Manhattan just beyond. From there we simply had to fly across the dark waters of Newark Bay to downtown Manhattan, then wing our way up Broadway above the great spires of the city and we would be home. We just had to keep flying on.

CHAPTER 14

And then again, I have been told;
Love wounds with heat, as Death with cold.

—Ben Jonson, "Though I Am Young and Cannot Tell"

Long-distance flying changes the balance between intellect and instinct. The body takes over, using its wings and muscles, and relieves the mind of overseeing behavior. Thoughts are freed to wander as the physical self takes control. Now, as Benny and I headed eastward at treetop level, the wide highway below and the stars above, I was cut loose from all bonds to earth, but not liberated from the conflicts inside my heart.

For years I had tried to live a solitary life, and during those decades of shunning human contact and refusing intimacy with either human men or vampire males, I retreated into a shell where I felt I could not be hurt, and where I, who had done so much harm, could not destroy those I cared about. Then against my will, a spymaster—my *mother*—had dragged me into commerce with the world to become a protector, rather than a destroyer. The shell had cracked and I had allowed the other Darkwings—Benny, Cormac, and the late Bubba Lee—to enter my heart. And most of all I had loved Darius.

Unfortunately, with Darius I had chosen not wisely, and not well. Self-knowledge hadn't stopped me from making the same old mistakes once more. I was smart enough to know that my attraction to Darius was directly linked to my former liaison with Lord Byron. I just wasn't strong enough to resist it, as I had not resisted Byron over a century ago. I remembered all too well what happened after I had helped him escape from the Pisa prison and began the journey back to my villa at Montespertoli.

With the adrenaline that had coursed through my veins subsiding, I realized nothing good could come of our rekindling our torrid love affair. We hadn't finished our brief coupling in the doorway, but when Byron again made a move in the jolting coach, I pushed him back and moved away.

He called me a tease and said, "My lady, your heart is like the sky; it changes night and day. Now o'er it clouds and thunder are driven, and darkness is on high—"

"Your lines are very pretty," I had cut in. "They are not, however, going to change my mind about letting you seduce me. I hate inconstancy. Once we reach my villa, write your little mistress to come fetch you and begone." To tell the truth I was jealous of Byron's other lovers, and I had no right to be. Why should he have been faithful to me for these ten years? In England, I sent him away with no promises. It was I who was inconstant. Even while I was insisting that I would never see him again, I had run to his aid.

Looking annoyed, Byron turned away, threw himself back against the seat cushions of the swaying coach, and stared straight ahead. "What you call inconstancy is nothing more than admiration of some favored object, as in a niche I see a lovely statue I adore. I would rather stay with you. You are my soul's twin. We are two damned creatures who see others for what they are—shallow, vain, and in general very stupid. My behavior is not inconstant. I am very consistent. I drink to escape. I eat to sate my appetite. I sleep to forget. And I rut mindlessly to distract myself. All cats look alike in the dark, you know," he said, and closed his beautiful eyes. Long lashes cast a shadow over his cheeks.

I felt a wave of tenderness toward him. I reached out and took his hand with its strong fingers in mine. "George, unleashed, our passion would be the instrument to destroy us both."

He opened his eyes and looked at me, and in his eyes I could see the depths of his soul and his despair. "How much better it would be to die upon your breast than take a last shuddering breath amid the filth of a dungeon or atop the trampled mud and blood of some battlefield. I have never betrayed your secrets, Daphne," he said, gently raising my hand to his lips and softly kissing it. "I have never penned a word that would disclose who or what you are. Every other woman I have mocked in verse, even as I told her I adored her."

"You are incorrigible. But what of your fight for Italian freedom? Don't you wish to return to it?" I said, abruptly disengaging my hand from his. "Men die more often for causes than for love."

"Say you'll let me fight for your love, and I'll abandon all else," he insisted.

"Show me you mean it by not leaving me," I said. I wanted to believe him. Feeling the heat of his flesh, the touch of his breath, the sweetness of his presence had brought joy back to my empty life. As Byron might write, "The ashes of our hopes is a deep grief."

We had been back at my villa for only a few short nights when a letter for Byron arrived from my former lodger, Pietro Gamba. It had been delivered while Byron and I had slept during the day. When the maid carried it to him, he and I had been sitting behind the kitchen in the rustic dining hall that sports the swords and armor I disliked so much. After a long day of rest, we were eating our first meal, our breakfast as it were, around seven in the evening. Putting aside the sweet roll he had picked up from the tray on the table, Byron broke the seal of the missive and began to read. He face grew serious; his brow furrowed.

He looked up at me. His linen shirt hung open to his waist; his hair was all curls like a wild child's; a day's growth of beard cast a shadow upon his cheeks. He looked as beautiful and guileless as an angel when he said, "I have to leave tonight. Please forgive me."

I sat there, emotions colliding within me. "Why? Was your vow to give up all for love just empty words?"

"No, no. I will come back in a few days. By then, my part in the Carboneria's schemes will be finished. Dear lady, I am obligated to do this one more task and say my farewells to those who gave me their friendship and trust. It is a matter of honor; please understand."

"Is the Countess Guiccioli part of your 'one more task'?" I said bitterly, getting up and walking to the open door that led out into the gravel courtyard, where the scent of rosemary perfumed the night air.

Byron came up behind me, lifted my hair, and pressed his lips to the back of my neck. "She is a child who knows nothing of what you and I feel—and do—together. I must make a quick journey to Pisa; that is all. It will take me less than a fortnight. When I come back, it will be forever. I will become your husband, if you wish to risk ending our sweet dalliance by marrying. We both know that passion in a lover's glorious, but in a husband it's called uxorious." He turned me around to face him and pulled down the top of my gown from my shoulders. He kissed both breasts. He kissed my throat. He lifted my skirt.

Weak creature that I am, I let him take me there on the

flagstone floor of the dining hall where any moment a servant could walk in. Again, with hard stone behind my back and the hard body of Byron pressing into me, I felt desire, rage, and bloodlust surge forth in me all at once. Suddenly my teeth grew long and sharp. Lost in rapture and with my emotions torn between anger and passion, I was close to biting him. He—or I—was saved by the sound of horses entering the courtyard.

Byron rose off of me. He stroked my cheek with his hand. He brushed away a tear that escaped despite my efforts to not cry. "I am coming back, sweet lamb," he said. "This idyll of ours will not end. How have I loved the twilight hour and thee!"

Moments later he was gone. Days later I received word from my mother that Byron and Pietro Gamba had boarded a ship and were sailing to join the revolutionaries in Greece. My heart nearly broke before the shell around me closed and became harder than before.

History repeats itself. Darius, another tormented poet who embraced war and ideals more passionately than he embraced me, had made me believe that he truly loved me. Now I suspected that he had used me. He certainly had misled me, and with his former girlfriend—who had tried to kill me—he had finally betrayed me.

I thought he was a better man. In fact, this assassin Gage had a lot in common with Darius—both were former Special Forces members and both were executioners, for Darius had been a vampire hunter when we met. Gage was being sent to kill a man with ideals; Darius had snuffed out my dream of a lasting relationship, one that could have been eternal once I had made him a vampire.

Just then, in a cold flood of understanding, what Fudd had said became clear. Gage was "weird, not human weird."

Maybe Gage wasn't human, and if he was not, what was he?
A vampire? A twisted, gut-wrenching thought occurred to me
then. Had Darius not been an ocean and a continent away, I
might not just ask him about Gage; I might accuse him of
being the assassin himself. The very thought of that accusa-
tion made me sick, and I couldn't continue to think it. I knew
it wasn't true. I just wanted to think the worst of Darius because I hurt so much. After all, Tallmadge could be Gage as
easily as Darius could—and Tallmadge was a more likely
suspect. It would be a kick in the ass if Tallmadge had been
recruited to investigate himself.

But I did believe Darius might have a good idea who Gage
was. The community of navy SEALS and army Rangers was
small, selective, and tight-knit. I really needed to ask him.
Yeah, sure, I do. I was just thinking up a reason to contact
him, wasn't I? Our relationship was over, wasn't it? I needed
to move on, forget Darius, and see if I could work things out
with Fitz. The way Fitz reacted to my revelation that I was a
vampire made him a guy in a million. Heck, he was one in a
trillion. I was a damn fool if I didn't count my blessings and
get Darius out of my system.

And just how many women had been damn fools for love?

With all these thoughts winging around in my brain, I flew
on with Benny toward home.

With just one brief stop to rest—when we hung upside down
from the lofty steel arch of the Bayonne Bridge over the Kill
Van Kull—Benny and I followed the Jersey coastline past
Elizabeth, Newark, and Jersey City to New York Harbor,
where we flitted over to Manhattan. We arrived back on the
Upper West Side well before the first rays of morning got
close to the horizon. I landed on the ledge outside my apartment, and she blew me a kiss as she continued uptown.

To say I was dead tired was an understatement. I'd have to say I was undead tired, but I had responsibilities and couldn't just tumble into my coffin. Jade needed to go out, and she deserved a walk. She wasn't like a little Yorkie who can do her thing on newspaper. Even the Sunday *Times* wouldn't work for a malamute. Dragging my rear end but determined not to give in to my desire to lie down, I threw on a pair of jeans, an old gray sweater, my heavy Frye boots, a jacket—and an attitude.

While I dressed, I told myself I really had to wake up and smell the coffee. I was acting like a moping, melodramatic teenager—probably because my body was forever stuck in my late teen years. With each button of my jacket, I chanted a mantra: *Screw Darius* (button); *screw Tallmadge* (button); *Screw J* (button). Maybe I shouldn't have lumped J in there, but he was no prince. *Hello, Fitz* (last button).

I wondered how the Fitzmaurice clan would react to a wedding in a crypt, with organ music straight from Transylvania, and an invite to the whole Dracula clan (they still do live in Romania, you know). I jest. But I knew Fitz was the kind of guy who would bring out a big white diamond and propose if we started having sex. Any woman can tell the level of a guy's commitment from about the first date. It's usually obvious if he's the kind of man who refuses to spend the night after making love, or a lover who's willing to move—but keeps a separate bank account, his own telephone number, and the option to split when the spark goes out. Then there is the guy who has decided he wants to settle down. You'll know this immediately because you will meet his mother before you meet his friends.

That was Fitz. He was wearing his heart on his sleeve and made no attempt to hide it. Daphne Urban Fitzmaurice? DUF for a monogram? It could be worse. With Darius I would be

Daphne Urban della Chiesa, or DUD. And the way I had acted lately, with Ducasse for instance, DUM would be a better fit.

My dog broke into my silly fantasies by butting her big head against my leg. She danced around excitedly when I got her leash. She looked into my eyes with her warm brown ones, and I loved her fiercely and with all my heart. Gunther's squeaking said he wanted to come along, and he scurried into my pocket as the three of us left the building and hit the bricks, or more precisely, the cement sidewalks of Manhattan.

It was the quietest time of the night, the hour right before the earliest risers got up to start their day. The windows in the apartment buildings were still dark. Nothing, not even a breeze, stirred on the street. I started out walking briskly, then broke into a jog, deciding to head east instead of west, and turning left to run on Broadway, where the energy hums and the city really never does sleep, but throbs with lights and the noise of all-night delis, careening Yellow Cabs, rumbling subways, and chuffing city buses.

My buddies and I covered a couple of blocks at a good clip, and Jade's tongue was lolling happily out of her mouth when we made another left to start home. I wasn't paying much attention to the vegetable delivery van that came cruising up alongside us until Jade exploded into a barking frenzy. A man in a stocking cap had hopped out of the passenger side and rounded the front of the van with a gun in one hand, and a leash with a muzzle in his other. A second man was opening the driver's-side door. He didn't get far, because I landed a kick so hard on the door that it flattened the guy against the door frame. The air went out of him with an *ooofff,* and I heard his ribs crack. At the same time Jade had ripped her leash out of my hand and barreled into the gunman, knocking him flat on his back. He lost his grip on the pistol and it caromed off the curb. Meanwhile he was crabbing his way sideways with Jade growling and holding on to his ankle as if it were a snake she was going to shake to death.

He was lucky his sneaker pulled off. Freed, he scrambled on top of a parked car and rolled across the hood into the street. Jade was set on racing around the car, but I grabbed her leash. When I stopped her, she howled with a sound that raised the hair on the back of my neck. I dragged her over toward the driver, who had slid down against the door frame of the van and sat like a broken mannequin on the ground. He was out cold. I ordered Jade to sit. I swear she gave me a dirty look, but she obeyed as I patted down the guy's jacket and found his wallet. I stuck it in my pocket. Somebody must have called 911, because I heard a siren over on Broadway. I wasn't up to talking to the boys in blue, so I told Jade to come and we took off down the block.

As if I hadn't enough shit to contend with right now, some sick cookie was out there trying to steal my dog. Just when you think you can't get any more pissed, let me tell you, you most certainly can.

I woke up Sunday night feeling surly and out of sorts. The flight back to Manhattan had sapped my energy, and my fury at the attempt to take my dog left me tossing and turning when I should have been deep in slumber. Ergo I clomped around the apartment in an old T-shirt and bare feet, a coffee mug in my hand, casting a baleful eye at the dust bunnies and directing a particular feeling of pissiness at Darius, Tallmadge, J, and Tino Leguizamo.

The latter was the van driver from the aborted dognapping. I had looked at his wallet before I climbed into my coffin last night. A driver's license gave his name and an address on Thirty-seventh Avenue in Jackson Heights, Queens, which is the largest Colombian neighborhood in the city. Maybe I was jumping to conclusions, but I was convinced that this incident was somehow tied to drugs and Jade's previous owner, a South American shaman who was an expert on *susto,* an illicit methamphetamine-type stimulant from the Amazon. And I figured there were at least two rival groups involved, since somebody had murdered the guy in the baseball cap who had been stalking me.

Threatening my dog, and attacking me as well, made this situation personal and a top priority for me. Sure, I knew that national security and all that good stuff was at stake in the Darkwing mission, but when push came to shove, I wasn't a very good spy. Right now I felt like cutting the meeting with J and going after the jerks trying to grab Jade. I wasn't really going to do that, but what I *was* going to do was withhold the information about Joe Daniel's drug habit. I didn't have to do much thinking about it or wrestle with my conscience. I knew what my gut was telling me. I wasn't going to be a rat.

I realized that being a spy in itself made me an informant. Maybe it's my Italian blood, but to me an informant is the lowest form of life. I had rationalized from the moment of my recruitment that it was okay, even admirable, to pass on crucial information about terrorists and killers. But help the reigning politicos run a smear campaign against Daniel, like J. Edgar Hoover had done with Martin Luther King Jr.? No way, José. I had my secrets, and I'd let Joe Daniel have his.

I showed up at our Twenty-third Street office on time, for a change. The dossier on the countess was tucked into my backpack. I hadn't dressed to kill, but my mood noticeably improved when I put on a pair of really hot jeans by 7 for All

Mankind with Swarovski crystal designs on the front and left back pockets. I topped the jeans with a fitted brocade shirt jacket with tiny pearl buttons. On my feet I wore well-made but functional black boots with a small heel. I wore the same midweight distressed-leather jacket I'd been using the whole month. Looking good always helped me feel more in control—leading from a position of strength, I called it—especially when dealing with J, who played mind games like a master.

J was sitting in the dimly lit conference room at the head of the table, as he usually did. He was going over some files when I came in. A pair of crutches leaned against the wall, and his foot was in a cast, but he appeared alert and unimpaired.

"What do you have for me?" he asked without preamble.

"A couple of things," I said. I set my backpack on the table and took out the countess's folder. I stayed standing, getting ready to drop my bomb in the quiet room. "First off, we have a situation. It concerns Tallmadge." I proceeded to give a heavily censored account of Benny's abduction, our escape from the rural estate, and my suspicions about Tallmadge's complicity in the plot—although not his motives, which I might guess at but didn't know.

"In summary," I finished, "Tallmadge has a long-standing relationship with the Countess de Ericé, and I suspect some kind of working alliance with her. Whether it concerns espionage or just some personal deviance, I don't know."

J's face was frozen in a frown. "I didn't want Tallmadge brought into this operation. He isn't a team player. I'll bring the situation under advisement. Anything else?"

"I also should put on the table that I believe there is a possibility that Tallmadge is Gage." My words were met by a deafening silence. J just stared at me.

"I have information that Gage may be a vampire," I added.

"So do I," J said, his face unreadable. "And I should put on the table that your boyfriend, Darius, has been seen here in the city."

My knees started to give way. I sank down in a chair, but tried to keep my emotions off my face. "So?" I said.

"What's he doing here? I was told he was assigned to hunting terrorists in Europe," J replied.

"Why ask me? I don't know. Ask your contacts in his agency."

"I would think you'd have the inside information. If you don't, I have to ask myself why he's appeared this week, at this time. I did a computer check. I can't account for your boyfriend's whereabouts anytime there's been an assassination by Gage," he said, and I sensed a smugness in his tone. It got my back up.

"And if I did a computer search on you—assuming I knew *your* name—would I be able to account for *your* whereabouts? Would you be able to track mine? Of course not. Darius works under deep cover. Nobody but his handler can tell you where he is and why, and I'm sure he's not about to do it. And bottom line, J, Darius hasn't been a vampire long enough to be Gage."

"He's on our list of suspects," J said.

"Well, your list is full of shit," I countered.

Just then the door opened and Cormac came in. "Am I late?" he asked.

"No," I said. "I'm early. How are you?" I turned my attention to my comrade and turned my back on J.

"I feel like a million bucks, to tell the truth," Cormac said. He spotted the dossier I laid on the table. It was clearly marked FILE BOX 6. "That reminds me. You going to share what you found in the stuff from Opus Dei?" he asked.

"I have no problem with that. The boss might, though," I said, jerking my head in J's direction. J was silent, so I went on. "The boxes held files. Dossiers on hundreds of vampires. There were also records of kills by vampire hunters. Mostly the boxes were the Catholic Church's big to-do list for killing vampires."

"Was my file in there?" Cormac asked, turning a shade paler than he had been a minute ago.

At that moment, Benny pushed through the door. "What file are you all talking about?" she chimed in.

"The vampire files held by Opus Dei," I said.

Benny looked confused. She just kept standing in front of the door without approaching the table.

"I'll fill you in on the details later," I assured her. "Basically the Catholic Church has kept files on all of us for the past thousand years or so. My mother got her hands on some of them. Mine was there. I don't know about you and Cormac. You'll have to ask J." I nodded toward our handler.

"They were there," he said. "Now they're not. We're getting off the subject here."

Benny's color flashed red in a millisecond. "I think whether or not I'm on a master list to be offed is a mighty important subject. I can spit without opening my mouth, but I ain't stupid," she said. "Can you tell me I'm out of danger? What if the Church has another set of files?"

"I can't tell you anything," J said, "except that the Vatican had these files. They handed them over to Opus Dei, who may, and this is just supposition, be the organization that trains and runs the vampire hunters. We removed the files from their possession. Is there another set? I don't know. You might want to take that up with Daphne's mother. It's her area of expertise. Now, we need to get back to the matter at hand."

"Which is?" Benny asked as she primly pulled out her chair and sat down at the table.

"The identity of Gage," I said. "We think he's a vampire. I think he's Tallmadge. J has suggested he might be Darius."

Benny's eyes were wide. Cormac looked surprised. "Where is Tallmadge?" he said.

"Not here," I said.

Benny added, "He vamoosed last night. I wouldn't be surprised if he's making a run for it. He has to know I feel like killing him, after what he and the countess did," she said with an edge to her voice.

And she doesn't know the half of it, I thought. "He helped the countess, the one from the vampire club, abduct Benny Friday night," I explained to Cormac.

"So Tallmadge might not have anything to do with the assassination plot? This could be a personal thing?" Cormac suggested.

"I think he's got something to do with the assassination threat," I said firmly.

"I don't," J said. "According to Marozia, Tallmadge may be a loose cannon, but he's not a traitor. He's worked for the secret services since Washington was president. Personally, I don't like the man. I don't think he should be on this team. But I don't believe he's an assassin."

"Well, just for the sake of argument," I said, "say that Daniel becomes the Democratic candidate as well as running on the Green ticket. He's got a good chance at winning the presidency, and that puts a dove in the White House. That's not going to sit well with conservatives or the religious right. So what if the hawks in the government right now have decided to eliminate him?"

"But this administration sent us to stop the assassination," Benny argued.

"How do you know *who* is sending us to stop it? I don't. And even if this administration has ordered us to protect Daniel, who's to say that a faction, or even a powerful individual, disagrees with that stance and ordered the hit?"

"This is all speculation," J cut in. "What isn't is this: Gage is probably a vampire—and there is at least a possibility that vampire is Darius della Chiesa."

I started to protest. J held up his hand. "We have no proof of that. But get it out of your head that Tallmadge is an assassin. We do have a solid basis for believing Gage is a vampire, however. That makes him difficult, if not impossible, to stop. You three are Daniel's best hope. Now let's get a plan in place to keep him alive."

"I think we should set up surveillance at both Madison Square Garden and the Central Park location every night between now and Friday," I said, remembering what Fudd had explained about a hit man's modus operandi. "There is a high probability Gage—whoever he is—will be taking a last look at the site of the hit before finalizing his plans to carry out the assassination. Most assassins hang around the location they choose. I think we might be able to nab Gage at that point."

"The NYPD already has that angle covered," J said flatly.

"Well, sugar," Benny cut in, "the police are looking for a human assassin. I don't think they're going to be watching for a bat to drop out of the sky. And you're not about to tell them to do that, are you? Because even if you do, they're not going to take you seriously. Daphy's right. We have to be there."

"I second that," Cormac affirmed.

J looked at each of us, obviously making a decision. "All

right. I see your point. Cormac and Benny, you handle the surveillance."

"I'll take the Garden," Benny offered. "Being in the park will give me nothing but bad-hair nights."

"Sure," Cormac said. "I'll watch the park."

"You," J barked at me. Any good feelings between us had turned sour. "Stick with Daniel. See what you can do to get him to secretly alter his plans. Change the time he shows up at both locations. Change the way he's getting to the rallies. And at the last minute, change where he's standing. Anything to make the assassin change *his* plans at the last minute and make a major mistake. Understand?"

I did. It was a damned good idea. I nodded. "I'm supposed to meet with Joe Daniel and his campaign manager, LaDonna Chavez, tomorrow."

"What about Tallmadge?" Cormac asked. "Should we be looking for him?"

"That will be taken care of," J said. "It's not your problem."

"Are you all planning to terminate him?" Benny said in a low voice, knowing all too well the warning each of us had gotten when we were brought into the Darkwings: *If you run, we will find you. And you will die.* Benny's hands were clenched and her knuckles were white. She had slept with the guy. I had . . . well, only fooled around with him. She might have issues with Tallmadge right now, but she also might have feelings for him. Besides, if she wanted payback, I knew Benny. She was planning on getting some herself.

"I have a problem with killing a vampire because he wants a job change," I said before J answered. "I can't go along with it. If I find out that's what's in the works, I tell you right now, you can take this job and shove it."

"Is that a threat, Agent Urban?" J said, challenging me.

"No. It's a fucking promise." I glared back at him. He turned his eyes away first.

"I'll be in touch with all of you," J announced. "If nothing breaks, we'll have our next team meeting Thursday night." He stood up on his good foot and grabbed his crutches, then hopped into his office and slammed the door behind him.

Cormac, Benny, and I sat for a moment exchanging glances.

"You know," Cormac said, "from where things stand right now, it doesn't look good for Joe Daniel to live past Friday night."

"You don't think too highly of our competency," I said, but smiled to soften my words. In truth, I agreed with Cormac.

"I think we'd have a better chance if we really did know who Gage was and could track him down before he attempted the hit. That he's a vampire opens up a whole lot of issues. How do we kill him? I can't stake one of our own through the heart, and even if I had a gun that fired silver bullets, I don't think I could use it," he said, his voice quavering.

What Cormac just said brought vividly to mind Bubba's death. I remembered the shots—*bang bang bang*—the car speeding away, Bubba gasping out that he was hit, then inexorably crumbling into dust. It was a terrible memory. I knew from the look in Cormac's eyes and the way Benny was touching Bubba's ring that they were thinking of it too.

"I know I can't do it," Benny said. "I'll stop the sucker, but I won't kill him."

"I feel the same way. Killing one of our own kind goes against everything I've been taught all my life," I said. "And Darius is *not* Gage!"

To me, the other two waited a beat too long before saying anything.

"Of course he's not. He's in Germany anyway, right?" Benny finally said and squeezed my hand.

"Maybe not," I murmured. "He might be here."

"Well, if'n he is, sugar, he came back to see you, that's all," she said.

Cormac didn't say anything. He shook his head, then said, "You want to grab something to eat and talk more about what we have to do?"

I didn't, not tonight. I wanted to get my ass out to Jackson Heights and find out who was after my dog, so I said no. Benny wanted to go, though, so she and Cormac got up.

"You go on ahead," I said. "I need to clear my head a minute." Benny gave me a hug before they went out. I sat there staring at the table. I pulled the countess's dossier over to me, thinking to put it into my backpack. I opened it for no good reason and stared at the attached photo of her with its label, COUNTESS GIULIETTA ARIADNE GIUSEPPINA DE ERICÉ. I kept staring at it. What was her relationship to Tallmadge, and what were they up to? Something had bothered me about the two of them from day one. I was missing the obvious; I knew it.

Maybe if I hadn't been fantasizing about a marriage between Fitz and me, and me having the monogram DUF, I never would have seen it. But suddenly a shudder made my body shake as if I had palsy, and the truth hit me between the eyes. *G*iulietta *A*riadne *G*iuseppina de *E*ricé. GAGE. Holy Mother of God, the countess was Gage.

I jumped up. My knees were shaking, and I momentarily gripped the table to steady myself before I walked over and started pounding on J's door.

He flung it open. He was leaning on a crutch. "What do you want?" he barked. "The meeting's over."

"Look," I shouted, and shoved the folder at him. "Look. At her name."

He took the open folder in his free hand, glanced at it, then looked up at me blankly. "So?"

"Look at the initials," I said, stabbing my finger at the photo. "GAGE. She's Gage, God damn it. The assassin isn't Darius. It's the countess," I screamed at him. And in that moment I knew something else that was obvious: My mother already knew it.

CHAPTER 15

"Change everything, except your loves."

—Voltaire, *Sur l'Usage de la Vie*

I left J standing there in his office and rushed out of the Flatiron Building wound as tight as one of those cheap plastic gorillas that does back flips the minute you let go of the key. As soon as I exited the lobby I walked up to the corner, where I stopped to take some calming breaths. Adrenaline had my nerves doing a crazy dance, and my head felt as if it were in a vise. I counted breaths in; I counted breaths out. As soon as I was calmer, I called Benny's cell phone. She had a right to know what I had figured out. She didn't pick up, but I left a message for her to get back to me.

The March night was cool, but clear. People walked by me as I stood on the street and flipped shut my cell phone. Nobody noticed me. Nobody stared. I appeared no different from anyone else. No one could tell I was a vampire. No one could see the weight on my shoulders or the clashing armies assaulting my emotions. And I couldn't see into anyone else's interior life. John Donne got it wrong. Every man *is* an island.

I didn't move for several minutes, staring at the traffic lights changing from green to yellow to red, and tried to get my thoughts straight about Gage. Where was the countess now? She and Tallmadge seemed already to have fled from her country estate in New Jersey before the end of the hunt.

She couldn't have gone too far, though, since the assassination was set for the end of this week. I wondered if I needed to go back to the vampire club and see if I could get a lead. I had my reservations about returning there. Hell, I was scared shitless to test myself that way. I felt good about the way I handled the hunt. I had controlled my urge for blood completely. Maybe my rage had trumped my hunger. How would I react when that anger receded and hunger took the upper hand?

As I stood there on Twenty-third Street, where Broadway and Fifth Avenue converge and cross, I saw those city streets as a symbol for this moment in my life. Which path would I choose? I had to know how powerful my hunger for human blood had become. I needed to understand how far gone I really was. The shape of the rest of my life and who I chose as a mate depended on it. Would I soon be living in the netherworld of the vampire, where my power would be unchecked, humans would be prey, and a mate like Tallmadge or, God help me, Ducasse would be at my side? Or could I rise above the dark urges of the vampire race, and if I couldn't live in the light, be a seeker of it nevertheless?

The question was huge. I didn't have any answers. Instead of being frozen by indecision, I focused on my original plan to go out to Jackson Heights and see what I could find out. I intended to "ask" the guy I had crushed in his van door about who was trying to steal Jade. If Tino Leguizamo thought he was having a bad day, it was about to get much worse.

I have leaped before I looked plenty of times in my life. That doesn't mean I'll always confront a risky situation without covering my back. Before I took the subway out to Jackson Heights, I decided to call my mother.

I hit the speed dial. She answered her phone on the second ring.

"You knew about the countess, didn't you?" I said after she barely got a chance to say hello.

"I'm fine, thank you for asking," she said sarcastically. "As for Giulietta, I had her on my short list of suspects. That's why I wanted her file. Once I filled in some blanks in my own dossier, I was able to add two and two. So did you."

I could have told her the real reason I wanted the file—because I was worried about Benny—and I could have told her I hadn't had a clue that the countess was Gage until a few minutes ago. But I didn't. Let her think I'm a genius. Don't look a gift horse in the mouth, I always say.

"I told J," I confessed.

A long sigh came through the receiver. "I specifically told you to keep the information confidential."

"Yeah, well, it was an accident. Why don't you want him to know, anyway?"

"I *do* want him to know. I just wasn't ready to disseminate the information. There are ethical questions here that humans wouldn't understand. The countess is one of us. That raises an issue about her termination."

"How have other rogue vampires been, uh, 'terminated'?" I asked.

"They weren't. Not by any of us, anyway. The countess is killing humans. Her motives for doing so are immaterial. All vampires kill at some point in their lives. And some do it on a regular basis. It's a vampire's nature, not a crime."

"Maybe you don't know it, but at her country estate, the countess nearly killed Benny—and she might have if I didn't show up."

"The point is, she didn't. Would she have? We don't know that for sure. In any event, the Darkwings need to stop the countess from carrying out the assassination. I'm not sure how. And I don't know what we should do with her if we catch her. It's not a black-and-white issue."

"Here's another thing," I said. "Tallmadge is gone. Do you know about it?"

"Yes, I know."

"Is he working with the countess?"

"Anything's possible."

"Why do I feel you're withholding information?" I said, frustrated.

"Are we done with this mother-daughter chat? I have people coming over, and the hummus isn't made," she said, and I couldn't psych out what she was thinking at all.

"Give me another minute, will you, before you get back to saving the world?" I filled her in on the recent attempts to grab my dog. She listened intently, asking for a few points of clarification as I told about each incident. True, she probably knew something of the situation, since I had alerted J. My mother—who has never stopped meddling in my life—also keeps my building and me under surveillance. I'm not paranoid, but I suspected she even had me shadowed from time to time. Was she also monitoring my phone calls? I knew she would if she could. However, from the kinds of questions she asked about each of the three attempts to get Jade, I had the feeling she didn't know much about what was going on now.

Mar-Mar offered to send somebody to go with me when I went looking for Tino Leguizamo. I thanked her for the offer, but didn't see the need. I also knew that the minute I hung up the phone, she'd be using resources of her own to investigate. I might not need whatever she dug up, but as they say, "It doesn't hoit."

It took me a little over thirty minutes on the number seven train to arrive at Seventy-fourth Street in Queens. I walked out of the station into the section of Jackson Heights called

Little India. I passed Patel Brothers, a sari shop, and the famous Jackson Diner before I started looking carefully for the number that matched Tino's driver's license among the brick apartment houses that lined the street.

When I found it, I saw that his building was no dump. It was clean and neatly kept; it even had a defunct fountain in its courtyard. Maybe the fountain actually worked in warmer weather; anyway, there weren't any McDonald's wrappers in its basin. On the roster in the entryway I found a T. Leguizamo listed next to 3D, and I rang enough buzzers saying, "Pizza delivery," to get someone to ring me past the front security door.

The minute I stepped off the elevator, I could hear a man and woman arguing in Spanish. The angry voices were coming from 3D. Just then the door opened and a woman, her face flushed and her eyes red from crying, ran out, mumbled, *"¡Perdone!"* as she moved past me into the elevator, and kept hitting the buttons until the door slid shut.

I went over to the door and rapped softly.

"Luz! *Lo siento*—" a short man with a bruised face started to say as he flung open the door. He took one look at me and tried to slam it shut again. I stopped it with my shoulder and pushed my way in. He was reaching for a baseball bat when I grabbed his arm and twisted it behind his back. My strength surprised him as he struggled to escape. Getting behind him I twisted harder, and it must have hurt his busted ribs, because he dropped to his knees and started to scream.

"Shut up!" I ordered. "Just answer a couple of questions and I won't hurt you."

"No hablo inglés," he said belligerently.

"Sure you do. You were screaming in English for me to let you go." I put my lips right next to his ear and hissed into it. "Now listen to me very carefully, sucker. Who wants my dog?"

He didn't answer; he just tried futilely to struggle out of my grip. I took my free hand and grabbed his hair, tipping his head back as far as it could go, so that his face was right below mine. I looked him in the eyes. "I'm going to count to three. Give me a name or on three I snap your neck." I started adding pressure. "One . . . two—"

"Gilberto!" he choked out. I let up.

"Gilberto who? I want his full name," I snarled.

"Gilberto Orejuela. Orejuela," he gasped. Orejuela was a well-known Colombian drug lord.

"You're a liar. Orejuela's in jail."

"*Sí! Sí!* I tell you the truth," he whined.

"Why does he want my dog?" I demanded.

"*Brujería*. Magic. He needs *brujería* to get out of prison."

"My dog is just a dog," I said in a low, threatening voice. "Tell Orejuela, or whoever is behind this, that my dog is not magic. But I am. And if anyone tries again, I will send the devil to avenge me. *¿Me entiende?*"

The guy didn't answer.

"*¿Me entiende?* Do you understand me?" I demanded again, and I smiled a terrible smile, showing him my sharp vampire teeth.

His body trembled under my hands and he pissed his pants. "*Sí!*" he cried out. "*Sí!*"

"*Guevón*," I cursed at him, and tossed him against a wall. His back hit hard and the air went out of him as he slid down onto the floor. His eyes were doing a jiggling dance when I let myself out.

Once I was back in Manhattan I had some other *guevóns* to deal with. I had made up my mind to go to the vampire club and see if I could track down Tallmadge. From what I could tell he lived there, or at least stayed there most of the time.

Finding Tallmadge was the reason I was going there, or so I told myself. In truth, the confrontation with Tino had hyped me up. I was high on adrenaline—excited, not nervous. I wouldn't admit it to myself, but I wanted blood, and I wanted it badly.

When I rang the bell at the mansion on Irving Place, I was admitted without hesitation. Cathary greeted me and asked what he could do for me this evening.

"I'd like to see Tallmadge."

"I'm very sorry, but he's not in," Cathary responded politely.

"Has the countess been back to the club—since the hunt, I mean?"

"Yes, she was here earlier tonight, but she too has gone out," he explained. "She did mention that if anyone asked for her, to say—and she told me to word this exactly—to catch her if you can. It's a private joke, isn't it? She laughed when she said it."

It was no joke. "Did she say anything else?" I said as sweetly as I could. "I think the message was for me, you see."

"Hmmm, yes, she said I might say that she had some 'new insurance.' Is that what you meant?"

My brows came together in a frown. New insurance? Had the countess grabbed someone else as a hostage? I'd check on Benny and Cormac as soon as I could, but I didn't think it was likely she had either of them. I hoped not, but I feared I'd find out soon enough what the countess had done.

"Miss Urban?" Cathary asked as I stood not speaking. "Will you be staying? Can I take your coat?"

I focused my attention back on him. "Uh, no. Thanks. I'm not staying. I was just trying to get in touch with Tallmadge; that's all." I turned and was about to go when a figure appeared at the entrance to the drawing room. It was Ducasse— beautiful to gaze upon and so very dangerous to me.

"Mistress," he said softly. "I may be able to help you find Tallmadge."

"You know where he is?"

"I might," he answered, and stared at me with his silver eyes. Without a sound Cathary slipped away. I didn't see him go. Ducasse walked over to me. "I saw Tallmadge after the hunt," he said.

"Where?" I asked, feeling anxious, thinking I should go, but wanting to know what Ducasse knew.

"Here," he said. "Come sit down. It's uncomfortable standing in the hall. Come. I'll tell you the rest." He took my hand in his.

"No, I'd rather stand." I tried to look away from him, yet I didn't. His face was so handsome. His lips were smooth and sensual. I wasn't thinking rationally, I knew that, although I didn't seem able to break free of his gaze.

"You want to sit down, don't you?" he coaxed, guiding me into the darkened drawing room and shutting the pocket doors behind us. Pulling together my last ounce of strength, I stepped around him and started to push the doors apart. His hands on my shoulders stopped me. "Stay," he whispered in my ear. "Stay. Just for a moment. You have a moment, mistress. Stay; let me tell you about Tallmadge."

I turned around and faced him. "Okay, tell me, and be quick about it. I want to go."

Ducasse slipped his hands onto my waist, talking as he did it. I knew he was touching me, but I didn't move away. I wanted to, but I couldn't somehow. "He came back here. Around three. He asked Cathary if the countess had been back. Then he went to his room."

"Did he stay there?" I said, thinking I should move Ducasse's hands off of me, but feeling too dreamy and disoriented to do it.

"No. He came down a short time later and left. He was carrying a long case. Like one that holds a rifle."

"Oh," I said, wondering what that meant. Was it the countess's rifle? Ducasse had stepped closer to me. He was picking me up in his strong hands and pulling me against his body. Unbidden, my arms went around his neck.

"You're hungry, aren't you, mistress? You are hungry for my blood. Why not drink?"

"No," I said, but I was so hungry. So thirsty. I wanted the taste of blood in my mouth. Suddenly my nails dug into his back. He groaned and took me to a couch, where he sank down, pulling me with him. I was lost. My teeth were growing sharp and long. My lips sought the pulsing blood vessel in his neck. My instincts winning out against my will, I bit down hard and tasted what I so longed for. I growled an animal sound and drank, drank deeply, drank my fill while Ducasse sighed and held me tight.

I could tell he was very weak from loss of blood when I stopped. He looked up at me with glazed eyes as I lifted my head, his blood running in thin streams from my mouth. "I think," he said in an exhausted voice, "that soon I will be one of you. I bless you, mistress, for giving me what I have wanted for so long."

I looked down at him in horror. What had I done? I was creating another monster, and this one, this Ducasse, I feared would be a monster indeed, a scourge upon the world. I wished I could kill him then. Could I? I had killed before by taking too long a drink. Those times had been accidents, but if I drank from Ducasse again, would he die? Part of me said to stop, not to do this. But a harder, crueler voice told me I must. If I wanted one good thing to come of my compulsion, it should be to kill this monster now.

I lowered my face to his neck. He didn't stop me, but

groaned with pleasure. I didn't have to think about what I was doing. I just had to let my dark side reign. I sucked hard. I drank deeply. I felt the life leaving the creature below me as ecstasy flowed through my veins and filled me. If Ducasse could have become a monster, I had to admit I already was one. I took every drop of his blood for my pleasure; then, satisfied, I rose off his lifeless body. Did I feel remorse? I wish I could say I regretted what I had done. But in that moment, filled with sweet blood and more satisfied than I had ever felt before, I just laughed like the demon I was. "Too late, Ducasse," I said. "Too late. You thought you could outwit a vampire. Well, you paid for your folly."

I left Ducasse's body there. I walked to the door and didn't look back. It was only when I was again in the fresh air and on the city streets that the horror hit me. I was foul. But perhaps—just perhaps—I was free. Ducasse had seduced me. Not once had I gone to him willingly. He had hypnotized me with his eyes. And he had experienced the consequences. Why should I feel guilty? I began to walk the streets, distancing myself from the vampire club and from the deed I had done. Was I free? Or had I opened the doors to my dark side so wide I'd never be able to close them again?

I kept walking. I realized that no one could ever undo what had been done. Ducasse was no innocent. He was probably not entirely human. He had manipulated me and used me. Why should I care about dispatching him from this planet? I mentally steeled myself. I put what had happened behind me. What was done, was done. So be it.

I kept walking. With every step I was farther away from Irving Place and the vampire club, firmly believing it was the last time I would ever enter that little piece of hell. I had been wandering through the streets for a while, feeling calmer and better about myself, when my cell phone rang. I answered thinking that it was Benny, and wanted to tell her to meet me. I wanted a girlfriend to talk to, to tell me I had done the right thing. To my surprise, it was Fitz.

"Hello, Daphne?" I heard him say. I took a moment to get myself together, to be sure I had come back to myself from the creature I had become. "Daphne? Are you there?"

The sound of his voice gave me heart and hope. Here was Ducasse's opposite. Here was nothing evil or cunning. With Fitz, perhaps I could turn away forever from the dark world where I had been.

"Hey, I'm here," I said with a smile in my voice. "What's going on?"

"They're letting me go home. I just wanted to tell you," he said.

"When?" I said, stopping on the sidewalk and putting one hand over my ear so I could hear him better.

"As soon as I can call a cab," he said.

"You're going to take a cab? Don't you have a ride?" I said, concerned.

"Only if I wait until tomorrow. Even if I have to take the bus, I'm getting out of here tonight. I've had enough of hospitals."

"Look, don't do anything. Wait there. I'll come right over. Who's at your apartment to help you?"

"Uh, nobody. But it's just for tonight. I can get someone to come in tomorrow. I'll be okay," he said.

"Like hell! You'll come back to my place tonight. Now, don't you dare move. I'll be there in ten minutes," I ordered, and terminated the call.

I hailed a taxi and pulled up at the hospital with time to spare. I told the cabbie to wait and tossed him a twenty. Fitz was dressed and waiting downstairs by the emergency room exit when I hurried in. He was leaning on a chair, but he hugged me with one arm and kissed me lightly on the cheek.

"Look, I don't want to put you out," he said. "You can just take me home."

"Oh, shut up." Just seeing him was making me feel good and whole. "This isn't negotiable. It's my way or the highway." I grabbed his overnight bag. I slipped my other arm around his waist, although surprisingly he didn't lean on me much as we walked to the waiting cab.

"You seem pretty strong to me," I observed as I climbed in the cab after him.

"I told you I was okay." He smiled at me then, catching my eyes with his and melting into them, and all of a sudden we were both lost in feeling.

I spoke first. "I'll feel better if you spend the night with me there," I said softly. "You probably don't have anything to eat in your apartment, even if you were feeling well enough to make yourself something."

"I can always order Chinese," he responded, never taking his eyes from my face. "But it's sweet of you to care, and yes, I'd be glad to stay over at your place if you really want me to."

That last sentence was loaded with double meaning.

"I *really* want you to." I took his hand. "Just don't even think about us doing anything that can bust open your stitches."

"Hey, I can't bust anything if I just *think* about it," he said, and laughed.

We rode in companionable silence all the way uptown. When we got to my place he paid the cabbie the remaining fare, and we started for the apartment house. We had our arms around each other holding tight, mostly because I feared he wasn't as strong as he said he was, but I admit I enjoyed feeling his body against mine.

We were almost to the door of the lobby when it opened.

His face lean and craggy, his golden hair pulled back into a ponytail, his jeans as tight as a second skin on the hard, toned muscles of his legs, Darius stepped out onto the sidewalk in front of me. Involuntarily I gasped.

His face darkened. He stopped close in front of us and looked into my face, ignoring Fitz completely. "So *this* is what I disobeyed orders and came back from Germany for," he snarled. "To find *this*. I guess I'm just some kind of fool—and you're just a two-timing bitch!" Then he turned on his heel and stormed away before I could even say anything, although I don't know what I would have said even if I could.

My head felt like it just got whacked by a two-by-four. I stood there stunned.

"Are you all right?" Fitz was saying.

"Yes, yes, I'm fine," I said, fighting to clear my thoughts. "Let's go in."

Fitz didn't move. "Look, Daphne. It's better if I go on home. You have some things you need to take care of," he said, not sounding angry, just a little sad.

I looked at him hard. "St. Julien Fitzmaurice," I said. "The only thing I need to take care of is getting you upstairs and into bed. I told you, Darius and I are history. I didn't ask him to come back. I didn't *want* him to come back. It's over between us. And I'm going to feel a lot worse if you walk out on me tonight."

"I-I wasn't walking out, Daphne. I just don't want you to be with me if you have feelings for somebody else. Really. I understand. When Jessie left, I was hurt so badly I wanted to die. I've been there, remember?"

"I remember, Fitz. And I know what I want. I want you, if you're sure you want me. Look, if you've changed your mind, this is an easy out for you. No more having to deal with a vampire for a girlfriend," I said, harshness creeping into my voice.

"Daphne," Fitz said, and pulled me close to him. "I am sure this is what I want. I never doubted it." He kissed me there on the sidewalk, and it was long and sweet.

I didn't try to tear his clothes off in the elevator, as I had done with Darius. For one thing, when I put my hand on Fitz's shirt, I was reminded that his stomach was still swathed in bandages under his clothes. I didn't know what kind of pain he was in, but I figured he was in some. And I confess my heart hurt like a son of a gun. I never expected to run into Darius, and it raked up a lot of emotions. I lied when I told Fitz I didn't *want* Darius to come back from Germany. That he actually did and showed up here did a number on my head. But it didn't matter now. Darius had seen me with Fitz, and that finished things between us whether I wanted it that way or not. Maybe it was for the best. It forced me to give up on hoping Darius and I could work things out. It simplified the situation. It just hurt so fucking much.

After we got inside the apartment, I helped Fitz get his jacket off and then made the introductions with Jade and Gunther.

As he patted my dog's head, I asked Fitz, "Are you hungry? Can I get you anything?"

"I'm fine," he answered.

"Then come with me," I said, and took his hand. I led Fitz into my bedroom, not the secret one behind the bookcases, but the one with the king-size bed and cool, fresh cotton sheets. I stood in front of him. He put his hands on my shoulders. I had made up my mind what I needed to do. I reached out and unbuckled his belt, then unbuttoned and unzipped his pants. Inside his briefs, his staff was hard and waiting. His hands tightened on my shoulders.

"Are you sure?" he asked, and I could hear the hope in his voice.

I smiled up at him. "I think the better question is, 'Are you able?' "

"Daphne, I'd do this if it killed me—"

My eyes widened and I started to speak when his fingers touched my lips.

"—but it won't. It is all I've hoped for. All I've dreamed about."

I gave him a grin. "Saint Fitz," I said. "I'm not sure you dreamed about *this*," I said playfully. "I'm going to show you how a sinner makes love." With that I let myself down to my knees and lowered his trousers. Then I pulled down his briefs, releasing his manhood. Then I whispered for him to sit down on the edge of the bed.

He did.

Fitz was a big man, and his penis was long, wide, and admirable in every way.

I knelt between his legs. I felt the skin of his thighs touch my naked waist. He held me with his legs as I leaned forward. He groaned out loud as my lips slid over his staff and pulled him into my mouth. Deep, deep into my throat I took him, using all the skills I had learned long ago as a courtesan in the seraglio of a desert caliph. I felt Fitz's legs tremble as his hands gripped the back of my head. I sucked him until he was completely inside of me, filling my mouth and throat. He moaned as I pulled back gently, sliding up his shaft, using my tongue to tease him, making his already turgid member become rock-hard and throbbing.

"Don't," he said softly. "I'll come too quickly. Please . . ."

I didn't listen. I wanted to drive him wild. I pulled and

stroked, encircling the thick base of his member with my fingers becoming a ring I could tighten and loosen, pump up and down, and coax him toward a climax. He was groaning, pleading, pushing down on my head as he asked me to stop, then begged me not to. I felt him throbbing harder and harder in my mouth. With a quick move I thrust him deep into my throat as far as he could go. I heard him yell out and I felt him spill his seed, swallowing him in the way I had been taught, so that I didn't choke, but drank, drank him in, devouring his semen like I would have liked to, even now, be drinking his blood.

When I picked up my head, Fitz was gazing at me as if I were a goddess and he the supplicant. There were no words he could say. His eyes said everything.

"Lie down," I ordered. "The night is young. If you get too tired, tell me. I intend to please you tonight, sweet Saint Fitz, my Saint Fitz. Tonight you must relax and give yourself up to me. The fun has just started."

He put his head back on the pillow then and laughed. "I am the world's luckiest lad!" Then he grabbed my hand and pulled me roughly over to him, again showing me he was stronger by far than I guessed he could be. He took my face in one of his big hands, guided me down to his lips, and kissed me hard. My stomach did an unexpected flip.

"Listen to me, lassie. By all that's holy—or should I say unholy—I am crazy about you. And I can promise you, my love, that tonight you might be the one who calls the plays, but when I'm stronger I'll show you how an Irishman makes a lady scream," he said, his face all smiles.

"Shall we compete then?" I teased. "To see who can please the other more?"

"I'm a gamesman," he said. "I'm ready for the task."

"Are you ready for this, then?" I said, and stood. I went to my CD player, put on *All the Roadrunning,* the Mark Knopfler/Emmylou Harris album, and carefully selected the perfect song. I lit the dozen candles in a gleaming candelabra and extinguished all other light. The firelight licked its golden glow across my body. I hooked my fingers in my waistband and shimmied out of my jeans until I stood there in tiny black silk bikini briefs. Slowly, one by one, I undid the pearl buttons of my shirt. I could hear Fitz's breathing deepen and get ragged.

"You'll be the death of me," he moaned.

"I only fear that I'll be your undeath and your damnation."

"Damn me any way you please," he said. "I'd rather spend eternity in hell with you than a day on earth without you."

My eyes welled up with tears. This was what it was like to be truly loved. These were the words I had longed to hear. And I cried because I never heard them from Darius. With tears running unbidden down my face I stood stark naked in front of Fitz. The flickering golden candlelight caressed my flesh, giving it a patina smooth as satin.

Fitz's face was alight with hunger and longing. "I am a sick and wounded man, but either bring your beautiful self to me, or I'll risk doing damage to myself by coming there to get you," he growled, his voice turning low and sexy.

A hunger, an ache, an irresistible desire started in the core of me and spread outward through my veins like a racing flame. I came over to him and got onto the bed, and although I intended to be in control, Fitz was not a passive man. His strong arm came up around my neck and pulled me down on him. As his lips ground into mine, I didn't expect his strength. I didn't expect to want him so terribly much.

And before I realized what was happening, with a great exhale of breath, with a groan that was almost a lion's roar, his great, hard staff was entering me. Then, shocking me yet another time, he took practiced, teasing fingers and put them inside me, in the other door of desire, so that his fingers plunged in me, keeping a rhythm with his stiff, slippery manhood. Pleasure so overcame me that I arched up, my reason fled, I cried out in ecstasy for him to push still harder, rubbing the sweet button of my pleasure against his pubic bone. Desire became a spiraling storm building up and building up until I felt his member begin to throb, thrust and throb, and I screamed out, "Nowwww." He exploded inside me, and I climbed up over the top of ecstasy and came rushing down the far side, overwhelmed and overcome, moaning and crying and saying his name.

When it was done, and I cuddled under his arm, my face in his neck, him kissing my hair, I felt satisfied. Or almost satisfied. His salty skin was right beneath my lips. I licked his neck and tasted him. A blind need began to build in me. An urge flowed through me. I licked him a second time. But suddenly Fitz picked up my face with his hands. He kissed me and looked into my eyes.

"I know what you want to do," he said. "I don't fear it. But I am too weak. I lost too much blood when I was shot. And it's something we need to talk about. Should you bite me? Maybe someday, dear Daphne, but not now." He kissed me again and stroked my hair back. Then he lowered his face to my breasts and gently, teasingly bit me.

Exploring each other's bodies, we played without words. And before the hour was out, Fitz—no saint at all—took me again.

CHAPTER 16

Most folks are about as happy as they make their minds up to be.

—Abraham Lincoln

Near dawn on Monday, before I hit the sack, or more accurately jumped into my coffin, Fitz woke up from his night's sleep. I had done a lot of thinking during the hours before daylight. St. Julien Fitzmaurice was the best thing, as far as men went, that had ever happened to me. Our relationship wasn't primarily physical, although the sex was better than just fine. I didn't feel that over-the-moon breathlessness like I had with Darius. I also didn't feel that miserable sinking feeling I got after Darius and I fought, which was about every time we saw each other.

And I faced the truth: Darius was not a guy who was about to settle down and nest. Even though my bite had transformed him into a vampire, he was one hundred percent a soldier of fortune, a man who loved a life of high adventure and long stretches of time in places far from home. Whether he was a navy SEAL, vampire hunter, spy, or rock star, each of his chosen professions delivered that adrenaline high he craved. As for other women, for men like Darius there would always be an opportunity to wander, and he'd probably take it.

So when Fitz opened his eyes around five thirty in the a.m.—okay, so I nudged him until he did—I was sitting on the edge of the bed with a mug of hot coffee followed by a lazy, sweet wake-up fuck. It was a satisfying end to my night and a pleasant way to begin his day. When we were done and my eyes were sliding shut in weariness, I explained to him about my coffin room. He said I should go ahead and get my rest. He'd let himself out and call me later.

I wish I could say I had sweet dreams, but in one nightmare after another I was pursued by Ducasse's ghost, or I was chasing after Darius's vanishing figure as he headed into a battle raging on a field filled with red flames and yellow sulfur fumes. I guess the message was that I didn't have my head together quite as much as I thought I did.

After I slipped out of my coffin on Monday evening after sundown, I dragged myself to the Mr. Coffee machine, poured a cup, and found to my relief that there was a call back from Benny on my cell phone. I accessed my voice mail and heard her explain that she was "plumb tuckered out" last night from pub hopping with Cormac, but that they'd had a really fine time of it. They both had heard from J that the countess was Gage.

"Who wouldda thunk it?" Benny's excited voice danced in my voice mail. "Well, the sun don't shine on the same dog's tail all the time. She'll get what's a-coming to her. And I'll tell you what. I'm gonna do my damnedest to be the one to deliver it. Byeeee, and call me, girlfriend," she sang out, and hung up.

Some people have so much damned energy they wear me out. I yawned and listened to another message; this one was from Fitz, who was just saying hi, thanking me for *everything,* and asking me to give him a jingle whenever I had the time.

I hooked the phone up to the charger and went to take a

shower, hoping the water would wash away the lingering images of the dreams that kept me from getting a good night's sleep. I put the water on as hot as I could stand it. I got in and told myself I should be feeling good, not sliding down into a black hole of depression. *Yeah, right.* I put my forehead on the tiles of the shower stall and let the water cascade down my back while tears ran down my face.

Is there such thing as a good cry? I can't say I felt any better after I stopped weeping and stepped out of the shower; I smelled better, though. I padded on bare feet over to my closet and decided it might be time to put on something besides pants for a change. I found a flouncy, above-the-knee Dolce & Gabbana checked gingham skirt in black and white. It was almost too cute for a political interview, but I couldn't resist. So far I had shown up at Daniel's headquarters looking pathetically ordinary, first dressed like a tree hugger and then like a suburbanite going out for sushi. This time I wanted to make a statement. I pulled on a black scoop-necked sweater, shimmied into a pair of black tights, and slipped on black T-strap heels. I knew better than to wear fur to Daniel's headquarters—I guessed that many of his supporters were vegans—so I laid out a black midweight jacket with white piping to put on before I left.

I felt like a new woman, entirely feminine and pretty. Suddenly my mood lightened. I took a deep breath, looked in the mirror, and shook my hair around my head just to feel it swing. There was nothing to be gained by dwelling on things I couldn't change and that was the truth. I might as well enjoy myself and play some head games tonight. I did hope Moses Johnson would be there. I felt like doing some verbal sparring—and I already had the satisfaction of knowing something important that he didn't.

Fighting with words was the extent of what I expected to

encounter. I didn't intend to be chasing after bad guys tonight. I assumed I was just going to hang out at Daniel's headquarters, hoping to get a chance to talk to him and LaDonna. After all, we now knew who Gage was, but we still didn't know who had hired her. Maybe I could find out. And maybe I could convince Joe Daniel to alter his plans Friday night just enough to save his life.

Well, you know what they say about *ass*umptions.

A dozen people occupied the front room of Joe Daniel's campaign headquarters when I showed up around seven. Some had lists of phone numbers beside them as they placed calls urging people to register to vote; others stood at Xerox machines duplicating what I guessed were position papers, judging from the titles I could spot, such as "Global Warming—It's Nearly Too Hot to Handle," and "Stop the U.S. Appetite for Oil—Let's Fast!" The cocktails and partygoers of Friday night were absent. Tonight was all about the unglamorous shitwork of getting a candidate elected.

I spotted Joe Daniel sitting in the same place he was the first time Benny and I came here. He had made it into a mini-office. On a shelf behind him sat a pair of real combat boots—bronzed. There was an insignia for the paratroopers hung on the wall, and a plaque having something to do with Desert Storm back in the early nineties. Joe Daniel was preoccupied and didn't pay any attention to me. He had retreated into his own private world, practicing with his yo-yo. He had ditched the black one and played with an iridescent blue one made of aluminum. He was doing elaborate things with the string. I figured the yo-yo hobby was a Zen thing for him, a version of walking meditation. I came close enough to get his attention and said, "Mr. Daniel? I mean Joe? Can I talk to you a few minutes? I have some things to go over with you about security."

He smiled but looked at me blankly, trying to figure out who I was.

"Daphne Urban," I reminded him. "With the Protectors. Ginny said she'd tell you I needed a little of your time."

"Oh, yeah. The all-woman security service. Sure. Let's sit down over here," he said, then stood up and pulled out a folding chair for me.

I sat. He sat. He put the yo-yo down in front of him. I looked earnestly at Daniel. I was beginning to think that a flouncy skirt wasn't the best attire to get a VIP to take me seriously. Anyway, I plunged in. "Let me get right to the point. I have some good news. My colleagues and I have a strong lead on the gunman hired to kill you."

His face didn't betray much. He just looked at me politely, then stated the obvious. "But you haven't caught him."

"No. But we're getting closer to locating 'him.' However, we still don't know who's behind this threat. I'm sure the police have questioned you—"

"And the FBI. I told them all the same thing. I don't know. Some nut, I guess," he said dismissively.

"Joe," I said in the most serious voice I could muster. "Whoever wants you dead is no nutcase. We are almost certain it is not an individual, but a group, a powerful group. I need you to understand that even if we stop this assassin, if you run for office, chances are there will be other attempts."

"Maybe. Maybe not. I can't worry about that. When I was in the military I didn't go into battle thinking about whether or not I was going to get hit. I went in to do the best job I could and get my mission done. That's what I'm doing now. Anything else you want to ask me? I have an NPR interview in a few minutes."

"No more questions, but I have some specific instructions to give you. You have to know that a predictable routine makes you an easy target. You even have a printed itinerary for the entire week. I have a copy. The press has a copy. It makes you a sitting duck. I'm asking you—I mean, the Protectors are asking you—to make some last-minute changes in your schedule. Suddenly announce earlier starting times and make people scramble to get there, or be late. Take a different route. Switch your meeting rooms. Don't sit here in this same spot night after night. When you give a speech, make the sound guys move the podium at the last minute—even if it's just by a few feet. Switch around whatever you can. Understand?"

He regarded me with a look of more respect than he had before. "That makes sense. Sure. Look, I appreciate your efforts. But the best thing you or anybody can do is catch this guy alive. Then we can find out who hired him. Aside from that, I can assure you that nobody here knows a damned thing." He got up and put out his hand for me to shake. I did.

He looked at me, not as a come-on or an ogle, but with the kind of close inspection that lets a woman know a man thinks she's easy on the eyes. "Nobody would ever guess you're a rent-a-cop. I'll give you that. At least I don't have to worry about you being a damn government spy. Thanks again," he said, and walked toward an entourage of people toting National Public Radio equipment who had just come through the door.

I don't know if I really made an impression on him as far as his using some common sense, but I gave it my best try. I walked away and went looking for LaDonna. I had made up my mind about something on the way down here, and figured I'd drop some bait and see if she took it.

I found LaDonna in the back room, sitting at a card table,

thumbing through file folders filled with legal briefs. As I walked over, she took off a pair of reading glasses and looked up at me. She didn't look pleased to see me.

"Got a minute?" I asked. "I'll try to make it short."

"A minute is about all I can spare," she said curtly.

I placed myself right against the table where she was sitting. I leaned forward and put my weight on my hands until my face was just a little too close to hers to be polite. "Well, it's just this," I said in a very soft voice. "The cops think— and I think—that somebody close to Daniel is also working for whoever is trying to kill him."

"That's a load of crap," she said as she pushed her chair back to put distance between us. Now, here's a tip: Somebody honestly offended by my implication would have either held her ground or pushed her nose right in my face. Score one for me.

"Well, if anyone is, I think it's you," I said, adding an implied threat to my soft voice, and thus upping the ante.

"This conversation is over," she said. She jumped up, snatching her files into her arms. I moved a few steps and blocked her way. She couldn't get past me without some physical contact. So she stopped. Score two for me.

I stood face-to-face with her and went right on talking. "Hear me out. My organization knows who the assassin is, and we're close to finding *her*. It's only a matter of time before we know who is behind the plot to kill Joe Daniel. True, even after the shit hits the fan, there may be no way to trace this back to you. But I'm giving you a heads-up. I know. And you'll know I know. Maybe you should think about resigning."

"Are you finished?" Her voice was cold as a block of ice.

"Yes, and so are you." I stepped aside as she hugged her files to her chest and walked by. She tried to act huffy, but her hands were shaking so hard the stiff paper of the folders was rattling. Score three for me. I won.

I'm sure Moses Johnson didn't know exactly what I said to LaDonna, unless he was an accomplished lip reader. But he could read body language, and he had been watching our exchange closely from his station all by his lonesome next to the watercooler.

I walked over with a smile on my face. I wasn't about to tell him the hit man was a vampire. But I figured I'd throw him LaDonna.

"What do you think?" I asked.

"About what?" he said.

"LaDonna as the mole," I said, leaning against the wall next to him.

"Probably a good guess," he said, draping an arm over the watercooler. "Do you have anything on her?"

"All I started out with was a gut feeling about her change of heart when she switched from right wing to left wing. It didn't ring true to me. Then there's her brother's death. I wonder how she really felt about Daniel coming back and going peacenik. But what I ended up with was pay dirt. When I just confronted her, she got scared, very scared. She didn't deny anything. She ran away from me. Bam, *wrong answer.* I think she's a sure thing. Do *you* have anything on her?"

He didn't answer for a moment. "Some phone records. She calls Washington, D.C., a lot."

I wasn't impressed, and I let him know it. "Joe Daniel is still a Congressman. He has an office and staff there. That seems like a pretty legit place to call, to me."

Johnson looked at me with tired eyes. "The people she calls are strictly legit too. The problem is, all of them sit on the other side of the aisle."

"You want to name names?" I asked, suddenly more interested.

"No. And it wouldn't help if I did."

"Sure it would," I insisted.

He gave me a look that was part pity and part disgust.
"Look, Miss Urban, let me acquaint you with the facts of life,
in case you forgot them. Just because we have two and two,
it doesn't mean they add up to shit. Names aren't going to
help. What would help?" He took his arm off the watercooler
and grabbed a paper cup. He filled it. He took a sip. Then he
started talking again.

"How about a confession? Like, say, if Miss Chavez de-
cides to spill her guts out of a sudden feeling of remorse because Daniel's brains got splattered all over her power suit.
Then we would have something. What else might help? If
whoever Miss Chavez is reporting to is caught with his pants
down and his dick someplace it ain't supposed to be—and
that place is bad enough that he'll need to wheel and deal to
stay out of prison. Without somebody deciding to spill his
guts, we're never going to be able to prove anything. You
think people this smart and this connected are going to be
dumb enough to leave a trail of cookie crumbs? You think the
hit man is going to have a personal check with his employer's
name on it in a bona fide John Hancock?" He crushed the
empty paper cup in his hand.

Before I could come up with a snappy comeback, my cell
phone rang. I could see the number was Cormac's.

"Excuse me a minute," I said, and turned away to take the
call.

"Yeah, Cormac?"

"I was up at Strawberry Fields. The countess strolled by."

I could hardly hear him. There was a whooshing sound
drowning him out.

"Can you talk louder?" I asked.

"I'm airborne." That explained the poor reception. "I'm following her."

"Where is she now?" I was straining to make out his words clearly.

"In a black Town Car headed for the Lincoln Tunnel. Look, Daphne." He was practically screaming into the phone. "I can't fly fast enough to keep up with her. Benny said there's a house in Jersey. Maybe that's where she's headed."

"I'll get on it," I said.

"Take Benny with you. This is real personal for her," he said, sounding breathless.

"You bet. Call J, would you? Tell him what's going on."

"Got it. Got to go," he yelled over the wind.

I flipped the phone shut, and forgetting Moses Johnson, started for the door.

He didn't forget me. A strong black hand grabbed my arm. "Where you going?"

I looked down at his hand. He didn't remove it. He held firm.

"I have to leave," I said.

"I see that. But just a minute, Miss Urban. What happened to sharing? We made a deal, remember? I give you something. You give me something. I couldn't help but overhear both ends of that phone conversation. Who is the countess, and why do you have to follow her?"

"It's a long story. I don't have time right now," I said, giving my arm a little tug.

He tugged back and smiled without warmth. "Make time," he said, giving me a cold look.

I glared at him, but I didn't see any way out of telling him the truth, or a version of it, anyway. "I have to go to New

Jersey. I have a source who knows something about the assassin."

"You have a ride?"

"Ummm, no." He had a point. What the hell was I going to do, hail a taxi, take a bus? Fly?

"I do. So how about we use my car? I'm bored with this watercooler's company; she puts out but doesn't talk much."

"Isn't Jersey out of your jurisdiction?"

"I'm a U.S. citizen. I'm allowed to travel to Jersey. I just can't arrest anybody. Any chance of that?"

"No. No chance at all. It's just that . . ."

"What?" he asked, raising his eyebrows.

"Oh, never mind. Let's go," I said, and with him still holding on to my arm, Johnson and I started for the door. I stopped.

"What now?" he asked.

"We have to pick my girlfriend up at Madison Square Garden. I have to call her and tell her we're coming."

"Jesus. What is this, a fucking date? Are you sure you don't want to stop off and change into a cocktail dress?"

"That was a stupid thing to say," I said as we marched out into the street. His unmarked Ford Crown Victoria police car was parked at the curb.

He opened the passenger-side door. "Okay, I'm sorry. Now get in."

Benny was standing in front of Macy's practically jumping up and down when she spotted us coming across Thirty-fourth Street. We pulled up to the curb, and she dove into the backseat.

"Whooooeee," she yelled. "Time to do some rat killing."

Johnson turned around and gave her a sour look. "What's that supposed to mean?" he said.

"It's just Southern for taking care of business—and we're on our way to kick some ass!" she said, happy as a pig in you-know-what.

Johnson glanced over at me. "Maybe you'd better tell me that long story now."

I gave him a highly edited and very creative version of how the countess had kidnapped Benny because Benny rejected her advances, and how the countess held Benny captive at the country estate—where I found her during a party I was attending. Then I twisted the truth a little more and said that the countess was working with the assassin, a guy named Tallmadge.

Johnson grunted now and then while I told my story. I don't think he bought much of it. "You know," he said, "what I can't figure . . . I mean, what are the odds that the same lady who gets a crush on Benny just happens to be in cahoots with the assassin you're looking for? Did you leave out something?"

I ignored him and turned around to look at Benny in the backseat. "Did Cormac contact J?"

"Yes'm, he sure did. And J told him that he couldn't see why the countess would head for her own house in Jersey, since it's the first place anybody would look for her. He said she could be going to hole up in some motel, and he wasn't going to waste his time on a wild-goose chase. And I told Cormac to tell J that anybody might look for her at that there country estate of hers, but they sure ain't going to find her if she ducks into the maze.

"You know, I always thought it was sort of peculiar she'd go to all that expense to build that maze for a night of . . . entertainment. You know, I think there's more to it. I just have this feeling."

"Benny, I think you're on to something. This is a game to

the countess. She dared me to try to find her. I think she wants us to follow her out there."

Moses Johnson broke in. "Ladies. Reality check. If she is playing a game and leading you somewhere on purpose, you'd better believe she's the cat and you're the mice. It sounds as if we're walking into a trap."

"Oh, we're a lot smarter than mice, aren't we, Daphy? I think we can get the cat caught in the mousetrap. Don't you?" Benny giggled from the backseat.

"Well, there's one of her and three of us. So yeah, I think we have a shot at it," I said.

"What about this guy Tallmadge? The one you say is Gage. What happens if he's there?" Johnson asked.

"Are you scared, Detective Johnson? The odds are still in our favor," I answered.

"They're not if he's got a high-powered rifle with a scope ready to pick us off when we get out the car," Johnson said.

"The man has a point, Benny," I said.

"Yeah, he does," she agreed, putting a finger in her mouth and looking pensive. Then she took the finger out and tapped her lips while she said, "So I guess we ditch the car when we get there and sneak in the back way."

"I'm not exactly dressed for a search-and-destroy mission," I said, looking down at my T-straps and flouncy skirt.

Benny gave me the once-over. "You got black tights on, Daphy. Take off the skirt. You'll still be decent. You'll look like a cat burglar."

"Good point," I said, and sat back to play navigator while Johnson drove west on Route 78 toward the rolling hills of New Jersey.

CHAPTER 17

Her skin was white as leprosy,
The Nightmare Life-in-Death was she,
Who thicks man's blood with cold.

—Samuel Taylor Coleridge, *The Rime of the Ancient Mariner*

We had to drive only about fifty miles out to Somerset County, and before we got too close to Peapack I made Johnson pull into a Wawa. I ran in and came out carrying a big plastic bag.

"No coffee?" Johnson griped. "What's in the bag?"

"Something we are definitely going to need," I answered.

We left the Crown Victoria on the side of the road maybe a quarter mile from the drive leading up to Fantazius, the countess's estate. Like all good Boy Scouts and members of the NYPD, Moses Johnson was prepared. He pulled a Maglite out of the trunk. I grabbed my Wawa bag, and we started off, me freezing my ass off, since I was wearing just black tights to cover it. Once we got to the driveway, the three of us skirted the edge of the lawn, sticking to the tree line. The big white house looked deserted, its windows vacant, like lifeless eyes. We sneaked around back and passed the pool area.

When we reached the entrance to the maze, it was as bleak a structure as I have ever seen. High concrete walls stretched in gloomy sameness along either side of huge gates whose ornate ironwork depicted skeletons dancing in macabre positions, their skulls grinning down from overhead. The gates stood open—as an invitation or a dare?

I noticed that Detective Johnson had drawn his gun. I wondered how kosher it would be if he shot anyone out of his jurisdiction. Of course, if he fired his gun at anybody in this place, he might as well be shooting blanks, since bullets can't kill a vampire—unless Johnson was using silver bullets, which wasn't likely or even within the realm of possibility.

I motioned to my two companions to stop and whispered, "Wait a minute." I opened up my Wawa bag and took out the first roll of string—five hundred feet worth. I had bought every roll they had in stock. Even then, I worried that I wouldn't have nearly enough if we penetrated too deeply into the miles of twisting alleys. If we made it out of here at all, Benny and I could fly above the maze, but Johnson might be leaving like a bat out of hell—on foot.

I tied one end of the string to the gate and we started in. Benny whispered to me, "Should we go airborne?"

"I don't think so," I replied in a voice barely louder than a whisper. "The countess specifically said that the maze held hiding places you can't see from the air—and she said there's a tunnel, some kind of special underground structure with a 'surprise' inside."

"My money's on the tunnel," Benny said.

"Me too," I agreed. "I have the feeling we're in for a long walk."

We entered and immediately faced three alleys, which were hedgerows lining paths covered with a dark and grainy material, like black sand. Each alley led off in different directions. The three of us looked at one another. I shrugged.

Detective Johnson said, "As Yogi said, 'When you come to

a fork, take it.'" And he took the alley pointing straight ahead. Benny and I followed through the somber darkness of the hedgerows which grew higher than our heads. A peculiar odor permeated the air. It smelled like a combination of cat piss and blood, and its strong ammonia scent filled my throat and choked me. An unrelieved gloom hung over everything, and the only light was the beam of Johnson's Maglite. And not a sound pierced the stillness.

We walked quickly, and whenever the alley forked, we blindly took one or the other without pondering. We hit dead ends more frequently than not and had to double back, feeling more frustrated with each blocked path. Occasionally we passed small structures with entranceways flanked by pillars with friezes above them that made the little building look like a pagan temple.

Johnson shone his flashlight over the facade of the first we encountered. Its frescoes rivaled those of Pompeii in their profanity, depicting giant phalluses, supplicant females, and couples engaged in Kama Sutra poses. We attempted to enter that first temple, but quickly backed out. The interior was empty—except for a pile of bones and a stench of decayed flesh that reached out with a lethal miasma. Nausea overwhelmed me. Johnson retched. We backed away and hurried on.

After a very long time, when all of us began to grow weary and I was down to my last ball of string, we came to an open space and stopped. A larger version of the abattoirs we encountered along the way stood in its center, its open doorway a gaping maw of blackness. We heard a low, moaning cry from its recesses. I dropped the white plastic Wawa bag and cautiously approached this gateway into the unknown.

Once inside we found ourselves at the beginning of a great tunnel leading downward. From somewhere in the shadowy depths came the clinking of chains and a muffled scream. Moving close together we descended into the grotesque depths, Benny in the lead, Johnson between us, and me close behind. The passageway was arched just inches above our heads; the walls were black and smooth as glass. The floor beneath was stone, and black as lava rocks.

Down we went, and the farther we descended the warmer it became. I felt perspiration dripping off me like rain. Johnson pulled off his jacket and threw it to the floor. The clinking of chains recurred in regular intervals, along with a dull clunk, as if a great wheel or clockwork was turning one cog at a time. At last a red glow appeared at the end of the tunnel. We hugged the smooth obsidian walls and pressed forward, fearful of what lay ahead, for the screams were louder with each clunk and rattle of chains. Finally we beheld a terrible sight.

A torture chamber sat in a large, cavelike room. Shackles were bolted to the walls. Whips and knives were displayed on a bloodstained table. And Tallmadge lay bound in silver chains upon a great wheel designed like the torturous rack of the Inquisition. The wheel was turning just a millimeter at a time, but each turn stretched his body, causing sinews to screech and his bones to creak. Tallmadge turned a bleak look in our direction and choked out the words, "She's here."

A long case lay open on the floor near this horrible machine. I assumed it was the one he had carried from the vampire club a few days ago. Inside was no assassin's rifle. I could see the long, pointed stakes that were the mainstay of a vampire hunter's munitions.

Then we heard a voice. The countess stood beyond the torture machine and was flanked by two hellhounds, gigantic creatures with three heads apiece and a serpent tail. Their mouths dripped gore, and their eyes glowed with a terrible fire. They stood at either side of a huge wooden door, with the countess between them. She wore a shimmering silver leotard. Her lips were red. Her hair was white. Her eyes were glittering. "Welcome to my parlor, said the spider to the fly," she quipped, and trilled a laugh that rang out like iron bells.

The wheel turned again, and Tallmadge screamed.

"Let him go," Benny said fiercely. "Now."

"I think not," the countess said. "He intended to kill me."

"So do I," Benny cried, and rushed at the countess. The monsters leaped forward in response, and Johnson, displaying immense courage, emptied his gun into them with no effect. Brandishing the Maglite like a club, he rushed into the fight. I ran forward too, already wild with fury, jumping on one of the hellhounds and riding him. He thrashed and bucked to try to loosen my grip, all the while screeching a loud and terrible cry. I reached down beneath the monster's head and, with my nails that had become talons, I sought to rip out his throat. Also my long teeth bit deep into the back of his neck, not for his blood but to sever his backbone like a cat does with a rabbit caught in its mouth. He collapsed beneath me, and his great body began to disintegrate to dust.

Benny was wrestling with the countess, the two of them rolling about on the floor. Johnson was fending off the second Cerberus with his Maglite, but he was down and losing ground fast. I grabbed one of the sharpened stakes from Tallmadge's bag and rushed at the creature, sinking it deep between its ribs. The animal arched up and back, leaping wildly until its body went into a spasm in midair and it fell down, beginning to crumble even before it hit the stones of the dark floor.

Stake still in hand, I ran toward the countess, who was now straddling Benny, who bucked and flailed beneath her. I wanted to plunge the stake into the countess's exposed back but my hand froze. As if an invisible shield kept the stake from descending, I could not will my hand to move. I could not do the deed.

But Johnson could. He grabbed the stake from my hand and thrust wildly at the countess. She screamed and jumped back, hissing and holding up her hands as a shield. He raised his arm to thrust again, and she turned and jumped toward the great wooden door, which swung open on its own. Nothing but a void lay beyond, into which she leaped. And when she did, she vanished.

Benny went to follow after her, but I seized her arm and yanked her backward as Tallmadge, with a mighty effort, yelled out, "Don't!" And then the great door swung shut.

Benny picked herself up off her ass and gave me a dirty look.

"Hey, I probably just saved your life," I said.

She stared at me for a long second, then blinked and said, "Yeah, you probably did." Just then the torture wheel turned again and Tallmadge screamed.

"We'd better cut him loose," I said.

"Good idea," she agreed.

I took one of the deadly stakes and shoved it into the mechanism of the wheel, stopping its dreadful movement. Benny and Detective Johnson went about unhooking the silver chains that wound around Tallmadge's broken body. His teeth clenched and his eyes squeezed shut as Johnson lifted him enough for Benny to unwind his bonds. I held firm to the stake and was ready with another should the machine snap the one stuck in its gears.

After what seemed like an eternity, but was probably less than fifteen minutes, Tallmadge was free. It was clear he couldn't walk, and I'm certain he couldn't fly either. His body would heal with a vampire's rapid recuperative powers, but he was still grievously hurt, and it would take time.

Supporting him between us, we wended our way out of the loathsome tunnel to the surface, and as we broke into the night air, I felt we were emerging from a tomb. Because of his great pain, we had some discussion on the best way to leave the maze. If we transformed and flew, we could clear the walls and be back at the Crown Victoria in minutes, even carrying another person, instead of hours as we followed the string out of the maze. With daylight sure to come first, we had no choice. I turned to Detective Johnson.

"You're not going to like this," I said. "But we have to get out of here. I'm going to carry you out, and Benny will take Tallmadge."

"I'm a little bruised and scratched, but I'm not injured. I can walk," he said gruffly.

"We don't have time," I said, and truer words were never spoken, as we were about to find out. "Look," I said to Johnson, "what you're about to see may be a little, ummmm, unusual. Just go with it, okay? We really have to move, and move fast."

The detective just looked at us, perplexed, but cooperated as Benny and I helped Tallmadge transfer his weight to Johnson, who stooped down and took him in a fireman's carry. As soon as Tallmadge was set, Benny and I looked at each other, stripped down, and let the energy rip—lights, camera, action. I couldn't watch Johnson's face during the change, but I'm sure his expression was priceless. It certainly was when Benny and I emerged from our vortexes of light as huge batlike creatures.

"Son of a bitch," I heard Johnson say. "I knew there was something about you two that wasn't right."

"Forget the accolades," I said. "Help Benny get hold of Tallmadge; then get on my back."

"What? Not on your life," he snarled.

"Look, I can't tell you how I know, but I know something is going to happen. Like animals who know a tsunami is about to hit the beach. We have to get out of this place, so shut up and listen to me for once. Just move it!"

I'm happy to say he stopped jawing and did as I asked. In the middle of getting Tallmadge onto her back, Benny yelled over to me, "Take that there sack from Wawa and carry our clothes, will you? I ain't riding back to Manhattan naked as a babe."

Then with some difficulty she jumped into the air and beat her wings against the backdrop of the moonless night.

I quickly scooped up our duds, then got down on all fours for Johnson to climb on. He did it, mumbling all the while, "Nobody is ever going to believe this. Hell, I'm not telling anybody. It would be worse than saying I spotted a damned UFO." Once he settled on my back and held on to my shoulders, I too soared skyward, but it took a tremendous effort. Tallmadge was slender, at least, but Johnson was no lightweight.

"You've been eating too much KFC and Big Macs," I complained as I strained to get over the top of the walls.

"So charge me a double fare," he said into my ear.

I had no sooner gotten clear of the wall than I heard a crackling sound behind me. I glanced backward and saw the black sand of the maze's alleys starting to glow red; then as tongues of flame swept over the paths, they became rivers of fire, quickly setting the hedgerows ablaze. Within seconds the maze of Fantazius was an inferno, its heat so great I feared it would ignite my pelt if I didn't fly faster.

"Holy shit!" Johnson yelled, and gripped my shoulders

tighter as I thrust forward with all my might to escape to cooler air. I was out of breath and my chest was heaving when I landed next to Johnson's car. Johnson climbed off and got Tallmadge into the backseat as Benny and I moved down the road a little and changed back to human form.

Once we did, I could see that she was pretty beat up. She had some deep scratches on her hands and arms from her fight with the countess, one of her eyes was swelling shut, and her lips had turned puffy. "Are you hurt badly?" I asked.

"Nothing a bath won't fix," she said, starting to sound funny talking through her big lips.

She got into the backseat with Tallmadge, I sat in the front, and Johnson floored the accelerator and fishtailed back onto the paved road. In the distance we could hear the fire sirens going off.

On the way back to New York, Tallmadge filled us in on how the countess had discovered that Benny had escaped and left the hunt while everybody was having fun and games. He followed her back to the vampire club, where he confronted her, telling her he knew she was Gage and that he wasn't going to let her kill Joe Daniel. She just laughed at him and left. A few minutes later he went after her, carrying the case with the stakes.

I broke in at that point and asked him how he knew the countess was Gage.

"Marozia called me," he said.

"Oh, she did? Are you two friends?"

"Not exactly. But we've worked together in the past," he answered.

"How long ago in the past?" I said through clenched teeth.

"During the Revolution. The countess worked with us too, not that those two were friends. They couldn't stand each other."

Benny broke in. "Tallmadge, sugar, tell us what happened after you followed the countess."

He put his head back on the seat and closed his eyes. "She outsmarted me. After I got my bag of stakes and went hunting her, she led me down into that place of damnation and overpowered me, with the help of her creatures. Then she put me on the wheel. I couldn't escape. She said you would come, but there was nothing I could do to warn you. She was going to trap all of us in there while she killed Daniel. I'm sorry."

"Now, you don't have nothing to be sorry for," Benny assured him, and stroked his cheek. "You just rest, you hear?"

"One more thing, Tallmadge," I said. "Where did the countess go through that door? Do you know?"

He opened his eyes, lifted his head, and looked at me. "Don't you know?" he asked.

"Well, I could guess, but no, I don't know," I said.

"It's better that way," he answered, and put his head back down.

As Moses Johnson drove through the night, heading back to the city, he was talking to himself under his breath during most of this conversation. Sometimes he mentioned my name.

"You want to say something to me, Detective?" I finally asked him.

He glared at me. "I'm not saying anything to you. I'm not saying anything to anybody. As far as I'm concerned, this night never happened. You understand?"

"Sure," I said. "What about Joe Daniel? The assassin is gone. You going to call off the boys in blue?"

"Are you nuts? How the hell could I justify pulling men off this detail? I don't know where that lady went. I don't know if she was the assassin or not. The NYPD will keep protecting Joe Daniel as long as he's in New York. That's my final word."

And as he promised, Moses Johnson didn't say anything else the rest of the way home, even when he dropped each of us off—Tallmadge at his club, Benny and me on the Upper West Side. He grunted a couple of times, but that was all.

I dragged myself into my building feeling completely spent. I was glad this was all over. I pushed through my door and stopped dead. A zigzagging trail of blood covered the floor. A man's sneaker lay abandoned in front of the door. A lamp had been overturned. And my apartment remained strangely silent. No dog greeted me. When I called out for Jade, Gunther squeaked a reply from his cage. I ran through the apartment calling her name.

She was gone.

CHAPTER 18

It ain't over till it's over.

—American folk wisdom often attributed to Yogi Berra

Despair overwhelmed me. The coming light of dawn was too close for me to go looking for Jade. By tomorrow night she could be in Florida or on a plane to anywhere. Of course, I would go looking for her, but I didn't know if I had a snowball's chance in hell of finding her. I slowly went over to the couch, sank down, and put my head in my hands as grief overtook me.

Just then a sound came from outside my front door and a voice called out, "Daphne! Open up."

It was Darius's voice. I sat without moving. Facing him tonight was more than I could bear. If I didn't answer, maybe he'd leave.

"Daphne! I need you to open the fucking door!" he yelled, and kicked it with considerable force at the same time he called out, "I have your dog."

I ran over and flung the door open. Darius held Jade in his arms. Her body was limp, her head hung down, and she wasn't moving.

"No!" I gasped.

Darius moved into the hallway. "She's unconscious, not dead. They must have drugged her."

"Who? What?" I said as I followed him into the apartment. He put her down gently on the living room rug.

He looked at me with stricken eyes as he knelt next to Jade. "I don't know who they were. I came back here. I . . . I wanted to talk to you. About the other night, you know. That was a couple of hours ago. I was walking up your block when I saw two men leaving your building. They were pulling a dog crate behind them, and I saw them put it into the back of a van that was parked out front. Then they slammed the doors and got in to drive off. I had a bad feeling and ran up to the building, where I saw your doorman lying on the floor trying to get up.

"The van took off, but I was lucky and caught a taxi right away. I told the cabbie to follow. We went all the way to frigging LaGuardia airport. The van turned into the long-term parking lot. I convinced the cabbie to go in too. We got to them just as they were removing the crate. I barreled out of the cab, and then . . . well, I took care of them, you know. I got Jade out of the crate. I saw she was breathing okay, so I picked her up, put her in the cab, and came back here.

"What's going on? Who were those guys?"

"Some unfinished business," I said, with rage flowing through me like hot lava.

"Those two guys are finished now," he said. "They're not going to bother you again. Why did they want Jade?"

"Some Colombian drug lord has it in his head that she's magic. Because of Don Manuel, the shaman who used to own her, I guess. It's crazy," I explained.

Darius stood up and looked at me. "Maybe she is magic. She brought me back here to you." He moved toward me, his arms ready to embrace me.

I stepped back. "Don't," I warned. My heart felt as if it

would burst, but I had made up my mind. "Darius, it's over," I said.

"I don't want to believe that," he said. "I know you still love me. Why are you doing this? Is it that other guy?"

My voice was steady as I said what I decided I had to say. "No, it's not him. It's us. It just doesn't work. There are too many secrets, too many lies. I don't know who you are, not really. I don't know your family or any of your friends. I don't even know who you work for now—or who sent you to hunt vampires in the past. But one thing I do know: You're always going to leave." My voice quavered. "Oh, hell, we've said all this before." I covered my face with my hand.

Darius moved closer to me and pulled my hand away. He gently lifted my chin so that I had to look into his eyes. "Look at me. Listen. I know I've hurt you. I'm sorry. And I'm not being fair, I know that. I came back, true. But you're right: I am going to leave. I have to go back to Germany. And after that, who knows?"

Tears had begun to run down my cheeks. I did still love him, and I loved him so fucking much. I just knew I couldn't give in to him again. I shook my head. "I can't do this anymore. I just can't."

"Shhh," he said. "Don't cry. You're right. I have no business asking you what I'm going to ask you."

I closed my eyes so I couldn't see his face. I didn't want to hear this.

"I want you not to close the door all the way. Leave it open just a little. Someday I will come back for good. And someday I *will* come back for you."

"Don't," I said with all the firmness I could manage. "I need to go on with my life. Without you."

His voice was sad when he responded. "I understand that.

Do whatever you have to do. I'm not going to stop you. I just want you to know that for me, this isn't over."

"It is for me," I said softly.

"Maybe," he said, and kissed me on the forehead. "We're vampires. We have forever, and a lot can happen in all that time."

I just stood there and didn't say anything at first. Then I said, "Thank you for saving Jade. I mean it. I will owe you for that for the rest of my life."

Darius stood there for a moment, studying me, his eyes searching mine. It hurt me to look back at him. His lean cheeks were all planes and angles; his face was perfect except for the jagged scar that ran down his cheek. He was the man I would always want, but the one who would always break my heart.

"Good-bye, Darius," I said softly. "Take care of yourself."

"You too, Daphne. But then again, you always do." He turned, went to the door, and left. He didn't look back.

When I arose from my coffin on Tuesday evening, I was feeling guilty that I hadn't talked to Fitz since I saw him Monday morning. I didn't return his phone call, and it was the first thing on my mind that I had to do.

Then I saw Jade lying in front of my crypt's door. A rush of love for her poured over me. She was here and she was safe. I thought of Darius, of course, but I suddenly realized I hadn't dreamed about him. And at that moment, as grateful as I was that he had brought Jade home, I felt as if I had at last quit beating my head against a wall, and it felt good.

I went to the phone and called Fitz. He answered on the first ring.

EPILOGUE

None of us ever heard from Tallmadge again after the night Moses Johnson dropped him off at the vampire club. I certainly didn't go looking for him, but Benny did. She said he had told Cathary he'd be away indefinitely. I wondered if Tallmadge had decided to skip out from under the long reach of the intelligence service, as he had hinted he would. I asked Mar-Mar what she thought. She answered that she didn't know, but she imagined Tallmadge had other things he wanted to do. If he's running, I am rooting for him. I hope he never gets caught. It would let us all know that if we wanted to escape, it can be done.

Benny, by the way, quickly recovered from the roughing up she got in her fight with the countess. When I called her on Tuesday evening right after I called Fitz, I was surprised to find that Cormac answered her phone. He said he was pissed off that he'd missed all the action before he put Benny on the line.

In response to my query about her injuries, she just said, "I ain't too pert, but I'm a little better than common."

I translated that to mean she was feeling better.

I also took the subway back to Jackson Heights that night. Tino Leguizamo no longer occupied 3D, and so far there haven't been any other attempts to steal my dog. I still don't completely buy the "magic dog" motive. In my gut, I suspect it has something to do with getting a hold over me because I'm a spy. I'm vulnerable when it comes to Jade, and I had better keep that in mind.

And on the Friday night of that week when everything changed so much for me, in Strawberry Fields at the Imagine Circle in Central Park, Joe Daniel spoke about peace to a few hundred U.S. labor leaders, social activists, and dignitaries invited from around the world. As the spectators held lit candles, Daniel talked about the world John Lennon envisioned in his song, a place where human beings live together in peace and share the planet we all call home. It was a spiritual speech, not a secular one.

No gunshots desecrated this shrine to a man and an idea. Daniel's history-making appearance there ended without incident.

Later, at Madison Square Garden, Joe Daniel spelled out his plan to stop global warming, rehabilitate the environment, end worldwide dependence on carbon-based fuels, and stop America's involvement in the oil wars of the Mideast. Daniel pulled no punches, but he sounded a lot more like John Kennedy than Mohandas Gandhi. I know. I was there. At the end of the night the chairperson of the National Democratic Committee walked over to Joe Daniel and formally asked him to run in the presidential primaries as a Democrat. Daniel accepted the invitation. It was a historic moment. I hope he makes it unharmed to Election Day and, if he wins, that he lives to take office. I don't want to be overly pessimistic, but he still has a lot of powerful enemies.

The Monday following Daniel's speech, LaDonna Chavez

resigned abruptly from the campaign team, giving family problems as the reason. It didn't get much news coverage because the same day the headline story involved the resignation of a powerful conservative senator with strong ties to the military—his former company won almost all the defense contracts for the Mideast. I have no proof that this longtime friend of the religious right had anything to do with hiring the countess, but I don't believe in coincidence, and I do think it's entirely possible he was behind the conspiracy. I suspect we'll never know.

As for me, I was supposed to leave tomorrow night with Fitz and drive up to a party thrown by the Fitzmaurice cousins in one of those picturesque towns on Cape Cod. The huge bash is to celebrate the recovery and heroism of my "Saint Fitz." I got the feeling Fitz planned to have an engagement ring in his pocket. I might never know, because I have to cancel going along.

I checked my message machine after I woke up tonight and found out that the Darkwings were being called in for an emergency meeting. "Don't leave town," the message instructed.

I called J back. He picked up. "What's this all about?" I asked as I yawned and stretched.

"Hostages," he answered. "Teenagers, kids really."

I woke up fast. "No shit," I said.

"No shit. Get your ass down here," he said.

Suddenly I remembered an article in the *Times* yesterday about the daughter of a prominent banker who had been reported missing. The FBI had been called in. The news story revealed that nearly a dozen teenage girls from prominent families had vanished in the past couple of weeks. Like I said, I don't believe in coincidence. I think I have my next assignment, and I'm going to be too busy to get engaged in the near future.

Besides, I don't know if I'm ready to give up four hundred years of independence. To tell the truth, I don't know, in my heart of hearts, if I'm over Darius. I don't know what I'll say if Fitz asks me to marry him.

I may ask him to wait awhile. After all, if I turn him into a vampire, I'll have eternity to make up my mind.

Acknowledgments

I want to thank New American Library's editorial director, Claire Zion, for her clear vision about the kind of books that readers want and for her steadfast support of this series. I have long admired her as an editor and loved the books she has championed. Her enthusiasm for new ideas and quality writing stands out in the publishing industry, and her energy for making good books "happen" has been a tremendous motivator for me to dream bigger dreams.

My deepest appreciation goes to my NAL editor, Liz Scheier. Smart, and even more important, wise, she has helped me beyond measure. Her editing talent has made me a much better writer, and her advice is always right on target. I am so fortunate to be working with her, and to view her as a true partner in creating the Darkwing Chronicles. She is also, besides being a top-notch editor, an absolutely terrific human being.

But without my agent, John Talbot of the Talbot Fortune Agency, Inc., my manuscripts would still be in the bottom of a drawer instead of in book form and in readers' hands. He is always in my corner, and his belief in my writing spurs me on. I couldn't ask for a better agent or a truer friend.

Thanks also go to Allen Davis, Det. (Ret.), NYPD, for sharing his adventures on Manhattan's streets and for keeping me at least "in the ballpark" in my fictional descriptions of police work in this book. Any errors about the NYPD are strictly mine, not his. Good-natured and easygoing, Allen is nothing like my detective Moses Johnson except in sharing a sixth sense about people and threatening situations. Thanks also to Bernie, Allen's Saint Bernard, for the warm doggy welcomes whenever I showed up with yet another question.

Finally, I wish to again acknowledge the efforts of Bat Conservation International in combating the negative mythology surrounding bats and in showing us the wondrous ability, grace, and beauty of this unjustly maligned creature. Please visit their Web site at www.batcon.org.